THE
SILHOUETTE
GIRL

V.C. Andrews® Books

The Dollanganger Family
Flowers in the Attic
Petals on the Wind
If There Be Thorns
Seeds of Yesterday
Garden of Shadows
Christopher's Diary:
  Secrets of Foxworth
Christopher's Diary:
  Echoes of
  Dollanganger
Secret Brother

The Audrina Series
My Sweet Audrina
Whitefern

The Casteel Family
Heaven
Dark Angel
Fallen Hearts
Gates of Paradise
Web of Dreams

The Cutler Family
Dawn
Secrets of the Morning
Twilight's Child
Midnight Whispers
Darkest Hour

The Landry Family
Ruby
Pearl in the Mist
All That Glitters
Hidden Jewel
Tarnished Gold

The Logan Family
Melody
Heart Song
Unfinished Symphony
Music in the Night
Olivia

The Orphans Series
Butterfly
Crystal
Brooke
Raven
Runaways

The Wildflowers Series
Misty
Star
Jade
Cat
Into the Garden

The Hudson Family
Rain
Lightning Strikes
Eye of the Storm
The End of the
  Rainbow

The Shooting Stars
Cinnamon
Ice
Rose
Honey
Falling Stars

The De Beers Family
"Dark Seed"
Willow
Wicked Forest
Twisted Roots
Into the Woods
Hidden Leaves

The Broken Wings Series
Broken Wings
Midnight Flight

The Gemini Series
Celeste
Black Cat
Child of Darkness

The Shadows Series
April Shadows
Girl in the Shadows

The Early Spring Series
Broken Flower
Scattered Leaves

The Secrets Series
Secrets in the Attic
Secrets in the Shadows

The Delia Series
Delia's Crossing
Delia's Heart
Delia's Gift

The Heavenstone Series
The Heavenstone
  Secrets
Secret Whispers

The March Family
Family Storms
Cloudburst

The Kindred Series
Daughter of Darkness
Daughter of Light

The Forbidden Series
The Forbidden Sister
"The Forbidden Heart"
Roxy's Story

The Mirror Sisters
The Mirror Sisters
Broken Glass
Shattered Memories

The House of Secrets Series
House of Secrets
Echoes in the Walls

The Girls of Spindrift
Bittersweet Dreams
"Corliss"
"Donna"
"Mayfair"
"Spindrift"

Stand-alone Novels
Gods of Green
  Mountain
Into the Darkness
Capturing Angels
The Unwelcomed Child
Sage's Eyes

V.C. ANDREWS®

THE SILHOUETTE GIRL

G

GALLERY BOOKS

New York   London   Toronto   Sydney   New Delhi

G

Gallery Books
An Imprint of Simon & Schuster, Inc.
1230 Avenue of the Americas
New York, NY 10020

Following the death of Virginia Andrews, the Andrews family worked
with a carefully selected writer to organize and complete Virginia Andrews's
stories and to create additional novels, of which this is one, inspired by
her storytelling genius.

First Gallery Books hardcover edition January 2019

V.C. ANDREWS® and VIRGINIA ANDREWS® are registered trademarks of
Vanda Productions, LLC

GALLERY BOOKS and colophon are registered trademarks of
Simon & Schuster, Inc.

For information about special discounts for bulk purchases,
please contact Simon & Schuster Special Sales at 1-800-506-1949
or business@simonandschuster.com.

Manufactured in the United States of America

10   9   8   7   6   5   4   3   2   1

Library of Congress Cataloging-in-Publication Data is available.

ISBN 978-1-5011-6266-4
ISBN 978-1-5011-6265-7 (ebook)

THE
SILHOUETTE
GIRL

Prologue

WHEN I WAS a little girl, I often tried to run away from my shadow. I didn't like being followed. My father thought that was very funny, but I didn't laugh or smile along with him. My mother looked worried about it and tried to get my father to worry about it, too, but he never did.

My shadow wasn't there when I looked in the mirror, and when I awoke in the morning, I turned quickly to see if my shadow had gone to sleep with me.

"Where does your shadow go at night?" I asked my father once.

He looked at my mother and thought and thought about it.

"Good question," he said.

"No, it's not," she said. "It's spooky."

He shrugged. "Well," he said after a few moments. "If you look outside at night, you often see bigger and longer shadows, right? That's where your shadow and my shadow and your mother's shadow go at night. They go to join their shadow family."

"Stop it," my mother said.

My father leaned toward me when she turned away.

"When you lose your shadow," he whispered, "you lose the best friend you'll ever have."

Pru

SOMETIMES I ANTICIPATE an ominous dark gray mist in a patient's room before I enter it. The mist would be billowing in from the walls and ceiling as if there was a fire just outside the windows, but unlike smoke, it would have no odor, and it wouldn't burn my or the patient's eyes. For these patients, seconds that passed would be more like years rushing by. The earth would spin faster on its axis. They would sense time was slipping through their fingers. It was easier to hold a cup of water in your hand. Troubling thoughts would seep through their minds, staining every hope with the inky reality of a curtain persistently closing.

I didn't need to take a blood pressure or use a stethoscope to hear heartbeats slowing and ponderously pounding with desperation. Whenever I did and saw and heard the results, I feared my forced smile would speak volumes and put the patient into a panic, which would only make things worse. But I never let that happen. I was good at being soothing, being hopeful, and even trickling in laughter that lifted my spirits, too. To be a truly dedicated nurse, especially a cardiac nurse, I'd always have to help my patients believe there was room for hope. Pessimists in a hospital are like nonswimmers in a lifeboat. They are a constant reminder to the others of just how desperate the situation is.

When my father first heard me say I wanted to be a nurse, he nodded and said, "You're a good enough actress to pull it off, Pru."

"Why is it important for a nurse to be an actress?" I asked him.

"Oh, it's especially important for a nurse. Even if you dislike someone intensely, you can still make him or her feel welcome, comfortable, and you can give optimism even to the terminally ill, even if it's only getting them to believe they will live longer than their doctor has predicted. So much of life requires us to pretend to be someone we're not and say things we don't truly believe. That's a discovery you'll make daily, Pru. Don't fault yourself for it. For good or for bad, that's what it means to be an adult."

"A bit of a phony?"

"A bit of a phony," he said, smiling. "We all can't be a Sagittarius like your mother was and always say what we believe regardless of the consequences. For her, a friend was a potential victim."

I didn't laugh. My father rarely joked about something that he thought would impact on my future. He was intent on delivering his wisdom to me as I grew older, especially after my mother passed away. At one point, I sensed his panic, his fearing that I was nearing the age when I wouldn't value what he had to say as much as I had when I was younger and vulnerable. I know he felt that being a single parent to a girl on the cusp of becoming a woman made everything he said to me more important, almost desperate. He was afraid I'd become just another teenager full of herself, with an unseen umbilical cord tying me to my smartphone. My eyes would be stuffed with text messages. I'd make easily avoidable errors. *I should have listened* would be tattooed on my forehead and visible in every selfie.

But in the end, he would blame himself.

However, today I had no need to assume a false face and play a role in a tragedy. I saw no dark gray mist. If anything, the room I was entering was brighter than the sunshine splashing down from a nearly cloudless California spring sky. The ceiling seemed to have a halo. Unseen angels were holding hands in a circle, their feet gleaming with toes of diamonds as they danced with joy above us.

Douglas Thomas's life had been saved. He was well into his recuperation, and now his parole had come through. That was the way most patients saw their discharge from the hospital, a release from a different kind of prison. Illnesses prescribed the length of their sentences. I was the gentle jail keeper whose dainty hands wove tubes and wires, changed IV bags, and dispensed medicines with unpronounceable names. Some looked at me as if I was performing magic.

I stopped in the doorway to watch Belinda Spoon, one of my nurse's aides, help Mr. Thomas into the wheelchair, not that he needed much help now. She squatted to adjust the footrests.

Maybe more intentionally than everyone assumed, Belinda had a tendency to leave two, even three buttons of her blouse undone, revealing a cleavage that would easily swallow all of Douglas Thomas's long fingers right up to his palm. It was like dipping into chocolate pudding to find the rich dark cherries submerged like secret promises of pleasure. I had overheard her proudly refer to her ample breasts with that image herself. Right now, Mr. Thomas looked so mesmerized by the fantasy that he didn't see or hear me enter.

His cardiac surgeon, Dr. Simon, would probably tell me it was a healthy sign when a recovering bypass patient showed interest in sex. For Dr. Simon, interest in it was an indication of anyone's recovery from anything. Using that as a standard, the doctor himself was in perpetual recuperation. It was a wonder that he could get his mind off sex long enough to operate successfully.

Douglas Thomas had so wanted to walk out on his

own steam. For any patient, being able to do that was the reaffirmation that he or she was nearly completely healed, but I had explained that hospital policy and insurance concerns dictated that he be escorted in a wheelchair to his waiting taxi at Cedars-Sinai in Los Angeles. He was disappointed, but I rarely had a better patient when it came to following my orders like a child obeying his parent.

I didn't especially like to think of myself that way, but nurses do take on something of a motherly image, and patients, regardless of their ages, are often more like children. Men especially become little boys, and when they are past danger and discomfort, they want you to know they are back to being men. That twinkle in their eyes and the lust in their smiles reappear. At minimum, an attractive woman is sexually harassed in their thoughts.

"Cleared for takeoff," I said, holding up and waving his discharge papers.

He turned to me and with his long, spidery thin fingers brushed back his gray-spattered, dark brown hair, smiled, and straightened up in his chair. He had un-remarkable walnut-brown eyes, so dull that I imagined they were on some weak backup battery most of the time he was here. Just recently, they had begun to pull up some more energetic light. He was close to six feet tall, but only one hundred sixty pounds. From his chart, I noticed that he had lost a little more than six pounds during his stay. That wasn't much, but I asked him if he had been doing any dieting before he had been diagnosed. He said no, so I assumed he was always a slim man, with a narrow, tight face exaggerating his jawline. All the clothes he was wearing looked a size too large, but they had looked that way when he was admitted.

"Maybe I'll start eating more sensibly now," he told me on the first day he was out of intensive care and I had remarked about his weight. "My mother was always after me to put on some pounds. You'd be pleased if I did, too, wouldn't you, Nurse Dunning?"

"I rarely have the opportunity to tell a patient to gain weight. It's usually the other way around," I said, and he laughed.

"Maybe the first time you see me on the outside, you'll advise me to go on a diet."

Why would I see him on the outside? We lived on the opposite sides of one of the world's biggest cities. Accidentally running into each other at Starbucks or the grocery store was unlikely. He was obviously flirting, even in his relatively still weakened condition, but I tried to do nothing to encourage it. Too often, young women unintentionally send the wrong messages and get blamed for anything that happens. In this culture, it seems innocence is reserved only for men.

Right now, I nodded at Belinda and squeezed my own blouse closed at the collar. Message was delivered. She stood and buttoned hers, but not without a smirk, the expression clearly accusing me of being a prude and embarrassing her.

"Nurse Dunning," Mr. Thomas said, flashing a wider, healthier smile of delight, the sort of smile that makes a man look more like a little boy full of anticipation on Christmas morning, "I was afraid you wouldn't be here for the launching. I left something for you."

He nodded at the table beside the bed. There was a small gift-wrapped box on it.

"What is it?" I asked, well knowing.

"A token of my sincere appreciation," he said, looking more impish.

"That wasn't necessary, Mr. Thomas."

"I think by now you can call me Douglas, Nurse Dunning." He turned to Belinda and pointed at me. "This is the woman who saved my life."

I looked at Belinda, who wore that habitual tight frown on her face that she had whenever she was in my company. Her dislike for me was obvious. We were about the same age, Belinda twenty-four and I twenty-five. There was no question in my mind that if Belinda had enjoyed the opportunities I had, she would have become a fine nurse. She was practically one now, educating herself on the job.

But it wasn't jealousy that motivated her to be even more disapproving at the moment. Six days ago, just before I had begun my rotation, I had stopped in Douglas Thomas's room impulsively, like someone with a premonition. He was asleep, and Annie Sanders, the nurse I was relieving, a nurse who had been at Cedars four years longer than I had, had not woken him to take his medication, thinking she would return after she had tended to her remaining three patients. I had almost missed it, but the color of the pill caught my attention, and I pounced, waking Mr. Thomas in the process.

"What's going on?" he asked when I had scooped it up. He was in his second day out of intensive care. Bypass patients usually remained in the hospital for a week, some a bit longer. He saw the way I was looking at the cup with the pill.

"I think this is a mistake," I said. "I'll check on it, Mr. Thomas."

"What mistake?"

"Just relax, Mr. Thomas," I said, and started to turn. He reached for my arm. I was surprised at the strength of his grip around my elbow, the tips of his long fingers and thumb nearly touching each other.

"What is that pill?" he demanded.

"It's for enhancing blood clotting. You're on a small dosage of blood thinner," I said, and immediately regretted the revelation.

His eyes widened. "That might have killed me."

"I doubt this one dose would, Mr. Thomas," I said,

giving him my best reassuring smile, "but let me see what happened."

He took his hand away, and I hurried out to the nurses' station.

My informing the patient didn't go over well with other members of the staff. They thought I had spoken too quickly, maybe deliberately. As it was pointed out, all I had to say at the time was that there was a patient medication mix-up and not identify the pill and introduce the idea that we might have killed him. A recent estimate of death caused by medical errors in hospitals was at 210,000 a year. Some of the patients admitted were almost as anxious about that as they were about their illnesses as it was.

I regretted what I had told Mr. Thomas, but as my father often said, "You can't put the toothpaste back in the tube." Disapproving glances still floated my way in the hallways. Where was the loyalty to my associates? Cops don't expose other cops, and doctors dislike testifying against other doctors for malpractice. Why shouldn't nurses behave in a similar manner?

Belinda had pushed Douglas Thomas a little forward and was turning to wheel him out the door, but Mr. Thomas put up his hand to tell her to stop.

"I want to see her face when she opens that," he said, nodding at the small box.

"I got other patients to look in on," Belinda muttered.

"You ain't the only one bein' released today, Mr. Thomas. They're anxious, too."

"Just one more minute, please," he pleaded.

Reluctantly, she waited for me to go to the table and pick up the gift, the corner of her mouth so deeply tucked in that it looked like she had a finger hooked there and was pulling it open wider for a dentist to examine a molar.

"Go on. Open it before I'm shoved out of here," he said, giving Belinda a stern look.

I tore away the gift wrapping. There was no clue by looking at the plain white box, but I anticipated jewelry and not the usual box of chocolates.

That it was, an akoya pearl necklace. Thanks to my mother, I knew jewelry. This was no small gift and far from a token.

"Oh, I can't take this, Mr. Thomas. It's way too expensive."

"Hey, if I'm gone, what good is my money?"

"But you're not gone. You're going to live a long life." I sounded more like a gypsy fortune-teller than a nurse.

But he was only in his mid-forties with a good prognosis. I liked to know the basics about my patients, more than only their medical history. Douglas Thomas was a bachelor, never married. From the very small number of guests and the one relative who had signed papers, I thought he was quite a loner. I knew he was an accountant at a firm in Sherman Oaks. By his own admission, his interaction with people during his workday was limited, and from what I could tell, he had no romantic affair going at the moment, if ever.

I didn't pry with questions. However, he had been quite talkative here, mostly with me after the pill incident. I quickly learned that his father was in assisted living, suffering from early dementia, and he had lost his mother to heart failure three years ago. Like me, he was an only child. He was keen on finding similarities between us, which was not unusual for a man who looked past my uniform or maybe through it. Something in common was always a good launching pad for longer conversations. I tried not to have too many.

There was always such a fine line between being personable and being too personal when it came to how we nurses interacted with our patients, whether they were male or female. Sometimes I felt like I was on tiptoe, weaving constantly through a maze of mother-daughter, mother-son, and husband-wife relationships, because they were so emotionally naked when one of them was on a sickbed, possibly waiting for life-or-death decisions. I could see the panic in their eyes and smiles of hopeful expectation when I entered the room.

I dreamed of having the power that came from the laying on of hands. I might have saved my mother. That was a dream I cherished.

"Those pearls were my mother's," he said. "She'd want you to have them. It will make me happy and speed up my recovery just knowing you'll be wearing them, and when you do, I hope you'll think of me," he said.

"But, Mr. Thomas, a string of pearls like this? I don't know. Surely there is someone in your family, someone else who . . ."

"No one in my family saved my life."

"That's a little of an exaggeration, Mr. Thomas," I said, glancing at Belinda, who was shaking her head with disapproval icing her eyes.

"Not to me. Now, you listen. You were here when Dr. Simon advised me to avoid stress," he said, scowling. "If you don't take it, you'll be guilty of murder. Belinda is a witness. Right, Belinda?"

She looked at the ceiling, the impatience washing over her hefty body.

I sighed. There was no giving this back, I thought, and why prolong this? He looked like he would continue to argue about it and literally wouldn't leave the room or really would have another near heart attack if I refused to take it.

"Thank you, Mr. Thomas," I said.

He smiled like my father smiled, starting on the right side and then completing it with the spread of his lips. He put his hand over his heart.

"I'm happy you're pleased. Home, please, James," he

told Belinda. She didn't laugh. He looked back at me as they were going through the doorway. "I'm not through thanking you, Nurse Dunning. Get used to it," he said.

Strangely, that sounded more like a warning than a promise of something nice.

With the box in my hands, I felt obligated to walk behind them to the elevator and say good-bye to him there. Every employee stopped to watch us go by, their conversations put on pause. I pressed the box of pearls close to my breasts, not that I didn't expect everyone to learn about them as soon as Belinda had returned from delivering Douglas Thomas to his taxi. With the speed I knew she'd spread it, she might as well put it on the bulletin board at the nurses' station or do a PA announcement.

The smallest things could have great consequences, especially in hospitals perhaps. I had no idea at the time, but it was early days on the road to a far more serious, nearly tragic mistake than a single dose of the wrong medicine.

And this time, the mistake would be mine.

Like my father would say, "In the end, you own your own future, sometimes unaware you had taken possession of it."

Scarletta

AS USUAL, I ignored the steps, leaped off the school bus, and ran from Mr. Tooey's shout of disapproval booming behind me as I jogged down the block to turn into our light-gray-tiled walkway. Almost always, he threatened to tell my parents and have me barred from riding his bus. He never did. Once, I looked back and saw an irresistible smile under his bushy gray mustache.

I held my book bag under my arm like a receiver on a football team holding the ball and broke my personal record for sprinting the half block to our front walk. No one happened to be outside his or her home to witness my long strides, not that I would have paused to say hello or waved. I thought some of the neighbors were snobby, not caring to know us.

Because of the curly black line in the middle of each tile running to the edges, the walkway looked like a thin stream of ink flowing toward the front steps of our family's light-blue-shingled restored Victorian home in Pinckney, South Carolina.

The original house had been burned down during the Civil War. Ours was the third structure built on this lot, a lot twice the size of anyone else's in this residential neighborhood. We had gardenia hedges around the front lawns and Thuja Green Giant evergreens bordering the back of the property. The cloudless sky and early-spring sun had everything glittering this afternoon. At night, the antique pewter pole lights lining the walkway flickered like gas lamps from the days of Jack the Ripper. That was how my paternal grandmother disdainfully described them after my mother had replaced the far simpler and economical LED lights.

Our property had the tallest and oldest oak trees on the street, too, one on each side of the front of the house. My father had named one "The Duke" and the other "The Duchess." My mother never understood why.

"That's ridiculous. Neither," she said, "shows any sign of being masculine or feminine, Raymond. They're trees."

Daddy, however, claimed the Duchess had more curves and smoother leaves. I never said it in front of my mother, but I agreed with him.

Our home had been my paternal grandparents' house, and from the day my parents had inherited it when my grandparents moved permanently to their retirement home in Clearwater, Florida, my mother was renovating it, rebuilding from the inside out. She changed wallpaper, repainted rooms, ripped up flooring, and replaced all the light fixtures, even the one in the kitchen pantry. Every appliance in the kitchen, whether it was old or not, was switched out, including the sinks.

A seemingly endless army of construction workers and technicians marched in and out through our front door, usually over a wide swath of brown paper to keep the bottoms of their shoes and boots from touching our new floors. By the time I was eight, she had exchanged every piece of furniture with whatever fit her fickle taste. It was fickle, because some pieces hadn't lasted a month. When she had considered them over four weeks or so, she decided that they were either too dark or too light. Some were bigger than expected when they were actually placed in the room.

"You can't truly anticipate how something or even someone will look within four walls of your house," she said. "For most, it's too late, and they're stuck with their choices, but it will never be that way for me."

All this drove my grandmother crazy, not simply because she had spent so much money on everything that had been removed but because my mother's choices for replacements weren't all one style. She liked eclectic, something my grandmother called chaos. I never said it, but chaos might have been the better description. The dining room was far more modern than the furniture in the living room or my mother and father's bedroom. And the library-den looked like it had been lifted completely out of one in Scandinavia, minimalistic, with black bookshelves, black and white chairs and settees. It was a clean look but also a cold look. My mother claimed she wanted to enjoy a different feeling in different rooms. "Most houses," she said, "are monotonous."

My mother had decided to transform most of the landscaping as well, tearing out bushes and flowers, even small trees, creating rock gardens, and bringing in a fountain to be placed on the front lawn. She chose one that was a bit too large, with a cherub spewing the water from her mouth. My grandparents hated it when they first saw it, but my father didn't side with them. "It's Doreen's choice," he said, "and her choices are mine."

My grandparents left a day sooner than they had planned and rarely visited us afterward. My mother wasn't upset with their disapproval. I thought she even enjoyed it. It was as if she wanted to erase any evidence that anyone else, especially my father's family, had ever lived here.

I once heard her tell Daddy that she didn't want to be constantly in anyone else's shadows. "I make my own silhouettes," she had said. She was determined that the air would be scented with her flowers and the house would not remember the footsteps made by anyone previously. Old creaks were gone, and the wind would have to find new ways to invade the replacement windows, the new white shades with pink circles and velvet ruby-red curtains, everything too ostentatious for my grandmother's taste.

"This house is you and me mostly now, Scarletta," my mother told me. "Everything that came from your father's family is practically gone."

She didn't even want their paintings and old family photos displayed. The attic had become a cemetery. I never went up there because it was full of the angry dead. Sometimes, on wintry nights, I thought I heard moaning from above. Everything stored was abandoned like old people who were shoved away somewhere to be forgotten in a world where the living were dead before dying.

But despite all this, I loved my house. I loved the way it stood out on our street, and not only because of its age and size. There was something important about it; it was there for so much history. Even the postman paused to look at it a little longer than he gazed at other houses. It commanded respect, and on July 4, with the flag prominently placed over the porch, it resembled the lead ship in an armada proudly sailing across the country, the Star-Spangled Banner woven in the wind that powered it. Surely strangers thought that whoever lived in this house were special, very important people. I always thought we were.

There were only three steps to the front porch. With

a running start on the walkway, I leaped over the short stairway and landed on the recently restored hardwood floor, my feet slapping down with a solid thump. I thought I might have shaken the house, even though at fourteen and five foot six, I barely weighed one hundred ten pounds. However, I was already the second fastest on the varsity track team. Some said I resembled a deer leaping over obstacles, my long legs opening like scissors to cut the air.

If my mother saw me fly over the steps, she would have shouted her disapproval, calling me "unladylike, as are so many of those unsophisticated women who walk like men to show their defiance."

I paused to smooth out my pleated plaid skirt and straighten the right strap of my bra, which had slipped off my shoulder when I ran and jumped onto the porch. I buttoned up my sheer blouse as well. Teresa Golding had told me that sometimes I looked like a nun trying to smother her sex; so when I was in school, I undid the top two buttons, revealing the entrance to my deepening cleavage, where promises welcomed the fantasies of boys. My mother had seized my hand as if I was drowning and practically dragged me out of the house to buy me two bras the moment she had seen the buds formed on my chest when I was almost twelve. Right after she had purchased my bras, she warned me about permitting a strap to show.

"It makes you look cheap," she said.

"Why cheap?"

"I mean lower-class, like poor white trash, Scarletta. No matter what I do, that's the way your father's family thinks of me, so I won't have you looking like that. They'd expect me not to teach you the finer things, and we're never going to let them be right about me. Ever!"

That comment about my grandparents surprised me. Was that really how they saw my mother? Years later, when the storm clouds had thinned and gone, my father would tell me that my mother actually thought she was better than him and his family. That was really what she was always out to prove with a vengeance, and not vice versa.

Nevertheless, restoring my clothes to the way they looked when I had first left in the morning was something I always did before I entered our house after school or after track practice. It was as if our community still had debutante balls and I was about to be presented to critical society. Those festive occasions were rarer now everywhere, but I often imagined older women with their noses moving like the noses of sniffing rabbits, lined up on both sides of our entryway waiting to judge me and decide if I was ready to participate in social events and even find a steady boyfriend.

My mother hated it when I looked disheveled and unconcerned about my appearance, no matter how old I was. My father claimed even my diapers had looked like fashion statements. "Even when you were only seven, she made your appearance the subject of an important lesson."

He wasn't wrong, but he never sounded that critical about it. Most of the time, he sounded proud.

My mother pulled me to her side when I was only a little girl to watch her do her makeup and her hair at her ivory marble vanity table with what I used to imagine was a magic mirror, its ivory frame embossed with doves. I didn't have to be forced to watch her work on herself. It was fascinating. She sat down wearing one face, and in minutes she had put on another.

She trimmed her eyebrows and penciled them in; she added fake eyelashes to lengthen hers, and she used makeup to make her eyes almond-shaped, exotic. She instructed as she worked, talking about foundation, the right amount of blush, and the way to put on lipstick, even though it would be years before I could do what she was doing.

When she was finished, she turned to me and said, "Imagine a frame around you when you leave this house, Scarletta. Everyone is looking at you, so you have to be the prettiest you can be. Whether we like it or not, that's how women are judged in this world. We never stop being debutantes."

From then on, whenever my mother saw me looking less than what she would consider perfect because something I was wearing was out of place or I hadn't brushed my hair well, she would shake her head and say, "Frame."

My father had no idea what that meant. When he asked my mother, she said, "Girl talk, Raymond. You wouldn't have a clue."

"You could say that again, Doreen," he replied, but smiled. The sharper she spoke to him, the deeper and wider that smile would be.

However, the mystery continued for him until he couldn't stand it any longer. He took me aside one day when my mother wasn't home and asked me.

"What does she mean when she says 'Frame,' Scarletta? You can tell Daddy."

I didn't see any reason not to tell him. My mother didn't tell me to keep it a secret. It was just that I wasn't sure how to explain it, so I drew it and showed him.

"Of course," he said. "Of course. How dumb of me not to have realized."

"You're not dumb, Daddy," I said.

I was old enough to believe that a man who owned his own furniture-manufacturing company and employed more than two hundred people couldn't be dumb, even though he never had gone to college like my mother had. He had inherited the company from his father. My aunt Rachel, four years younger than my father, didn't want anything to do with the family business, even though my grandfather tried to get her to be a bookkeeper.

Instead, she attended Bennington College, pursuing a major in liberal arts, and then married my uncle

Benjamin, who had just begun his dental practice in Raleigh, North Carolina. They had two daughters, Tess, who was now eighteen and in college, and Nora, who was fifteen. We rarely saw them. My mother told me that my aunt was a snob and looked down on us, "because she was married to a professional, and we wouldn't have the money we had if your father didn't inherit the family business. I wouldn't have married the man she married even if he was real royalty. Your uncle Benjamin is dwarfish," she said.

My aunt was a few inches taller than her husband. She wasn't half as pretty as my mother, and Uncle Benjamin, besides being much shorter than my father, was nowhere nearly as handsome.

My father was six foot three and lean like a champion tennis player. He was a tower of strength to me. He could lift me with ease and, when I was very small, sit me on his shoulder and walk with me riding him like some Indian princess on an elephant. I loved being up there and looking down on people. Eventually, my mother thought I was too old to be carried like that. She had to say it only once, and when she did, my father brought me off his shoulder quickly, almost too quickly, because I landed like someone whose parachute hadn't opened. My ankles hurt, but I didn't complain.

"You're messing her up," my mother snapped.

My father knelt to fix my blouse and then looked up

to see if my mother was satisfied. She didn't smile; she just kept walking. Of course, now I had to walk, too, but it wasn't far. We were going to a restaurant "just to get out of the house," my mother had said. She had chosen my clothes and my shoes and brushed my hair.

Sometimes I felt like a doll, a toy my mother had decorated with this outfit or that, but then, when I turned eleven, she suddenly stopped doing it.

One evening, before we went out to a restaurant, I went to her room to ask her how I looked. Her approval was always the ticket to the outside world.

"You're at the age when you should be in total control of your appearance," she said, surprising me. "Especially with all I have taught you, Scarletta. What if I wasn't here? You had better start working on your self-confidence. A woman is never more vulnerable than when she lacks it."

I didn't know what that meant. Did she think I was already a woman? I was simply hoping for some compliment for the outfit I had chosen and the careful way I had brushed my hair, the same coffee-bean color as hers. There wasn't a strand out of place. Instead, she turned away and concluded by saying, "I have enough trouble looking after myself now."

I knew what she meant by that. She would burst out in howls when she discovered a new wrinkle in her skin or one growing deeper. My father told her she was putting her plastic surgeon's kids through college all by herself, but if she gave him that sharp, hard look, focusing on him with her unusual brown eyes with gray specks that looked like minuscule diamonds, he would retreat like a smacked puppy.

I had my mother's eyes, too. She told me so, making it sound as if I had escaped some horrible fate by looking more like her than I did my father, even though I and most of my friends thought my father was handsome, a George Clooney look-alike.

"We both looked up at the night sky as soon as we could and captured some of the glow of stars," my mother had told me. She made it seem as though we had been touched by angels at birth. I liked that. Everyone I knew thought my mother was beautiful, even if they didn't like the way she spoke to them. At Janice Lyn's house once, I overheard her mother talking about mine. She concluded by saying, "You have to give the devil her due. The woman is stunning."

I believed that and tried to imitate everything about her, even how she sat, held her fork, sipped from her glass, and especially her posture when she walked. Whenever we went somewhere, it was as if she was strolling down a fashion runway, modeling some famous designer's latest creation, her eyes forward, oblivious to the stares of admiration or curiosity she collected as she stepped forward. Sometimes I would let go of my father's hand and run to catch up to her and hold my head the same way.

"Both of you look like you think the world was created just for you," my father said once. It wasn't a criticism, even though my mother looked like she thought it was. He quickly added, "But why shouldn't you? I think it was."

As I grew older, I really was beginning to look more and more like her. Whenever anyone said so, my father would smile and agree. He'd say, "I don't know if I had anything to do with her. Maybe it wasn't a birth but a cloning."

He really wasn't upset. He was happy. "I've been blessed twice," he'd say.

My maternal grandmother was annoyed with him often, even before we had moved into my grandparents' house and he had approved all the changes my mother was undertaking. I heard her bawl him out for what I thought was a strange thing: worshipping my mother. He never said prayers to her, but she made it sound like he went to his knees and lit candles every night in front of the large portrait of her above our fireplace before he went to sleep.

My father had paid a famous artist from Florida nearly seventy-five thousand dollars to create the painting from his favorite picture of her in a gown she had worn to their fifth wedding anniversary celebration at the Carolina Country Club. Her dress was a tailored embellished silk and taffeta gown nipped in at the waist, with a voluminous pleated skirt. The bodice was French lace with shimmering paillettes. She wore the string of natural pearls and matching pearl earrings he had bought her for the occasion. I dreamed of someday wearing it all. It was the sort of gown that would never be out of style. It still hung in her closet, everything else kept away from it, as if another dress or a blouse would contaminate it.

Her portrait was really the most beautiful picture in our house and proved how true and important what she told me to think about myself was. "Capture your beauty in front of your own mirror first, and then share it with the world," she had said. Her declarations always did sound biblical. If anyone worshipped her, I did.

Imagining the frame around me now, I opened the front door and stepped into our wide entryway with the slate-tiled floor my mother had installed a few years ago. She had bought and hung a large antique oval mirror framed in walnut across from the coatrack. Daddy's soft full-grain black leather topcoat hemmed at the top of his thighs was hung there. It was a birthday gift my mother had given him nearly seven years ago, and he wore it so much, even when it was too warm to wear it, that it had begun to look like a second skin. At least, that was what my grandmother had said.

My mother's coat wasn't there.

Why was my father home so early from work at his factory? He was never home this early.

I heard a muffled cry and looked into the living room. He was sitting on the sofa, a duplicate of a Chesterfield sectional he had custom made in his own factory to my mother's specifications. He was leaning forward, his elbows on his knees, his face buried in his hands.

"Daddy?"

He looked up slowly. His tears were still trapped in his eyes, but they looked like they would soon drown him.

"She left us," he said.

The words made no sense.

"Who left us?"

"Your mother," he said, and leaned farther to pick up an envelope. "When I returned to the office after lunch, there was a message from your mother waiting for me. 'I left a note on the kitchen counter. Don't expect anything more.' So I hurried home and found this," he said, holding the envelope up but not really offering it to me. "A printed-out good-bye note. She's gone," he said.

"Where did she go?"

He shook his head. "She doesn't say, but she makes it clear that she is not returning. She took most of her clothes and shoes and almost all her jewelry. She mentioned someone else."

"Someone else?"

"She loves someone else," he said. "She'd rather be with him. I think they left the country."

Left the country? And forgot about me? I thought. Just like that? I had no clue that she was in love with someone else, and from the way my father was reacting, neither had he. How could she leave all this, us, the home she had rebuilt? Everything had her signature on it, especially me. She had practically molded me out of clay.

"Who did she leave with?"

He shook his head, and then suddenly, his tears broke loose, and his body trembled. I thought he would shatter right before my eyes. For a moment, I couldn't move. I rushed to his side. He put his arm around me and buried his head into my small shoulder. I was holding on to him as hard as I could, clutching him as if I thought he would disappear.

He caressed my cheek with his lips and held me as tightly and as closely as I was holding him.

"Now we have only each other," he whispered in a voice that sounded like it came from a stranger. "But every time I look at you, I will see her, Scarletta. I promise. I will see her."

From the tone of his voice, I wasn't sure if that was a good thing or not.

Pru

THE MOMENT I entered my second-floor apartment after work, my eyes went to the small dark-walnut stand to the left of the door in anticipation. As I had feared, it was there again.

The answering machine was blinking.

I knew the message wasn't from my boyfriend, Chandler. Before I had left the hospital, he called to tell me he was coming over with Chinese. He was quite aware that after an afternoon shift, I wanted to get home and have a warm soak and then a glass of Pinot before dinner. We went out only on the nights before my days off. He rarely suggested otherwise. After nearly five months of dating, we practically knew when each other held a breath.

I was holding one now, practically mesmerized by the blinking light. Of course, it could be a number of other people or businesses who had left a message. There were so many annoying promotions and giveaways. Why should I always expect the worst?

Nevertheless, I touched the playback button as if it was red-hot.

Hi. It's Scarletta. I'd love to borrow that beautiful pearl necklace someday. I look forward to seeing you wearing it. How are you going to explain it to Chandler? Men are so susceptible to jealousy. That's why they're the weaker sex. Maybe you shouldn't wear it. Maybe you should flush it down the toilet.

I think I would if I had a catch like Chandler.

The message ended with a small sound, like a swallowed laugh.

There was something vaguely familiar about the voice, the accent, but not enough for me to confidently identify it. She never called when I was home, and she never called my mobile. All I had as far as contact with her were these phone messages. Was that deliberately her plan? How did she know when I was gone? Was she out there, watching my apartment building, just waiting for me to leave? Why was she afraid to talk to me? Even if I left to buy some groceries or fulfilled another chore on my day off, a message would often be there when I returned. It was more than infuriating. It gave me nightmares.

After listening, I stepped back as if the machine was about to explode. This particular message convinced me that it had to be someone at the hospital, even though I couldn't recall anyone named Scarletta. But I didn't know every employee on every floor, of course. There were more than two thousand physicians and around ten thousand employees. Maybe it was time to tell the police or at least reveal it to Chandler. Of course, that was probably what she wanted, though, commotion. Bringing the police to the hospital, especially the cardiac floor, to interview other employees would surely not endear me to them, especially now.

The hospital was no place for the dramatic intrigues of the employees anyway. There was enough with the patients. All those nurses and assistants who were still angry about how I handled Douglas Thomas's wrong medication would amplify the derogatory talk already going on behind my back. I certainly didn't want any of them to know I had this problem. They'd giggle about it for sure, spreading the idea that I had somehow created this situation for myself, which they thought was typical for me. To most of them, I was a born loser, despite my efficient, professional, and intelligent nursing, but then again, I made sure they didn't know that much about me and certainly nothing about my social life.

More than one member of the staff implied that I was a little too familiar with my patients. They believed that I was too worried about being more popular than everyone else. No, I thought, if they found out about this, there'd be no empathy; there'd be no compassion for me. In fact, if they realized how anxious I was and how this was upsetting my life, their eyes would drip with satisfaction. Some of them could easily have their picture next to *bitch* on Wikipedia.

I had no doubt that once he found out about these deliberately vexatious messages, Chandler would be as intense about it as he was about anything else he deemed important. Talk about someone being anal, if he was fixed on something, it practically consumed his every breath and thought. Were all attorneys like that? He'd surely insist that we involve the police and might even worry about my being alone, here or anywhere.

He'd say something like "Stalkers today cannot be ignored. There are no pests, just perverts." He'd surely try to put the fear of God in my heart. He'd have me studying every shadow, listening to every footstep behind me. The whole thing would take over my life completely, which I was sure was just what Scarletta wanted. I'd never give her that satisfaction. Daddy often told me that when you act like sheep, they act like wolves.

No, I was convinced I was doing the right thing. This was something I had to solve myself. The police, even Chandler, should be the last resort. I was an independent woman, proud of my ability to take care of myself. I wasn't compensating for any inferiority complex, either. My parents wanted me to be self-sufficient. My father taught me that most mistakes are made because we're too dependent on this one or that one. And my mother's advice was "Bring a man into your life slowly. Compromise is certainly important in a relationship, especially marriage, but don't surrender your self-respect. Don't be too reliant. Always be in charge of yourself, Pru. Any man who doesn't respect that is not the man for you."

If I pointed out how reliant she really was on my father, she'd say, "Do as I teach, not as I do."

Her advice resonated even more now. Her words streamed across the walls of my apartment like breaking news on an electronic billboard.

I hadn't lost my self-confidence. One time, this telephone stalker would make a mistake, I thought while I was erasing the message. Hearing it once was enough, and right now, I didn't want anyone else, especially Chandler, listening to it and telling me she sounded insane and not simply malicious. Admittedly, he'd be saying what I was thinking but keeping buried and locked up in some chamber in my mind for now.

Don't let it take over your life, I told myself. *That's exactly what she wants, to get inside you so you carry her everywhere you go.*

Anxiety and fear quickly metamorphose into rage. I felt the heat rising from my stomach, up through my breasts and to my face, which I was sure was crimson. One time, she'd leave a call-back number, or maybe she'd get enough nerve to ask for a meet and suggest a location. I'd meet with her. Oh, yeah, I'd meet her, but with a hatchet. The more she called, the more vicious my fantasies were.

I knew that when I eventually did reveal this, the obvious questions would be asked. *Don't you have an unlisted number? Why didn't you change your number?*

Yes, I had an unlisted number, but what good did that do you these days? Those robocalls still came through, and whenever I put my number down for a purchase or something that required it, some company sold it for as little as a dime, along with the numbers of other customers. As far as changing my number went, I had done it since the calls began, explaining it to Chandler by telling him that I was getting annoying robocalls. He was getting them, too, so there was no doubt or question about why I had.

The solution to this was far beyond something as simple as changing a telephone number anyway. I wanted to catch her on my own and confront her, now maybe in front of other employees, and really embarrass and destroy her. I hoped she would continue to call. I prayed for it. I just had to be patient and wait for her to make a mistake and say something that made her identity clear.

I took off my dark-blue cashmere hoodie, one of my Christmas gifts from Chandler, hung it on the coatrack hooks attached to the light-blue-painted wall, and looked around my one-bedroom West Hollywood apartment in a building off Santa Monica Boulevard.

I had a living room furnished with a dark blue U-sofa sectional and a matching Empress armchair. The apartment came with a brown-ebony carpet, dramatic sheer white drapes on the two windows facing the street, and a large brushed-bronze ceiling fixture. I had an arc bronze floor lamp standing at the right corner of the sofa. I'd been living here nearly a year and had not yet put a picture on the living-room walls. I had none on the walls in the small dining room and none in my bedroom. There was a calendar on the one available wall in the kitchen. It wasn't that I didn't like art. I just had trouble making some personal decisions. It was as if I had two people inside me always disagreeing about what was beautiful and what was trite.

When I looked around, I realized that my mother, if she were alive, would throw a real shit fit right now. I had left a plate with the remnants of a turkey and cheese sandwich on the coffee table and a nearly empty glass of wine beside it. A copy of *People* magazine was on the floor, torn-open third-class mail splattered over the table, and the curtains on the windows half open on one side and wide open on the other. The windows needed to be washed. The room cried out for a good vacuuming, too. You could smell the dust. I kept talking about ripping up the carpet and putting down a wooden floor. My lease permitted it, and I could certainly afford it, but I hadn't yet worked up the energy and enthusiasm to shop for a new floor.

Sometimes I thought I was deliberately being untidy, like some recalcitrant, spoiled teenager who hated to be told what to do and would often do the exact opposite for spite. Why was I doing that now? Could you defy your mother even though she was long gone?

I started for the bedroom, paused, and turned to clean off the coffee table and pick up the magazine.

"Satisfied?" I asked the image in my mind.

That wasn't the end of it. The sight of the dinner dishes in the sink stunned me for a moment. What did I do, black out last night? Lately, I was so bad when Chandler wasn't able to see me. I couldn't blame it entirely on a late shift, either. At times like this, I wondered if I should give in and either move into his place or have him move into mine. Ironically, I, who was someone who took care of needy people at work, needed more taking care of than I'd admit. But commitments had been a serious issue for me for as long as I could remember. Whenever Chandler proposed something like it, I felt myself start to tremble inside. I'd smile and shake my head, mumbling, "Not yet. Give me time."

I knew he didn't need any more time. He could have moved in with me or asked me to move in with him only weeks after we had first met in the hospital cafeteria. I instantly felt how drawn to me he was the moment he had seen me. His sapphire eyes brightened when he turned his head quickly to look at me after getting his food.

I held his gaze and smiled to myself. What woman wouldn't admit, at least to herself, that she was flattered when a man looked at her like that, even a fat, ugly, old man? You still felt like a star, someone tracked by a spotlight everywhere you went.

He followed me to my table, and after I had sat, he asked, "May I?"

There were plenty of empty seats around us. I almost pointed that out, but instead, I shrugged and said, "Sure."

I could have promised him a new kidney or something from the way he reacted, quickly taking his seat before I could change my mind. I had nearly laughed. He was as exuberant as a teenage boy. It made the hospital cafeteria feel more like a high school one.

He was handsome in an interesting way, I thought. His chestnut-brown hair looked recently trimmed but not conservatively so. It was longer in the back than the hair of most of the professional men I knew. He had the front almost puffed into an old-fashioned pompadour, and his sideburns were just a little long. I thought he was easily six foot one or so and very fit-looking in his dark blue suit. It looked custom made. His cobalt-blue tie had tiny white beads. When he smiled, his firm lips hardly changed. If there was any imperfection to be noted, it was that his nose was a trifle too sharp. But it was like complaining about the potato chips when you were given a seat on a private jet.

"Chandler Harris," he said, and offered his hand. I gave him mine, and he held it a second longer than I had expected.

"Pru Dunning," I said. "Visiting?" I didn't think he was a doctor. If he had anything to do with the hospital, he was probably in management. That had been my initial guess.

"Yes. An important client," he replied. "But it's not only that. I really like the old guy. He had a stroke, I'm afraid."

"Sorry. Who's his doctor?"

"Cutter."

"Yes, a good man. Why is the patient your client? What do you do?"

"Lawyer. Not like in *The Good Wife*. I'm mostly boring business stuff, but sometimes an exciting negotiation. What floor are you working?"

"You make it sound like prostitution," I said, and he laughed.

"Sorry."

"Cardiac," I said.

"Well, it's not hard to see how you could win someone's heart," he quickly replied.

Maybe I blushed. I didn't feel it. I remember thinking

he was sincere. This wasn't just a pickup line. So I smiled, thanked him modestly so as not to seem arrogant. I knew I was attractive. I remember my father telling me that any attractive woman who acts startled and surprised when she's given a compliment is a true coquette, a flirt who knows how to do more than bat her eyelashes or put an invitation on her lips. "The trick is to walk the line between conceit and appreciation. Don't act like you get the compliments daily."

"So what drew you to nursing?" Chandler asked me. He held his smile, usually the facade of someone making small talk, but I thought he was really interested. "It is one of the most altruistic professions. No big money."

I raised my eyebrows. Actually, he sounded like someone doing a research paper now. I remember feeling a little disappointed.

"Money's important, but sometimes I think it was just part of my nature to become a nurse. It was inevitable. As a child, I hated to see anything suffer, even ants that had invaded our house."

All my life, I had been sensitive to the way most people rattled off questions just to fill uncomfortable silences. This man wasn't one of those people, I thought. Rarely did I reveal anything very personal about myself. But I recalled how much I wanted to back then.

"Once, when I was only about five, my father cut his hand fixing a pipe under the kitchen sink. He was handy that way. I saw the blood and, unlike others my age, didn't panic or freeze. I rushed to the cabinet above the counter where we kept our first aid, hopped up, took out the antiseptic solution and Band-Aids, and was at his side in seconds. He was rinsing it off. I'll never forget the look on his face. There was surprise, of course, but he could see something deeper in me. He let me clean his wound, dry it, and apply the Band-Aid. I remember the self-satisfaction, the feeling of accomplishment that comes from doing something really worthwhile. When I was older, I studied first aid more seriously, and from there . . ."

"To cardiac nurse," he said. "I'm impressed. Someone for whom her work is truly who she is and not simply a means to an end—end meaning a way to make a living."

"So you don't look down on idealistic people?"

"No, no."

"Most lawyers I know do."

He laughed and kept his smile. His eyes twinkled. Everyone wears armor when he or she first meets a stranger. It's only natural to be self-protective, to be careful about what you didn't and did reveal about yourself. His armor was falling away fast.

I remember thinking that I could fall in love with a man like this.

"How long have you been in nursing?" he asked. When I hesitated, he added, "You look like someone who just graduated."

"Almost three years," I said. "Two before I came to Cedars. And what about you?" I asked. "How or why did you become an attorney?"

"Not as romantic a reason as you have for a career, I'm afraid. My father was an attorney, a divorce attorney. I admired him, but I thought the work he was doing was more in the sewer of the legal world. Satisfaction was in the money, of course, but also in how well you could screw the other guy or girl. I wanted to be in law, too, but something different.

"I'm also afraid my parents were the stereotype story," he continued. Yes, the armor was falling.

"Meaning?"

"My mother was one of his earliest clients, previously married only two years when she hired him to handle her divorce. Soon after, they had an affair that turned into an engagement and another marriage for her. My mother had just started her teaching career when she filed for divorce. From the way she talks, my father was an unexpected bonus."

"Your father must be a charming man."

"He's a persuasive guy," he said, and smiled. I remember wondering if he was smiling with pride or just acknowledging that he had a slick dad.

"And then you were born?"

"Not right off. I'm the youngest of three. The other two, my sisters, are both married and live on the East

Coast, Julia in New York and Lydia in New Hampshire. We all grew up in California. Julia is married to a psychiatrist and has two teenage daughters. Lydia married a broker. They have a son, Clifton, who is in his second year at Yale.

"Three years ago, my father retired. My mother already had. They now live in the Hamptons."

"New York?"

"Yes. My father's younger brother, Winston, lives on Long Island, too. Let's see, what did I leave out?" he asked, pretending to really think about it.

"Blood type."

He laughed and nodded simultaneously, like someone who was confirming what he had instinctively believed before he sat across from me.

"Figures a nurse would say that. Are you from here?"

"Maryland," I said. "My father sold dental equipment and was on the road a lot until my mother contracted breast cancer. He worked in the company office then and remained there after she died."

"Oh, I'm sorry."

"Double sad ending, I'm afraid. My father was killed in a car accident a year after. Trailer truck jackknifed on him."

"How terrible. Brothers or sisters?" he asked quickly. He obviously wanted to know if I had to bear the burden of such tragedy myself.

"No, just me. I had an aunt in California who for a while was a surrogate mother, my mother's younger sister, a poster woman for spinster. Even an amateur psychiatrist could diagnose her sexual paranoia."

"So she's no longer your surrogate mother?"

"She passed away last year. A brain aneurysm."

"I'm sorry."

He looked lost for words after hearing such a stream of tragedy.

"I wasn't that close to her. She wasn't excited about my coming to live with her. People who have lived most of their mature lives alone develop pretty firm habits. A teenage girl can easily disrupt them."

"I bet. You're not married, I see," he said, nodding at the absence of a ring.

"I came close but no gold ring or silver," I said.

"Anyone in the running presently?"

We had told each other so much so quickly. At least for me, it was unique. I felt like putting on the brakes.

"I think I'm beginning to feel like I'm on the witness stand," I said.

"Oh, I'm sorry. I'd claim habit, but it's more than that. I really want to know more about you."

I didn't miss his meaning.

"What about you? I don't even see an imprint on your finger."

"Similar. Close to being close, but I'm too much of

a workaholic. At least, that's what I've been accused of being."

"Ditto," I said.

"Romance happens only by accident for people like us, or at least me, for sure. I doubt that you like to be fixed up. I don't."

"Spontaneity has its charm," I admitted.

"Like right now?"

I laughed. A laugh was such a simple way to avoid a commitment.

"Where do you live?" he asked. I described it.

"I'm leasing a place in Brentwood," he said. "Live alone?"

"Yes. Why?"

"I find it easier when there isn't a roommate."

"What exactly do you mean by 'easier'?"

"Asking you out," he said. "Otherwise, there's the roommate who's either jealous or deliberately too critical until she gets a date."

"You sound like too much of an expert," I said. "I'm just a helpless single woman with limited romantic experience, struggling to make a life in the City of Angels."

He kept his smile. He was looking at me more intently. "Why is it I doubt that? I think you're keeping your secrets."

I shrugged. "My father used to say when you lose the mystery, you lose a great deal of the passion."

"Sounds like a wise comment."

"But mystery has become more dangerous these days," I said. "Some people wouldn't have considered my comment about blood type off the mark. People are down to learning their prospective date's DNA before agreeing to meet."

"I'm willing to take a chance only on the little I know about you," he said. "Can I call you?"

No lack of self-confidence in him, I thought, but I hadn't felt a single negative note flowing my way from the moment I set eyes on him. Maybe I was more careful than most women these days, but even though he was handsome, charming, and obviously successful, I forced myself to be cautious.

I gave him my phone number but made it clear that I would only meet him for lunch sometime.

"Baby steps," I added.

"Why? You're not in maternity?" he joked, and then he put up his hands quickly. "I'm not greedy. Lunch it will be," he said. "I have confidence you'll fall in love with me."

Another safe laugh was my response.

Recalling all that fondly now, I scraped off the dish from the living room and began to rinse it and the other dishes before loading them in the dishwasher. My mother had taught me to do that.

"Dishwashers don't get it all. Nothing gets it all."

Despite my wishful defiance, her instructions haunted me. Sometimes I'd swear she was at my side, giving me that critical look, shaking her head and muttering, "What am I to do with you? Hope you marry someone so wealthy that you're surrounded by servants, even someone to help you dress in the morning? Princess Pru," she'd add. Funnily, it didn't sound like something critical. It was almost as if she wished it would come true for me.

After I turned on the dishwasher, I started for the bedroom and then stopped. Ever since I had started nursing at Cedars, I had made it a point never to wear my uniform into the bedroom. Chandler swore he never had smelled that aseptic hospital odor, but I did. Funnily, it never bothered me at work, but when I was out of the hospital and especially at home, it reeked and practically turned my stomach. I never told anyone that. It wasn't something they would recommend you say when applying for a nursing position or when you're trying to please patients.

I stripped off my uniform and brought it to the washing machine in the nook off the hall and dropped it in. Then I took off my shoes and deposited my socks. I'd wash it all later with other things that were piled in the clothes basket. It was teeming over, which was another sight that wouldn't please my mother, but I ignored it.

I went to my bedroom to take off my bra and panties. I hadn't made the king-size four-poster bed before I left for work. The oversize pillows looked trampled upon, and the pink blanket was still bunched and pushed to one side. It had been another restless night, but whenever I did make my bed, I made it almost military-style. You could bounce a coin off the top sheet.

I heard my mother's voice again, reminding me, "When you do something, do it right, or don't do it."

That was echoing in my memory this afternoon, so I didn't do it. I wasn't in the mood to do it right.

The only reason I would do it now was that Chandler was coming, and there was something about an unmade bed that discouraged sex in it for him. It didn't matter to me. I told him I could make love with him on bedsprings.

He kidded me about not being the best homemaker, but I suspected he wasn't kidding, as much as I wished he was.

"How can a nurse be so messy? Isn't immaculate built in to your work?" he asked.

"I'm a different person at work," I told him. "I'm sure you're a different person when you go to court or negotiate a contract."

"Maybe," he conceded, but no matter how I explained it, when I was compared to him, I was Miss Slob USA. He was one of the cleanest and tidiest men I knew. Of course, he didn't have to wear a uniform to work like I did and make sure that it wasn't rumpled and unkempt, unless I wanted to count his suit and tie as a uniform. Still, his clothing always looked pressed and cleaned, even at the end of his workday. My father was like that.

I put my purse on the dresser table and the gift box of pearls beside it. My telephone stalker had left a good question in her message. How would I explain it to Chandler? He was a Boy Scout when it came to procedure. He'd wonder why I didn't report it to the hospital manager or something. Wasn't there any rule about accepting gifts from patients? There had to be something, he'd say. Patients were so vulnerable and so dependent. People could claim that it was taking advantage of them to accept their gifts. There surely had to be guidance for things like this in the American Nurses Association code of ethics.

My head was reeling with all the questions. It actually felt heavier. My neck ached. Still naked, I went out to get myself that glass of Pinot. After I poured it, I went into the bathroom and started running water into the tub. I paused and stood before the full-length mirror on the inside of the bathroom door, something I had attached on my own, which impressed Chandler. I inspected myself like a pre–Civil War slave owner looking at prospects.

Despite the lack of real exercise, my figure was intact. My breasts were firm, full, shapely, helping to form this hourglass figure that was still quite evident when I wore my nurse's uniform. My stomach was flat, and I had the legs of a ballet dancer. Gravely ill men still looked at me with those judgmental eyes, especially the ones wearing oxygen masks. They looked like supersonic pilots. The mask emphasized their eyes following me about the room, making me self-conscious about my shapely bum. Surely they were thinking I was a ten.

What about them? Couldn't I put a number on my male patients, not for looks so much as for cooperation and respect? Mr. Thomas had turned out to be a ten for sure, but especially during the last few days, even he'd look at me with that "healthy male interest," as my mother used to call it, and see me more as a woman than a nurse.

Scarletta's latest messages were full of references to my figure and especially how I walked. "It leaves so little to the imagination. Stroking your ass would feel like smoothing out clay. I bet you'd love to feel my fingers between your legs. They'd feel like butterfly wings."

I could hear the real lust in her voice. She sounded like she was salivating over the possibilities. Where did anyone get the idea that I could have a boyfriend and also be gay or, as my father used to joke, AC/DC? It was just another way to intimidate me. I was sure of it. But admittedly, sometimes it stirred my sexual imagination. Was it only natural for a woman to look at another attractive woman and think of intimacy?

Maybe Scarletta hoped Chandler would get that idea and end his relationship with me. Maybe one of these days, she would call him and claim I had encouraged her. She might even make up assignations, cite some birthmark or dimple, and add some detail that would convince him. Shouldn't I prepare him for such an event?

Not yet, I told myself. I might still end all this without anyone knowing what had gone on. Then, later, I could accept the accolades. *How brave you were.* I could just hear some of them admitting that they wouldn't have had the courage.

I sipped more wine, closed my eyes, and took deep breaths to get myself relaxed, just the way I often instructed anxious patients to do.

In fact, I was so comfortable in the tub when Chandler arrived that I was almost asleep. I loved that easy space between consciousness and slumber, a space filled with nothing, no images, no threats, and no painfully sad memories. I was floating in true limbo.

It took a good few seconds for me to realize he was standing there in the bathroom doorway, watching me, that sexy grin on his face, his lips moist, the excitement brightening his eyes.

"I don't know how you can be a great negotiator," I told him once. "One look at your face, and I'd know when to demand more."

"I don't make love to my opponents," he had said when I suggested this to him.

"None you wish to? No pretty opponents?"

"The pretty women who negotiate are too unisex for

me. They all look like they would demand to be on top all the time no matter what, controlling everything, even when I can have my orgasm. 'Don't you dare have an orgasm before I say,' " he said, putting his hands on his hips and imitating an arrogant woman. "Some look like they'd give you a grade afterward."

"You'll always be A-plus to me."

"That's all?"

"How long have you been standing there?" I asked. He was leaning against the doorjamb now, smiling with just a hint of evil, like a boy in grade school teasing a girl he really wished would like him.

"About a minute, waiting for you to realize it. I do love watching you when you don't know I am."

"That's sly. And unfair." I sat up and laid my arms on the sides of the tub. I wasn't eager to get out.

"Only when you have something to hide," he said. I didn't reply. "Tougher than usual day?" he asked.

"Yes. We had three STATs on my shift, all involving defibrillation. One didn't make it. All occurred during the first few hours of my shift."

"Oh. You have to be so cool and strong to get used to that and continue working."

I appreciated that he didn't ask how old the expired patient was. Whoever died was someone's husband, wife, grandparent, or child. It was a loss that would take away a major reason for living, especially when it was a child, and sometimes as painful when it was a wife or husband of someone married a long time.

My father was fond of quoting Dante Gabriel Rossetti after my mother died. "Beauty without the beloved is like a sword through the heart." I thought of it at his funeral. It eased my pain to think he would no longer suffer a sword through his heart.

When I had told Chandler that, he actually teared up. I would never call him an overly sentimental man, but he did have his heavy romantic moments.

"I want us to feel that way about each other," he had said. I was afraid to agree. That seemed to be a bar too high, but I gave him just a smile and hoped it was enough.

He loosened his dark blue tie and took off his suit jacket.

"Coming in?" I asked.

"Does it snow in Alaska?"

I added some warm water as he took off his clothes. Men never think women can get hot watching them undress. Maybe it's a little true—maybe because they do it too quickly. They practically rip off everything so we don't have time to work up sexual excitement. They're so anxious to get it on. At least, most of the men I knew were. Chandler was different. Everything he did, even making love, had a grace to it, an elegance, even when he was a little overheated. His eyes always searched mine to be sure I wanted it as much at that moment.

Sex for a man had to have a resolution. There was such a clear and immediate goal to achieve. Sex for a woman was a never-ending journey. We could pause to sip some wine, even make a phone call. Maybe that was an unfair comparison, an exaggeration. We had the power of multiple orgasms. We had to wait to reload.

I believed that Chandler wasn't constantly thinking of all this. Underneath it all, he was really shy, although he'd hate to admit it or be accused of it. Masculinity required aggressiveness, not blushing and being tentative and unsure. Most of the women I knew expected that. Besides, confidence brought better orgasms.

Chandler was no virgin when we met, but I suppose the better way to describe him was that he was a man who would never trivialize his sex. If anything, he even took that too seriously. He reminded me of my father, who treated anything he had to do as if it was life or death. That was something that irked my mother.

"Why do you take so long to decide something so simple?" she'd complain. But he impressed me. Being cautious, analyzing carefully, paid off. Whatever persistence and ambition, whatever success I had really had been thanks to him. I don't think a day had gone by without his giving me some sort of advice. He was always so serious. It was truly as if he was my life coach, guiding me through every challenge, encouraging me after any disappointment.

"Don't be a woman who giggles after something she says that she's not sure of. It will warp your self-confidence and the confidence others have in you," he told me when I was barely more than twelve. "Sometimes your girlfriends sound like those old-time laugh tracks on television. They all giggle in unison."

But unlike my father, Chandler had a great sense of humor, sometimes too dry and sometimes bordering on sarcasm, especially with other people.

He tried to be oblivious about his undressing. The subtlety in his clever legal work carried over to his personal life. After all, he was a successful negotiator, catching his opponent off-guard, leading him or her into a trap, and bringing it to a satisfactory conclusion. I loved listening to him describe his strategies with an opposing attorney. When it came to sex, he would put on that innocent face for me, too. *Oh, am I getting you excited? Did I do something, say something?*

Naked, he approached the tub slowly. My apartment came with this very lengthy tub, more like a seven-foot-long bathtub for a queen. It wasn't all that deep. The fixtures were practically antiques. He thought there was something romantic about it. He said we were taking a bath together in the nineteenth century. He was right. At least my tub had character. The rest of the apartment was cookie-cutter but quite up to date with appliances.

Chandler had long, sinewy legs. He had been a star

soccer player at UCLA. He stepped in and lowered himself between my legs. I lay back, smiling. His sapphire eyes had a way of brightening like bulbs on a dimmer you could ease up slowly. His upper body was tight from years of exercise, swimming, and tennis.

"I got you your favorite, orange chicken," he said. "Lots of brown rice and fortune cookies."

"Will mine promise another unforgettable night?"

"Sure. I put that one in yours myself."

"Well, don't stop with putting things in there," I said, and deliberately exaggerated like a coquette, tapping my eyelids together.

He laughed, and then he leaned forward. I went halfway so we could kiss. His hands slipped under my rear end smoothly, and he lifted me like someone bringing a bowl of soup to his lips. He began by kissing my inner thighs and working his way up. I leaned back and moaned. His lips pressed gently as he touched me deeper with the tip of his tongue. My excitement twirled up my spine and had the room spinning. I had my hands on his head, holding him, keeping him prodding.

Then he pulled back and gracefully moved his legs under his body like a double-jointed gymnast, lifting my legs just enough to bring his erection forward like a torpedo. It made me laugh at first. He tilted his head, surprised, and then I moaned, and we began our slow, rhythmic motions. We had done it in pools, and we had done it before in my tub. He was extra gentle, because I wasn't leaning on something soft. There were men who made love, and there were men who made love with consideration, compassionately, and were just as concerned with your fulfillment as with their own. Chandler was the latter. Sometimes he also kept his eyes open and looked at me so hard that I stopped moving.

"What?" I asked the last time.

"You fascinate me. It's almost as if your face changes right before my eyes. I love the way you ride into ecstasy."

"Sounds like you're boasting," I said, and he laughed.

He watched me now, but then he closed his eyes and looked like he was the one riding into ecstasy. He looked so pleased that I was actually jealous.

"Hey." I shook him. "Remember me?"

He laughed. "I was just thinking that it probably feels this way in the womb," he said. We had both reached a climax.

"Are you suggesting male and female fetuses make love?"

"No. I just meant the warmth around us, the way I felt like we were floating. Leave it to you to come up with prenatal incest," he said, and I feigned being insulted.

He sat back. "Turn over, and I'll wash your back," he said.

I did. He moved the sponge over me sensuously, pausing to kiss me on the neck and shoulders.

"Have I told you lately how beautiful you are?"

"I'll check the DVD recorder," I said.

"Wise-ass." He reached down to stroke mine. Was he ready to go again?

I turned slowly. He kissed me but sat back instead and reached over the tub to pour some of the Pinot into my empty glass. After he took a sip, he handed it to me.

"The last time I was this pleased, I was in the womb," he said.

"You men are always trying to get back there."

I handed the wine back to him. He sipped and smiled.

"A nurse was probably the second person I saw in the delivery room. My father wasn't there. He was in court with a big divorce case, multimillionaire. And here I am again, with a nurse."

"Lucky you."

"I think every man fantasizes about making love to a nurse at one time or another. There's something about the combination of tender loving care and raw sex," he said.

Good time to bring it up, I thought. *Catch him at the right moment.*

"A patient gave me a gift today. I had to take it, or he would have had a setback from disappointment for sure."

"What kind of gift?"

"It's in a box in the bedroom. Pearls," I said. "Expensive pearls, a necklace."

"And you took it?"

"I told you. He was insistent. I didn't want to create a scene. This was the patient who was given the wrong medication. Remember? I spotted it before he had taken it. I told you about it."

He thought a moment. "This gift? It was on discharge?"

"Yes."

"Well, they can't get you on giving preferential treatment. Patients have left money to nurses in their wills and to their doctors especially," he said. "Still . . . I wish you hadn't taken it, Pru. Maybe you can report it when you go in and ask that it be given to a charity. That would be cleaner morally."

I nodded. And then smiled. "I knew you'd figure something out for me."

"How expensive do you think they are?"

"Thousands," I said.

His eyes widened. "Yeah, get rid of it. I mean, you can be appreciative, but . . ."

"You're not just jealous, are you?" I teased.

"Maybe," he said, nodding. "Should I be? How old is he? Is he good-looking?"

"He's forty-four. No. He's just a lonely guy who needed a heart bypass."

"What's he do?"

"Accountant."

"They can be lonely," Chandler said, and rose to step out of the tub. "I'm starving."

He held up a towel for me, and I got out, too. We dried each other's back.

"What about your day?" I asked.

"A boring estate negotiation, but my client was quite satisfied."

"We spend so much of our waking hours satisfying others," I said.

"As long as we satisfy each other."

I laughed, and he gathered his clothes and followed me to the bedroom. After we had put on robes, I reheated the food, and we sat at the dining-room table rather than in front of the television as we more often did. I could see Chandler wanted to talk.

I tilted my head, my eyes narrowing with suspicion.

"What?" I asked, watching him work himself up for some sort of revelation. "Something's up."

"I guess you can read me pretty easily. Remind me never to negotiate with you."

"Just give me what I want all the time. Okay, so what is rolling around in your head?"

"I think we have something special going," he said, "and I don't mean only because of the great sex, Pru. We have work schedules that would discourage most other couples, but we accommodate each other. We know the power of compromise. To me, that's special."

"Why is it I know you're leading up to something very big?"

He laughed but nodded. "That really is another thing that makes you special. And I don't mean your ability to read just me. But don't get overconfident. I pride myself on the ability, too. We each have a hard time hiding something from the other," he said. "It's futile to try."

I think I might have blushed, but not from a compliment, from fear. I know my heart started to thump harder. Did he somehow know about the telephone stalker? Had I left one of her messages on the machine when he was here and I was in the bathroom or something, and he had pushed the play button, perhaps out of curiosity or perhaps because he was afraid I was starting with someone new? Was this what it was about? I didn't care about the motives. I cared about him knowing right now, knowing too soon.

I paused, my chopsticks raised. On the other hand, maybe he was about to tell me he had slept with someone else? I didn't think him capable of being so loving and involved with me one moment and confessing to being interested in someone else right after, but I had learned something important in my young life: expect the unexpected, be a little cynical, and the shock of it won't be as intense.

"What is it, Chandler? We're eating. I'm worried about my digestion."

He laughed. "You know I've been with Taylor, Barnes, and Cutler for nearly five years now. They made me a junior partner, and I'm on the verge of becoming a full partner."

"Yes?" I said, lowering my chopsticks. Was my heart pounding? Was he going to propose, show me a ring, bring me to a yes-or-no moment? I was still not ready for it. I thought I had made that clear, and for this long, at least, he had respected that.

"We're opening offices in San Francisco." He quickly raised his hands, palms toward me. "I'm not moving up there permanently, but they've asked me to take charge of the setup. It's a quick flight back and forth. However, I'm going to be away a little more than I would be normally. The way you and I work, it might make for longer postponements."

"Postponements?" I smiled. "Lawyers. How much longer are these postponements?"

"Longer," he said. "I'm not ready to put a number on the days, but I'll work hard to be here around your schedule. And make weekends work when you're free, too. I suppose when you have some days off, you can join me in San Francisco."

"Time and distance test the strength of a relationship," I parroted. I was sure I had told him my father had said that to my mother when she complained about how much he was on the road selling dental equipment.

But did I mean it as a warning? Had I embellished it? He smiled and shook his head.

"I agree. Absence makes the heart grow fonder, but I can't grow any fonder of you than I am," he countered.

I scowled with skepticism. "What's to say they won't make you stay up there once you've set it up?"

"They already know I won't. Not unless you tell me you're working for a hospital there."

"Even if they offered you a partnership?"

"I've got a better one here with you," he said.

Who would be sweeter and more loving? I thought. I almost told him the secret of my stalker just to please him, but now I thought it would make him even more nervous to go away and do his work. Besides, I could handle it, I told myself. *Stop worrying.*

Couldn't I?

"Are you upset?" he asked.

"No. Yes," I confessed. "But I'll deal with it."

"Just don't consider it a STAT."

"I won't," I promised.

"Or fill the empty space with some other distraction, especially one that wears a jock."

I looked toward the front door and my answering machine. He looked in the direction I was looking.

"What?" he asked.

"I was just imagining you coming through that door after a postponement," I said.

He smiled and reached for my hand.

I didn't want to lose this. There was a promise of a better life coming.

She can't make trouble for me with Chandler, I thought. *Can she?*

Scarletta

DADDY CRIED THAT night. His sobbing woke me, or what sounded like his sobbing, so I got out of bed and went to my doorway to listen and be sure. I thought it might have just been a dream.

All our bedrooms were located upstairs. Our spiral stairway with mahogany banisters was one of the few things my mother hadn't changed. She did replace the dark brown carpet with a light brown twist pile that was softer, something that terrified my grandmother when she first saw it. "My heels could get caught!" My father had to walk her up and down when she went up to see the changes my mother had completed in their bedroom.

My father and mother's bedroom was on the east side of the house. She refused to use the bedroom my grandparents had, so now it was a room without furniture. She had removed all of it after my grandparents stopped coming to our house because they couldn't travel anymore, even for a short visit. She claimed she was going to order a new bedroom set for guests, but she never had, and since we never had an overnight guest, Daddy didn't pressure her to do so.

The room my mother had chosen for them was smaller, but there was no afternoon sun pouring through their windows. She didn't like keeping the curtains closed in the afternoon and said she would have to if she had kept my grandparents' room. She claimed the morning sun wasn't as intense, but you still had to be cautious.

"The ultraviolet ages you," she told me. "Even if you're standing inside and it flows in through windows, it still washes over you and damages your skin."

She didn't walk about outside with an umbrella on sunny days like other people sensitive to sunlight, but she always wore a wide-brimmed hat. She was famous for it. Her favorite was a Maison Michel stripe band fedora. My friends would tell me they were positive they had seen my mother because they had caught a glimpse of the hat when they had driven by some shopping mall or store. Sometimes they would just catch a glimpse of the hat as she was getting into her car.

"Scarletta's mom!" they would scream, as if they had just caught sight of a movie star.

Often she would wear it on cloudy days as well.

"The sun's rays still come through," she told me. "You're never too young to protect your skin. It has memory, and years later, it will remind you what you have done to it. I want you to protect yourself, Scarletta. You'll thank me when you're my age."

I knew my friends would laugh at me if I wore a hat anything like hers. At least she let me wear the hat that advertised our school's football team. It had a long enough brim to satisfy her, but many times she made me put on sunscreen, even to go out and play with other kids on the street or in their yards when she permitted it. If there was a smudge of it on my nose or under it, they'd groan and call it disgusting.

I continued to stand in my doorway and listen for what had awoken me. There it was again. It hadn't been a dream after all. Daddy wasn't crying loudly; it was more like moaning. I hadn't cried once yet. I was still in disbelief. It was inconceivable to me that my mother was gone forever. Only people who died were gone for good, but when I looked in her closet after dinner, I saw that the gown she had worn for the portrait wasn't there. That convinced me she was gone, more than anything Daddy had said. Yet I wondered, why take a gown you never wore again and probably never would? She might as well have put it in a glass display case like the gowns of kings and queens in museums.

I wanted to go to my father and get him to stop being so sad, but I decided he wouldn't like me to see him crying again. I was about to turn back to my bed when I was suddenly sure that I was hearing whispering. Was my mother back? Had it all been some silly mistake?

Full of hope, I tiptoed to the doorway of my parents' bedroom. The hallway was always dimly lit by two chandeliers my mother had bought. She had replaced the larger ones, declaring that the hall "looked like a shopping center." Both my grandparents had wanted it that way because of their failing eyesight.

My parents' bedroom door was partially opened. I pushed it softly so I could look further in. My mother believed in creating what was known as a feng shui bedroom, a room that would invite the harmony of sensual energy. I understood that my grandparents thought it was ridiculous, some sort of voodoo. Not many people knew about it. My father didn't talk about it, apparently, and my mother never brought a dinner guest upstairs to see the bedrooms.

I remembered her convincing my father of the changes by telling him their bedroom should invite a good night's sleep but also encourage the making of love, "something your parents rarely did." I wasn't sure what it all meant at the time, but I thought encouraging love had to be a good thing. Why wouldn't my grandparents have liked that? Weren't they in love?

My mother insisted that taking out the television set had to be done first. Daddy loved lying in bed and watching television, but if that was what she wanted him to do, that was what he would do. "Your mother is the captain of the ship when it comes to the house," he told me.

She then had him remove all the plants from the bedroom and put in an air purifier. The biggest change she made was to move their furniture around so the bed was not in line with the door. She stripped away their bedding and had the sheets, pillowcases, and blankets all changed to what she called skin colors, sort of pale white. She replaced the art with pictures that had men and women embracing and kissing. After a certain hour, she wouldn't permit any light but candlelight, except in their bathroom. I really didn't understand any of it but was afraid to ask any questions. She was still fuming from my grandmother's comments.

At breakfast one morning, I heard my mother complain about my father's leaving their en suite bathroom door open after they had both used it. If he came home late from some meeting and she was already asleep, he'd be quiet, but in the morning, she'd see he had left the bathroom door open and bawl him out for it.

"You're letting the positive energy escape," she said, her eyes big to emphasize how angry that made her. I remember thinking, *Is positive energy something you can see? Why can't I see it, too? Is it something only husbands and wives see?*

He apologized and promised to improve, but occasionally, he forgot, and she pounced each time, her voice louder, sharper. She accused him of not wanting passion and love in their bedroom enough. I recalled her doing that recently and wondered now if that was a reason for her finding someone else and leaving. All the positive energy was gone. Why should she stay with him?

When I gazed into the bedroom, I saw the bathroom door was closed, and I heard the air purifier running. I shifted so I could see the bed. At first, because of the angle, I saw only my father, but he was on his side and turned, bracing himself on his elbow so he'd be looking down at my mother as if she was there.

Was she?

I quietly stepped into the doorway to get a better view. I was surprised that she had left her favorite hat behind. My father had placed it on her pillow in their oversize king-size bed that he'd had custom made in an elegant gold oak. It was modeled on a baroque bed she had seen in Italy. He used to sing an old song to her: "Whatever Lola wants, Lola gets." She didn't care if he teased her as long as he did or got her what she wanted.

When the bed was delivered, I thought it looked gigantic, a bed for the Titans I had seen in movies. I could easily sleep between them, but my mother never encouraged that, even if I had a nightmare. She would simply send my father to sit by my bed until I fell asleep again. Usually, he did first, but I didn't tell on him.

What really surprised me right now was her pink lace

and chiffon nightgown spread down her side of the bed. For a moment, I thought she really might be there but quickly realized that it was only the gown. He had his hand palm down on the middle of it, and he was whispering. I thought I heard him say, "Doreen." Suddenly, he lowered his head and swung himself so that he was lying on top of the gown. He sounded like he was moaning again, and it frightened me.

I backed up slowly, instinctively knowing he would not like me watching him do this. When I was out, I turned and quietly hurried back to my room. I wasn't sure what it meant, but it kept me from falling asleep for the longest time. Before I did fall asleep again, I said another prayer, wishing that Mother would come home, that she would be there in the morning and apologize to both of us for giving us a scare. I dreamed it, too, and in the dream, I heard her footsteps, the way she would walk in those stilettos, sounding like she was poking holes in the hallway's oak flooring.

I was so sure of it that when I opened my eyes, I rose quickly and hurried out to my parents' bedroom. The door was closed. It hadn't been completely closed last night, so she must have come back, I thought, and knocked. After a moment, my father came to the door. He was nearly dressed, only his tie left to be knotted.

"Hey," he said. "I'll make us some pancakes this morning, okay?"

"Okay," I said, surprised he had an appetite. Wasn't that a good sign?

I tried to look past him.

"She's not back, Scarletta. I told you. She's never returning," he said. "She's gone off with someone. I'm sorry, sorry for us both. Go get washed and dressed for school. And do it all as if you expected your mother to be down there waiting to inspect you."

He closed the door.

I stood there, finally feeling that dreaded dark, cold sensation I had feared when I looked in her closet and saw her gown wasn't there. My mother was really still gone. No dreams, no wishes, and no surprise visit would change the reality.

There was something else to think about now. What would I tell my friends? Should I pretend this was not happening, pretend until someone's mother found out the truth and asked what I was telling everyone about it? The questions would surely come down on me like stinging hail.

How would my father deal with this? Would he tell his friends, his workers, his sister, and his parents right away? My grandparents were very old and sick. Both of them needed the visiting nurse's service. As far as I knew, he hadn't spoken to my aunt Rachel lately. She and her family hadn't visited us for nearly ten years. Would he call her now? Would Aunt Rachel even care? As people say, there was no love lost between her and my mother, or my father, for that matter. My mother said their Christmas cards were "deliberately plain and boring. Nothing was personal about them. They could have been sent to anyone, even their mail deliverer."

My uncle and aunt always sent me birthday cards with a hundred-dollar bill in them but never sent any to my mother or my father. I really doubted that my aunt and uncle would visit to see how we were when they did learn my mother had run off with some lover.

Maybe my father really was still hoping my mother would return, I thought when I left him, and that was why he wanted to be sure I dressed so as to please her? Perhaps he suspected that she would be here when I came home from school. He'd want to show her that just because she had left, it didn't mean he wouldn't continue to be sure I followed her directions for my appearance and behavior. All my life, he would tell me, "Your mother wouldn't like that," or "Do it at least to please your mother." Why would any of that change, especially after only a day or so?

I returned to my room. My mother had designed every inch of it. She had chosen the light brown carpet, had the walls and ceiling repainted a darkish pine, dressed my windows in dark brown blackout curtains, and then had my father custom-make my bed, dresser, and desk in a cocoa-tinted wood. These were the colors she liked for me. "For your age," she said, and just assumed I would not only not mind them but be appreciative as well. I suspected they came out of some book that assigned colors to moods and personality.

"Sometimes you grow to like something," she told me when I didn't look that overjoyed. "Don't judge things too quickly. Nice things, quality things, and beautiful things eventually become part of who you are. That's why I take my time even to pick out a doorknob."

If she did return, would I ever dare to tell her that I was still not crazy in love with my room? But what if she really was gone for good? Would I ask my father to change my room? *That's cold,* I thought. How could I even worry about such a thing? How could I even think it?

As far as I knew, no one else yet knew anything about my mother's leaving us. Maybe I'd go to school and act as if nothing was different. Maybe nothing would be different after another day. *Keep that candle of hope burning,* I told myself. When I was sad or afraid, my father had often said that dwelling on bad things brought them to life. Thinking about good things helped them to happen. My mother pooh-poohed that but did say, "I wish it were true, wish it was all that easy. Your father is a dreamer."

I stood at my closet, deciding on what to wear. My first question was always the same: was this something my mother would have chosen for me? Even long after she would make the decision, I favored dresses and blouse-and-skirt combinations that I knew she liked. I couldn't comfort myself by thinking that this morning she wasn't going to be down there waiting to see what I had chosen and judge me, not that I had much chance of choosing something she really despised anyway. She had bought everything in this closet. I never had asked her to buy me anything special. I was afraid to ask her to get me something one of my girlfriends had. When we went shopping, she didn't pause to see what I liked anyway. She would show me something and say it was what I should like, and if I didn't right now, I would.

She was always critical of what my friends wore. Either their clothes made them look cheap, or they weren't well coordinated. "Too many of your friends' parents care about what they look like only when they go out on special occasions," she told me. "Well, every day is a special occasion, Scarletta. You're always on the stage. I can't say it enough. People are always assessing you, rating you. I'm sure even your teachers are impressed with how I dress you."

They were, but that wasn't important to me. My friends weren't impressed with how I dressed. That was what really mattered. Most of the time, someone like Agnes Ethridge or Mindy Lester would make fun of me. I really wished we all had to wear school uniforms so I wouldn't have to worry about my clothes and whether my classmates or teachers would approve of them. Not one of my classmates really did, even though I occasionally was asked how much something I wore cost. I never paid attention to prices, and that annoyed them more.

"Scarletta looks like she belongs in a department-store window," Agnes told everyone at lunch one day. The laughter felt like bee stings.

"You know, she's right," Mindy said, pretending to really think about it. "Sometimes I see you standing and looking like a storefront mannequin. Why do you have to wear such expensive things all the time? You're afraid to move in them. A smudge is like a scar to you. Don't deny it. I see how you jump if someone brushes against you, and you squeal like a pig if someone steps on your perfectly polished shoes."

"She has to get dressed up for dinner, too," Jackie Hansford said. "Every night."

Jackie had been to my house for dinner, and my mother had been critical of how her mother had sent her to eat with us. She didn't hesitate to tell Jackie, who told her mother. Apparently, she was quite upset. She told me that what my mother had said made her whole family feel like people just off the boat or people without any taste.

"My father doesn't wear a tie to dinner, but Scarletta's does. Every single night, right, Scarletta?" she sang, her face full of glee.

"Yes," I said. What else could I say? It was true.

"Dainty, proper Scarletta the mannequin," she chanted, and then they all did in chorus, which made everyone in the cafeteria turn our way, most smiling and laughing. I wanted to shrink into my socks.

That night, I came up with an idea. I stuffed one of my sweater shirts into my book bag. Whatever my mother expected I would wear to school would not be coordinated when I put on this shirt. She didn't pick things out for me, but that didn't mean she wasn't ready to pounce if I didn't meet her expectations and shout, "FRAME!" I did this sneaking around with different shoes and socks, too. It seemed to please my friends and stop them from mocking me so much. I had to be excused to go to the bathroom right before school ended sometimes to change back, or I had to rush out fast, change, and just make the bus. Amazingly, no one noticed or maybe cared, but I thought that if I could keep my mother happy and my friends pleased, I was being pretty smart.

But then, one day when I was in the third quarter of the seventh grade, my mother made an unexpected visit to the school to get me. Her mother, whom I had seen only twice in my life, had died. Grandmother Natasha had been living in a mental clinic for the past fifteen years. When we were there to visit her, she didn't seem to know who my mother or my father was. She barely looked at me. I thought she must have been pretty once,

81

but now her gray hair was so thin I could see her scalp, and she was so underweight that my father thought a doctor wouldn't need an X-ray to see her insides.

"Just put a bright light behind her," he said. He shook his head, feeling sorry for her.

I didn't know immediately why I was being called to the principal's office, but the moment I saw my mother, I felt myself go into shock. I actually trembled. For a moment, I couldn't move. She was standing in the doorway of the principal's office and saw me in my deliberately disheveled clothes. Her eyes looked like they might shatter and fall like tiny shards of glass to her feet. How would I explain this? I thought, and then wondered why was she here calling for me anyway.

Before I could think of an excuse and ask why she was there, she stepped out, put her arm around me, and turned me down the hall as if she wanted to keep me from being seen by the principal's secretary.

"You didn't leave the house like this. Explain," she ordered.

My brain went into overdrive, desperately looking for an excuse, any excuse that would appear to make sense.

"We are doing a messy experiment in science class today. I brought this along to wear in case," I said.

She shook her head. "I don't have time for this. Your grandmother is dead. Go change back into your proper clothes and come out to the parking lot. Your father is waiting in the car."

"Which grandmother?" I asked.

"My mother. Your father's mother will outlive us all."

"Where are we going?" I asked. The word *dead* wasn't really registering in my mind.

"Where do you think? To arrange her burial. My father isn't here to do anything to help," she said. "Maybe he's dead, too."

Whenever she mentioned her father, it was said with such bitterness I half expected spit to follow. He had deserted her and her mother when she was only four. Her uncle George, her father's older brother, who was a rich investor, took care of her and her mother for most of her life. He provided her with private schooling and her college fund. He was dead now as well. His wife and children had inherited everything. My mother said his wife made sure of that. She claimed he had given her enough.

But she was finished with college by then, and she had met my father, so that didn't matter. She made it sound as if money and not love was the reason she had married him. Maybe that was why she had turned to feng shui. She thought it was time to bring love into their marriage.

I wondered why I had to go along to arrange a burial, but I rushed to my locker to get my bag and then hurried into the bathroom to change and fix my hair. I was still trembling when I stepped out of the school and ran to my father's car. When I got in, he turned around to smile at me.

"Hey," he said. He didn't seem to care about my having to change my clothes, but I was pretty sure my mother had given him two earfuls of complaints about what I had been wearing.

"Don't 'hey' her, Raymond. I've been teaching her how to properly greet people all her life." She looked me over. "Fix the collar of your blouse. It's uneven," she said. "Let's go. Let's get this over with," she told my father.

He might as well have been our limousine driver taking orders, I thought.

For some reason, my mother believed it was necessary for me to see her mother laid out in the undertaker's parlor. Usually, everything she made me do in my life was some sort of lesson for when I was older. What could this one be?

As if she could hear me wonder, she turned to me and said, "I want you to know what death is, really is, and what's involved when it's someone in your family. I don't expect you to shed tears for either grandmother, but especially not this one. Don't worry about that," she added.

She certainly wasn't shedding any for her own mother. For a passing moment, I was worried that I would grow up to be like her and not shed any tears for her. How terrible even to think it.

When we arrived and I looked at my grandmother,

I didn't think she looked much different from the last time I had seen her. Before I could stop myself, I said so. However, when my mother turned to me, she didn't look angry.

"Astute observation, Scarletta. She died a long time ago," she said. "It was just that no one told her."

I thought that was really a very strange thing to say. How could you not know you were dead? When I looked at my father, he shrugged. He had been relatively silent the whole trip and wasn't saying much now. It wasn't the first time he'd acted as if we were stepping carefully on thin ice.

"Say good-bye to your grandmother," my mother ordered. She pressed her hand behind my shoulder and pushed me closer to my grandmother's body. "We're not going to have any sort of formal funeral. Nobody who would know her cares, and most are dead. I don't want you missing any more school over this."

My father rushed forward to take my hand when he saw how shocked I was. I had heard dead people smell, and right now, her eyes were open. If she was dead, why weren't they closed? Maybe she really didn't die, but they thought she had. What if she suddenly turned to look at me with that strange angry and confused expression?

"Say a silent prayer," he whispered. "Like you do before you go to sleep."

Sometimes, I thought. *I don't pray all the time.*

I really had nothing to say when I looked at my grandmother, but I tried to appear like I was reciting a prayer.

"All right," my mother said. "My conscience is relieved. Just wait in the other room," she told me.

She had brought me to relieve her conscience? What did that mean?

My mother and my father went in to speak to the funeral director and left me in the room where coffins were on display with their price tags. I was afraid to look into any. Maybe a dead body would be in one and his or her eyes would be wide open, too.

I decided to step outside to wait. There was no place to sit, so I sat on the sidewalk and watched the traffic and people. To me, it seemed like everyone passing was avoiding looking at the funeral parlor. It was probably too much of a reminder of what awaited everyone.

"Scarletta!" my mother screamed when she and my father finally emerged. "How could you sit on the dirty sidewalk wearing that skirt? It cost more than two hundred dollars!"

I got up quickly, and she spun me around to inspect it. I felt her slap at it, hitting my rump sharply as she chased off the dust and dirt.

"Your father is taking us out to dinner on the way home," she said. "We don't have time to go home and change, Scarletta. That's another reason why you must always treat your clothes like holy robes. You never know where you'll be going and which people will be looking at you."

"Okay, Mom," I said. I didn't often call her Mom. I didn't think she liked it. The truth was, I did it mostly when I was angry because of something she had said or done to me.

She shook her head as if I was close to a lost cause, and we got into the car. Once we were away from the funeral parlor, my father talked about happier things, like how well his business was doing and his idea for a vacation for us all.

"Her sister-in-law won't contribute a penny," my mother said, ignoring him as if she hadn't heard a word. "I won't even bother to tell her she died."

"No problem, Doreen. We don't need her money."

She looked at him. "I bet when your mother or father dies, your sister won't bother to do anything, either, Raymond."

"My parents have all that arranged. Besides, we live with our own conscience and let everyone else live with their own," my father said.

"Oh, please, Mr. Forgiveness. It amazes me you make money in the cutthroat business world."

"You get more with honey than vinegar," my father said, smiling. She couldn't get him angry enough to say something nasty back to her, I thought, even if she stepped on his foot deliberately with one of her stiletto shoes. He might not even say "Ow."

My mother was silent, and then she turned around and peered at me. "You're lying about your clothes, Scarletta. I'll ask your science teacher tomorrow."

I gazed out the window, the tears icing my eyes. They were not tears of fear or sorrow; they were tears of anger and disappointment.

I would never please her, I thought.

"Well?"

"My friends make fun of the way I'm dressed," I said. "They think I'm some mannequin in an expensive store window."

"I thought so. Listen to me, Scarletta. Don't live to please everyone else, or you'll never be happy. Besides, you have higher standards now, my standards. Someday you'll thank me. Do you understand? Do you?"

"Yes," I said. I understood.

I understood my mother wanted everything done her way. She wanted me to grow up faster. The things she designed for me, the lessons she taught, were all more for a grown woman, I thought. I wasn't going to have a chance to be a real teenager. Why wasn't she able to see that? Why wasn't she worried about my feelings now? Why didn't she think it was important for me to have friends and be popular enough to be invited to parties? I wondered if she was ever really a teenager.

My eyes were glazed with tears; this time, they were warm tears of sorrow.

Mostly for myself.

I could even see myself lying where my grandmother was lying, my eyes as glassy, stunned that no one was really crying about me because I didn't have any friends.

How many times do you die before you die? I wondered.

Pru

CHANDLER COULDN'T RETURN the weekend after he
left for San Francisco. Things weren't going as quickly
and as smoothly as he had hoped, he said, and apologized. I had half expected this would happen. My father
was fond of quoting Robert Burns: "The best-laid plans
of mice and men oft go awry." He taught me to anticipate
disappointment. Nothing worried him more than my losing faith and hope.

   "Take every promise with a grain of salt," he advised.
He recognized that the danger was to turn me into a
cynic and pessimist. "It's a delicate balance," he said.
"You spend most of your life trying to find it. I'm afraid
that this applies to nothing more than it does to your
relationships with men. We're notorious liars but often
not deliberate and often unaware of what we're lying
about ourselves. Complicated," he said, smiling, "but
we're worth it. I'm just being honest, honey."

Was he? Could it be true that men were more honest about themselves with their daughters than they were with their wives? Nothing seemed that complicated for my mother. She lived in a simpler world and usually ignored anything that made it more complex. It was always black or white, this or that, and if she couldn't think that way, she would be silent. I suppose being that complacent made life more comfortable. I didn't think it would for me, or for Chandler and me if we ever did marry. I was too opinionated. Perhaps that courage to say what I thought came from my training to be a nurse. If you didn't show authority, patients would have less faith in you, even if they didn't like being bossed.

I was on duty Saturday, and with only Sunday off, I thought it best to wait another week rather than fly up and back within twenty-four hours. Chandler was disappointed.

"Even one day with you tides me over. 'It restoreth my soul,'" he joked.

Maybe it wasn't such a joke. People in love came dangerously close to worshipping each other, but from how I saw it, this was true for women more than men. My mother once warned me, "Don't be with a man who worships you, Pru. Once you do something that displeases him, it will be harder to get back to where you two were."

"I'll call you on Sunday every chance I get," Chandler promised, perhaps because I was so silent.

"Okay. I'll message you my schedule for the next two weeks so we can try to plan better."

"As long as you hold to it and don't trade shifts with someone for whom you feel sorry. I know you want to have more of the staff like you, Pru, but don't let them take advantage of you."

Like Scarletta? I thought.

"I don't care if more of the staff likes me. I'm not in a popularity contest, Chandler."

"Okay. You're working toward that two-week vacation in June, right?"

"Right. But it won't be much of a vacation if I go up to San Francisco to watch you work, Chandler."

"Oh, I'll be done by then, and we'll go someplace where neither of us has any distractions," he said. "Love you, Pru. Really."

"I know. I miss you, too. That's why I sound so angry at your being so ambitious," I confessed.

He laughed. He liked that. "Don't take it out on a patient," he joked. "Hey. What did you do with those pearls?"

"I pawned them."

"What?"

"Joke," I said. "I'm working on it. As you suggested, donating to a charity, maybe. Just trying to think of the right one."

I didn't want to admit that every time I looked at them, I postponed doing something with them. As I had anticipated, Belinda had told everyone on the floor about the gift. Annie Sanders came at me with knives in her eyes once she heard.

"You're really exploiting my mistake, aren't you?" she accused. "Expensive gifts."

"I didn't want to take the pearls. I was just avoiding a scene. I'm working on the best place to donate them."

"Oh, I bet you are," she said. "Like to your jewelry box," she added, and walked off.

I hated still having to defend myself for catching her medical error. I knew she had been questioned about it, and it might have gone into her file or something, but I wasn't going to feel an iota of guilt. The bottom line was that the wrong medication could have been taken by a recuperating heart-bypass patient.

As I watched her stomp off, I thought she could very well be Scarletta. I didn't know all that much about Annie Sanders. Fact was, I didn't hear her talk much about herself at all. I dared not ask any questions now, of course. It would look like I had it in for her or something. No one would side with me. But I made a mental note to be more observant and listen to her other conversations whenever possible.

"Okay," Chandler said. "Yes, a charity is probably the best alternative. Talk to you soon," he promised.

I didn't sleep well that night. I got up twice because I thought I heard my mobile ring, but it hadn't. The second time I got up, I also thought I saw the answering machine blinking and rushed over to it, only to see it wasn't. I chastised myself for being so uptight about it. *You're letting this get to you, Pru Dunning*, I told myself. *It will soon affect your health. Inform the police or Chandler, and get help. End it.*

I returned to bed thinking that was exactly what I would do in the morning, but when I awoke, I felt stronger again and more determined than ever to solve the problem on my own. If there was any doubt that most of my coworkers at the hospital would take some delight in my problem, that doubt was gone now that they all knew about the pearls. Most of them wouldn't know how to appreciate such a gift. It was truly "pearls before swine." But they'd still resent me for having it.

Anyway, when I had no messages for three straight days, I thought to myself that this Scarletta or whatever she called herself was finally getting tired of the game. Without actually talking to me, what was she getting out of it anyway? How did she know she was annoying me? Was she watching me at work to see if it was hurting my performance? If it was Annie Sanders and that was her goal, she was sorely disappointed. None of the other nurses received as many compliments from doctors and the relatives of patients on his or her work as I did, especially during those three days.

But I had a bigger surprise in store for me the following Wednesday. That day, I had the late shift. Trying to work my way back into the favor of others on the floor despite how unconcerned I had pretended to be when Chandler mentioned it, I traded some time with Sue Cohen, who needed the day off for a family matter. I agreed to change to her morning shift even though I had worked the late shift the previous day. Claudia Eden took mine. Sue thanked me profusely for helping to work it out, and it quieted some of my critics. Since it was one of those rare all-day rains in Los Angeles, I decided I'd rather work anyway.

The rain became a misty drizzle on my way home. Inclement weather had the effect of putting me in a sexy mood. I wished Chandler were here. I'd make love to him in special ways. Some men might complain, but Chandler enjoyed being teased. I hadn't done it yet, but I fantasized about dressing in a fresh nurse's uniform and pretending he was my patient.

"It's time to take your temperature," I'd say.

"Please do," he surely would reply.

Is this who you really are? he'd surely wonder.

So would I, but sex finds another you within yourself sometimes.

I stopped to get some groceries, and at one point, I

was suddenly thrown back to a world of memories in the aisle displaying cleaning fluids, powders, and equipment. My mother practically bought a new mop every week. She was neurotic about dirt. I didn't know why I went down this aisle. I didn't have to buy anything. I had so much left over from last month, but the visions I had of shopping with her and listening to her diatribes against germs were mesmerizing. I could feel her beside me now as I often did.

How ironic it was to think of her dying of cancer. All of it was an unending nightmare that trailed behind me, waiting for an opportunity to leap into the front of my thoughts and hold me hostage to fears of the unseen and the sadness of her being gone so abruptly. It was as if Death had snapped his fingers. This was the supermarket aisle of irony. It wasn't hard to imagine there was something carcinogenic in one of those cleaning fluids. From time to time, the EPA took something off the market. In my memory, I saw a woman literally scrubbing herself into the hands of Death. Wasn't that my mother chasing her own demons? It certainly wasn't me. Maybe that was why I wasn't America's Little Housekeeper. Or maybe all this was a convenient rationalization to defend my laziness.

I took so long choosing between things, pondering the ingredients in soups and the percentages of vitamins, sugar, and salt in everything else, that I ended up buying some ready-made salad and salmon for dinner. Since starting a relationship with Chandler, I couldn't get excited about dinners alone anymore. It seemed more like just another chore. Few activities emphasized how lonely you were more than eating by yourself. Everyone talked to himself or herself at one time or another, maybe most of the time, but it was never louder or more intense than when there was no one else there at dinner. You ate faster; you didn't really taste the food.

After I parked my car in the underground garage, I headed up on the elevator because I was carrying two somewhat heavy bags. It was an extraordinarily slow elevator. All the tenants complained, some afraid it would have heart failure between the garage and their floor. Ordinarily, I avoided it. I favored the exercise, despite how much I walked in the hospital. When the doors opened on the second floor this time, I nearly dropped both bags of groceries.

Standing there in a dark blue pin-striped suit and a light blue tie was Douglas Thomas. He was holding a bottle of Dom Pérignon champagne with a pink ribbon tied around the neck of it. His hair had been recently trimmed, and he looked much healthier than he had the day he was discharged. His cheeks were rosy, and there was far more brightness in his eyes. I thought he had even gained at least a half dozen pounds. He had obviously followed my and his doctor's orders when it came to his eating habits.

All of that aside, I was upset. Such a thing as a surprise visit at my home challenged my professional status. It was a crack in the imaginary wall I knew we had to maintain to keep our authority. I was never snobby about it; I was merely correct. You don't cross this line. It causes you to lose the magic, and a good nurse has to possess some magic.

"Mr. Thomas. Why are you here?"

"Hi there, Nurse Dunning. Maybe for today I can call you Pru?" he asked.

"I'd rather you didn't. How did you . . . you found out where I lived?"

"Didn't take Sherlock Holmes," he said, smiling. "A little bird whispered it in my ear. There are more of them than you know flying around in that hospital. Gossip transfusions," he added, smiling at how clever he thought he was.

"How did you get into the building?"

"Buzzed a few until someone answered, and I said, 'Flower delivery.' Saw it in a movie once. So much for security, I'm afraid."

"Why are you here?" I asked, my voice still quite formal and sharp.

"I wanted to share this with you today," he said, lifting the bottle of champagne. "I returned to work this morning following the schedule you and Dr. Simon outlined for me, but I made sure they understood it was for only a half day, each day for a week. My boss had no problem with that."

"But—"

He rushed forward to take one of my grocery bags.

"Forgive me for permitting you to stand there like that so long. I'm just so excited to see you."

I let him take the bag. Big mistakes begin with small failures of caution.

"They gave me this bottle this morning at the firm. It was too early to open it, and besides, I really didn't want to share it with them."

He stood there waiting for me to say something, do something.

"This is not—"

"Oh, let's not refer to rules or regulations or anything ethical written in some book of codes," he quickly interjected. "You did a wonderful thing for me, and I wanted to be sure to celebrate my restoration with you. That's all. I'm not asking you to do anything more," he said, smiling. He lifted the bottle again. "It's a harmless little gesture, don't you think?"

The irony we live with is that we do have pure animal instincts. Becoming civilized doesn't kill them completely, but we rarely listen to them. At the moment, mine were telling me to put a quick end to this. A voice inside me was saying that I should thank him for the thought but point out that I had a personal life outside of my work and the hospital. I didn't want to hurt his feelings, yet I wanted to make it clear to him that I had feelings to consider as well.

"I think you should have asked me about this first, Mr. Thomas."

"They wouldn't give me your number at the hospital, and you're not listed," he said. "I knew there was no way to get your mobile." He lifted the bottle again. He was depending entirely on his prop for this scene. "It was just a harmless spontaneous idea. The last person in the world I'd want to upset is you, Nurse Dunning."

He smiled that little-boy smile I had seen so often when he was recuperating.

"Please don't be upset with me," he pleaded. "I'll never forgive myself if you're distressed with something I do."

He did look helplessly sincere. It just wasn't in my nature to be cruel. I sighed and nodded.

"Thank you," he said.

"My apartment is a mess," I warned him. "I was going to attend to it this afternoon."

"A couple of clean glasses is all we need," he said.

I moved forward to insert my key. He stood beside me, close enough for me to feel his breath on my neck. I imagined him holding that little-boy smile, but now perhaps it was becoming something more. I felt I should make it perfectly clear to him that I was seeing someone, that I was in a serious relationship. But I also thought I might be assuming too much. He was so excited by this simple little gesture, he'd be surprised I had read anything else into it. I'd feel like a fool, too.

As soon as I opened the door, I looked at the small table and saw there were no messages on my answering machine. He didn't see me breathe a sigh of relief.

"Looks comfortable," he said, referring to my apartment.

"No matter what you say, I'm sure you keep your place nicer and neater than this," I said.

"Oh, no, Nurse Dunning. I'm no one to criticize anyone else. Mine might be condemned by the health department."

"Somehow I doubt that, Mr. Thomas," I said.

At least I hadn't left any dirty dishes on the coffee table, and there were no magazines on the floor. The kitchen was a whole other scene, however. Everything from breakfast was still on the table. Fortunately, there was room for my grocery bags on the counter.

"Just put it here, thanks," I said.

He did so. I started to unload my groceries and put away what needed to be kept cold before I went for some glasses. I actually had champagne glasses, something Chandler had bought for me when he wanted to celebrate our first date's monthly anniversary. Douglas stepped back to watch me rinse them out and then clear some dishes and the box of cereal off the table.

"We really should chill this champagne a little," he suggested. "It was cold at the office, of course, but by the time I got here and you arrived . . . I didn't know you had gone shopping after work, of course."

"You waited out there for more than an hour?"

"I knew you'd be back soon."

"But standing out there that long . . ."

"I'm fine," he said. "Accountants by their nature have lots of patience. Should we put the champagne in your freezer for ten minutes?"

"It's all right as it is. Let's open it here and have a glass in the living room," I said. Why prolong this? I was suddenly his nurse again, practically prescribing when he should breathe. He heard the authoritative tone in my voice.

"Whatever you say."

The living room was closer to the front door, I thought. I wanted to get rid of him as quickly as I could. His surprising appearance at my front door was still making me uncomfortable.

He worked on uncorking the champagne with obvious delight and determination. He really did look like a little boy. I felt guilty for being so severe.

"Have you been feeling all right, taking your medicine and getting good rest?" I asked him to change my tone.

"Oh, yes. Following your wishes right to the T," he said.

"It's the doctor who gives the orders, Mr. Thomas. When do you see him again?"

"Soon," he said, and the cork popped.

Some of the champagne ran over. He began to apologize profusely.

"I really don't do this too often," he said.

"It's all right."

I grabbed a washcloth to soak it up, and then he poured us each a glass. When he handed me mine, I stepped toward the living room. He followed with his glass and the bottle of champagne.

"I'm having only one, Mr. Thomas," I said. "Got to get some housework done, and I'm not a big drinker. This will surely go to my head. My boyfriend hates coming into a mess," I added, just to be clear.

"I knew a pretty girl like you had to have a beau," he said.

Beau? I thought. *Who uses that word today?* I started to raise my glass to my lips.

"Oh," he said. "Would you do me one more little favor first?"

"What's that?"

"Would you be so kind as to put on the pearls I gave you? I would just like to see you wearing them once. It will sort of make this toast and celebration special for me."

How lucky it was that I still had them, I thought. He'd be devastated.

"Put on pearls? With my nurse's uniform?" I said, smiling.

"Sounds silly, but it's not to me. I've envisioned you wearing them, but it's not the same as actually seeing you wearing them."

The instinctive surge of fear I had felt in the hallway when I first saw him standing at my door returned. He took a small digital camera out of his jacket pocket.

"I'll make a couple of copies so you get one," he said.

"Not for the Internet, I hope."

"Oh, absolutely not. I won't be sharing this with anyone, Nurse Dunning. I don't understand how people share so much of their personal life anyway. If something is very special to you, it could mean nothing to others, and most often doesn't. Please," he said.

Get it on and over, I thought, and nodded.

"Okay, but I will be very upset if I see it anywhere."

"No one else will appreciate the sight of those pearls on you. No worries."

I nodded.

Who knew what he would say if he learned I was planning on donating the necklace to a charity? Maybe I should try to return it to him, telling him it made me feel too guilty to keep it. I put the glass of champagne down on the table and went into the bedroom. I realized that

I hadn't even taken off my jacket. I did that and opened the box containing the string of pearls. Feeling really very silly, I put them on, glanced at myself in the mirror, and then started out, thinking how angry Chandler would be about this. It was another secret I had to keep from him. Knowing how hurt he would be didn't make me comfortable.

Douglas Thomas stood there with an exaggeratedly wide smile. He looked so pleased and happy that I felt guilty again even for simply thinking of denying him this moment or attempting to return his gift. He handed me my glass and then focused his camera.

"Just a little smile," he said.

I did smile, but I didn't think I looked that happy despite it. My eyes were surely giveaways. He snapped the picture, looked at it, and showed it to me. Oddly, I didn't think it looked like me. Maybe it was the lighting. The weakened early-evening sun struggled to pass through my yet-to-be-washed windows.

"I bet this would make your fellow nurses and especially Belinda Spoon unhappy," he said. It sounded more like the start of blackmail.

"It would." There was no doubt what the expression on my face was saying.

"They'll never see it," he promised. He lifted his glass.

"I do hope not. As I said, it would make me very angry."

"Promise, cross my heart and hope to die," he said. He looked at his glass of champagne. He cleared his throat. "Too many people take things for granted," he said, assuming a more formal posture as he prepared to deliver his toast. "They treat anyone in any health industry like their personal servants, like it's all coming to them just because they're citizens or something. 'Thank you' is an expression dying on the vine in our world today, but not for me.

"To a wonderful, caring, and dedicated young nurse, to whom I will be eternally grateful. My dearest and most cherished thank you," he said, and tapped his glass against mine.

We drank.

He laughed. "Those pearls look like they were made for you," he said. "I knew they'd be perfect."

"Champagne and pearls. This is all way beyond what we're supposed to receive for our work, Mr. Thomas."

"It's what's deserved," he insisted, and tapped my glass again.

Finish it and get it over with, I thought. I did.

"One more?"

"Oh, no, no," I said.

"Do you mind if I have another?"

Before I could respond, he poured it.

"You should have a better apartment than this, not that it's a slum or anything," he said. He drank his champagne. "I'm sure it's expensive rent, probably a bit more than a nurse can afford. Do you share the rent with your beau?"

"He has his own place for now," I said sharply.

He ignored the tone in my voice. "You're in a good neighborhood, and it's a nice building. I don't spend much time on this side of the city, but I've always admired it."

His eyes seemed to get smaller and then larger to me.

"Nurses aren't paid enough. That's for sure. I know some janitors who make more than you do. The priorities in this country are completely confused. My mother was a schoolteacher, and she was paid pennies compared to much less important people. Don't forget I'm an accountant, so I know about these things. What I see sickens me sometimes, but everyone else laughs and says, 'It's none of your business, Douglas. Worry about yourself.' "

He wagged his head and drank his champagne.

I had the strange feeling that he was swaying. After a moment, I realized it wasn't him swaying. It was me. He continued to drink his champagne and smile. He was saying something about the pearls, but I couldn't understand it. I thought he was mumbling.

What's happening? I wondered. The spinning increased. My body suddenly felt very heavy. My legs were weakening, and my hands felt like they had turned to tissue paper.

I heard the glass shatter on the coffee table and realized it had slipped from my fingers. I was sinking toward the floor. It was as though it was swallowing me and I was on my way to disappearing. I uttered a small cry of despair.

He put his glass down and then stepped toward me just as everything went dark.

Scarletta

"YOU KNOW WHAT we're going to do tonight?" Daddy said at our first breakfast without my mother. He paused with that Fourth of July excitement in his face that usually exploded with a sudden idea.

His behavior surprised me. I was preparing myself for the saddest and most depressing start of any day, but he was beaming. At the moment, I couldn't imagine being excited about anything. Smiles and laughter were like distant stars, light-years away. My mother was gone, maybe forever, as he had insisted. Didn't Daddy have as big a hole in his heart? Couldn't anyone see that his and my smiles would be masks and not real? I didn't want us to be constantly unhappy, but I looked at my mother's empty chair and wondered how we would not be.

However, I had something weighing on my heart that was an even bigger dread. My real fear this morning was that the second my classmates looked at me, they'd know something terrible had happened at our house. My face was usually an easily read road map to my emotions. For me, it would be a day of avoiding people, keeping my eyes down, and then, when I had to, dressing my face in what my mother called "plastic joy." How could I not be depressed all day? I couldn't imagine doing well at track practice and thought that by then, I might claim sickness and take the early school bus home.

On the other hand, Daddy looked like he would have no trouble conducting his work just as he had always done. When I thought about it, I realized he was really good at hiding his innermost feelings, especially with my mother. Any other man would probably have growled back at her more, but he was able to laugh or smile at almost anything and therefore diminish the flames that threatened to burn down our family.

But perhaps this time, they had come from another direction, one totally unexpected. Sly fires burn faster. The flames emerge in an instant around you. There is much less of a chance to snuff them out. Yet looking at him, how impeccably he was dressed, how hungry he obviously was, and now how excited, it was easy to see that he was contending well, perhaps too well. Maybe he believed he had to be this way. He was fulfilling his role as my father above his role as a husband, an abused and distraught husband. It was all for me.

This morning, he had made me what was my mother's

112

and my favorite breakfast dish, Swedish pancakes with blueberries. I realized that he must have gotten up earlier and mixed the batter, because all he did was get the skillet hot and open the refrigerator to take out what he had already prepared in the bowl. He had even set our breakfast-nook table. He would do all this normally on weekends. He was determined to show me that nothing had changed. Sometimes on Sunday mornings, he would bring Mommy her breakfast, and he and I would eat here without her, which was what we were going to do now. Could I close my eyes and imagine she was up in their room sipping her coffee in bed? Could I convince myself it was just that?

"We're going out to your favorite restaurant for dinner tonight," he said. "Dante's."

"We are?"

"Yes, okay?"

"Okay."

I didn't know what else to say. That wasn't my favorite restaurant. It was my mother's. I just pretended to love it as much, but to me it was stuffy, and there wasn't all that much I liked on the menu. If we were going to a restaurant so that we didn't dwell on being unhappy about my mother leaving us, why go to one of her favorite places? The maître d' might ask about her, or there might be people eating there who knew us and would wonder why she wasn't with us. Wouldn't that be more painful for him and for me?

"You look very nice this morning," he said. He smiled, looking out the window. "You remember how your mother would never come down to breakfast without first putting herself together, as she used to say?"

He leaned forward to whisper.

"I don't mind confessing to taking a little more time with my own appearance because of her. She was a very big influence on us both. We have to admit that, Scarletta."

He returned to the pancakes, sighed, and poured himself more coffee.

I remained quite puzzled not only by what he was saying this morning but also by how he was saying it. He sounded like she had already been away for years. He turned back to me. His eyes did not look anywhere nearly as sad as they had yesterday and even earlier this morning when I had gone to his bedroom.

Suddenly, he stood straighter and looked like Mommy did when she made one of her important announcements or decisions. His lips were tightly pressed together, his shoulders were back, and he looked past me as if there were other people in the room, an entire audience of listeners, just the way my mother often did.

"Breakfast, lunch, and especially dinner should never be treated with too much informality. It is at meals when we most secure our family relationships," he declared with an attempt to mimic Mommy's voice. It was Mommy's statement, word for word. Anyone else might think he was making fun of her, but I couldn't imagine him doing that.

He relaxed and looked at me for some sort of compliment, I guess. When I said nothing, he nodded.

"Your mother is gone, Scarletta, but it doesn't mean we won't remember the good things she taught us. She did teach us good things, right? Sometimes we resisted a little, but in the end, we realized she was looking out for us. We're not going to forget those things just because she isn't here anymore. Are we?"

It was as if my tongue wouldn't obey the command sent down from my brain. I stared at him.

"Right?"

"Right," I said. It was hard to say it, because it meant I agreed she was gone for good.

"Good." He served the pancakes and sat. "Anything special going on today?" he asked.

It was late April. He knew that I had track practice after school and took the late bus home.

"No tests, but I have track practice."

"Right, right, track. Your mother wasn't crazy about your being on the track team, but she wasn't much of a sports fan. Working with a personal trainer was as far as she would go when it came to exercise. She wouldn't even take up tennis when we first got married and I was playing regularly. Did you know that? She could be very,

very stubborn when she made up her mind about something."

He leaned forward to whisper again. Why all this whispering?

"I'd think 'worse than a mule,' but I'd never dare say it. I bet you thought of her like that, too."

I shook my head. Call my mother a mule? Never, ever, never.

He looked thoughtful. "You know what?" he said, leaning back and speaking louder now, loud enough for her to hear if she were still in the house, even upstairs. "Your mother took her best things; however, she left a great deal behind. Actually, she had far too much to take on a quick exit like that. I haven't touched a thing she left in that closet, but you're close to her size in almost everything now, aren't you?"

"Not everything, no."

"But you can wear some of her nice things. For dinner tonight, why don't you put on that blue dress I bought her last year? That was one of the dresses she left, maybe because I bought it as a surprise and she didn't want to explain that to her new lover."

New lover, I thought. The words seemed so out of place. I never even heard her give another man a big enough compliment to make my father jealous. At times, I thought she hated men. She had so many warnings about them for me. It was a wonder I wasn't afraid of just talking to boys. "Men are hunters; men set traps; deceit, lies, and false faces are part of their DNA."

"You can wear the shoes that match," Daddy continued. "She told me you were the same shoe size."

"I don't know," I said. I meant I didn't know whether I would like to do what he suggested, but I was afraid to be too contrary. I didn't want to add an iota of sadness to what he was already suffering. Maybe he could pretend he wasn't with strangers but not with me. No matter how he sounded, he was like a match that even rubbed gently would burst into a flame of rage.

When it came to clothes, the truth was that my mother never let me wear any of her things. She had told me that since we weren't exactly the same everywhere, my hips were a little wider, and I didn't have as big a bosom, I might stretch something or in some way cause it to lose its shape.

"You have your own clothes," she said when I had expressed a little more admiration for one of her blouse-and-skirt outfits than I usually did. "A mother should be a mother, not a sister," she added. "Those women who deliberately buy and wear the same outfits that their daughters wear are simply trying to look younger. They look ridiculous and pathetic most of the time, especially when they reach my age."

I knew she was referring especially to Janice Lyn's mother, who had come to parents' night at the school wearing the same dress Janice wore. Other mothers thought it was cute, but my mother ranted about it, calling it one of the most embarrassing things she had to witness a supposedly grown-up woman do.

"Some example she's setting for her daughter," she said. "Acting like a big fool. And the rest of us have to act like it doesn't matter."

All of that came rolling back at me. She'd hate for me to wear her clothes and therefore make them look like a younger person's fashion.

"I have that new lace chiffon Mommy bought me right after Christmas, remember? I wore it to a school dance in February and once when we went to that steak house you guys liked. That should be all right, Daddy."

He nodded, but he looked very disappointed. "Whatever," he said. "I'll make a reservation when I get to the office." He finished his coffee and rose.

Dare I ask? I wondered, but I really needed guidance.

"What are you going to tell people about Mommy, Daddy?"

He looked at me as if the whole situation had just occurred to him.

"I'm not sure." He thought a moment and widened his eyes. "No. I am sure. I'm going to tell people the truth, Scarletta. Your mother has run off with someone. She had a secret affair, apparently, and she's gone. I'll tell them about the note she left and that she took most of her things, too, which will convince them. I'm certainly not going to chase after her. A man has to hold on to his pride. Sometime in the future, she might contact us or me for money. You can bet your ass on that, but until then, I doubt we'll hear a peep from her."

"What would you do if you heard from her?"

"If she called and asked for money?"

I nodded.

"Get a lawyer. That's what I'd say. I have a prenuptial, you know. Thanks to my mother. I didn't want to do it, but she was relentless about it, and your mother didn't care, because she claimed she would never divorce me. She was more in love with me then, I guess, if she ever really was."

He was quiet, and then, like someone waking from a daydream, he said, "Whatever. Got to get organized and going. Big day at the factory today. Ironically, I have a lot to celebrate tonight. We have the biggest order since our family began the business." He smiled.

No matter how well his business was doing, I still couldn't understand how Daddy could be happy about anything. I remained so shocked and numb that I really didn't want to go to school. I didn't know how to tell him. It would spoil his efforts to be happy.

"Maybe I should stay home today. I wouldn't know what to tell my friends at school, Daddy."

"Friends? Er . . . don't tell them anything yet, Scarletta. If someone asks something about your mother, just say you don't know. You don't really, and if you do what I do, you're bound to be pursued with annoying questions. I'd rather you not repeat anything I say just yet. Of course, you should go to school. There would be more chatter about us if you didn't."

"But don't you care where she went? Who she went with? I know you're angry about it, but—"

"Yes, yes, I care. I hate to admit it, but I do."

He paused, thought, and added, "I have a private detective who works for the company. He mostly checks out financial things so we can be sure we don't get into business with shady characters, but I imagine he can do more, do something like this. I'll put him on it and see if he can pick up some details for us, okay?"

What was I going to say? Now that I had pushed him, did I really want to hear the details? Did I want to confirm that my mother had really left us, left me? I'd rather live in foggy hope, I thought.

"But meanwhile, once you tell people Mommy left us for another man, it will get to my classmates' parents, and the kids will be asking me for details. Some of them thought she was like a movie star."

"Did they?" He smiled with that look more appropriate for a memory from long ago. "She was beautiful. I imagine she could have been a movie star."

He thought a moment. And then he had an almost wicked smile.

"You know what I bet your mother would do if the roles were reversed for you? She'd just start to cry, and they would feel terrible asking her anything. Just like a great actress, she'd milk it to death." He nodded. "That's what you do. Be your mother at your age. It's a natural reaction, right?"

I started to shake my head. I didn't think I could cry at will, not as he was suggesting, and I really didn't believe my mother would ever do that. She'd rather spit in their faces.

He clapped his hands together as if I had wholeheartedly agreed.

"We'll get through this together, Scarletta," he said, and then leaned toward me to add, "Just like you and I always do whenever we're faced with any difficulty."

Just like you and I always do? It was as if he was saying my mother was always on the outside. It was an unvoiced alliance between him and me against her. He held his smile, waiting for mine. I flashed it and nodded.

"Good," he said. "Good."

I cleaned up after breakfast as I often did, and then, just before Daddy left, I went up to my parents' room to just look at it, look at the bed, and convince myself once again that my mother was no longer here. Daddy had made his bed, but my mother's nightgown was hanging over the headboard. She had never left it like that.

"'Bye," I heard Daddy call from below. "Don't forget

to lock up, Scarletta. And don't forget we're going to dinner tonight. Get ready as soon as you come home. I know you women. You take a dog's age to prepare yourselves."

"Okay!" I shouted back.

Despite what he had told me to do and say when I confronted my classmates, I wondered if I could cut school, maybe even for the rest of the week. Perhaps my mother would be back by then. Would he be called? If the dean's secretary called here, maybe I could imitate my mother's voice and say I was upstairs in bed with a fever. Or I could just anticipate it and call in imitating her. Tracey Gold was great at capturing her mother's voice. She even avoided tests she knew she might fail.

But when it came right down to it, I didn't have the courage. I finished getting myself ready and walked down to the bus stop. There were a half dozen young kids there and two senior girls, Shelly Myers and Bobbie Lees, neither of whom was a fan of mine. I knew in my heart that they would take joy in learning that my family was shattered. Like so many of the girls, because of how my mother and I dressed and my mother's admittedly condescending ways, they thought we were snobs.

"You have a few strands of hair out of place," Shelly said when I approached.

Bobbie laughed.

"You have a few brain cells missing," I retorted. This morning, I didn't feel like ignoring anything nasty. I think the look in my eyes frightened her. She huffed and turned away.

They're cowards, I thought, my mother was right about girls like them. Show them they were getting to you, and they wouldn't stop. Defy them with so much threat in your eyes that they feared you have no control of yourself, and they'd choose to retreat and ignore you. Ordinarily, it wasn't in my nature to be like that, but I reached deeper into myself to find a coldhearted, raging beast who had orbs woven with the flames of candles.

I was and would be the stuff of nightmares whenever I had to be.

Rather than look for confrontations, however, I kept my feelings and fears to myself. No one paid any extra or particular attention to me. I was doing well in school until lunchtime in the cafeteria. Daddy had told one of his business associates about my mother who had then told his wife. With Internet speed, it reached Janice Lyn's mother, who sent a text to Janice to see what additional information she could get from me.

At the time, I was sitting with Jared Peters and Phoebe Goldstein, who were considered the brains of our class. One or the other was destined to be valedictorian. Jared's mother was an African American, an executive at the water department. His father was an X-ray technician at the hospital. He had a younger sister in the seventh grade.

Phoebe was attractive with her reddish-brown hair and stunning violet eyes. She wasn't in any sport but already had one of the best figures of any girl in the school. Her mother, who was an attorney, was quite attractive, too. Her father was town manager, not especially good-looking. Any other girl who looked like Phoebe would have wielded her sexual power, which would have resulted in a trail of boys with tongues hanging out, but Phoebe was oblivious to it. Socially, she was a few years behind, perhaps. Some thought she was just too smart for boys in our school and probably had a crush on a college-age boy, maybe a friend of her older brother, who was in medical school.

I liked them both because they seemed aloof from the ordinary silly teenage chatter. They actually enjoyed talking about current events and scientific achievements highlighted in daily headlines. They were better than the evening news. They researched sound bites. Because I listened to what they said, I knew I achieved higher grades, especially in history class.

My mother once warned me about school friends. "The ones you make in high school especially will begin to evaporate the day you leave for college. Years later, you'll wonder what you ever had in common with them. Keep them at arm's length. Less disappointment on the horizon," she said. I thought this was especially true for her. I never heard her mention one friend from high school, and she only occasionally referred to any friends she had made in college.

I didn't make any special effort to have lots of friends. Probably that was what made some of my classmates think I was a snob. I figured my father was mostly right with his advice about it when he and my mother would discuss my social life, especially when I complained about being left out of a party or a trip other girls had arranged.

"Real friends will just naturally get into your orbit, or you'll get into theirs. Don't force it. That's like watching water boil. If you do, it seems to take longer, even though it really doesn't. Just let it happen."

That seemed to be true. One of my "almost friends" was Janice Lyn, who now suddenly made such a beeline for our table that all three of us stopped talking and looked up, half expecting she would crash into it and send everything on it flying. But there was never anything diplomatic or graceful about Janice Lyn anyway. She could bowl over one of the school's fullbacks on the football team with one of her stupid, thoughtless comments. Right now, it was easy to see she was being propelled by her girlfriends, who had launched her from their table at ours like a gossip missile.

Without any prologue and with the tone of a fait accompli, she asked, "Your mother ran off with a boyfriend?"

The facade I had so successfully maintained until then

crumbled and shattered like a mask of ice thrust into a microwave. I couldn't find my voice.

Although I had confided in neither, both Jared and Phoebe pounced on her.

"Even if that were validated, why bring her so much pain?" Jared asked.

Janice looked stumped by the word *validated*.

"Your meanness and lack of compassion are dripping with yellow bile," Phoebe added. "Go wipe your mouth with rubbing alcohol and see a veterinarian after school."

"Huh?" Janice said, looking at them. "What the fuck . . ."

I knew I was expected to say something.

"I don't know what to tell you, Janice," I said. And then I added a simple, almost childish thing. "Our hearts are broken." That was close to my father's advice, even though I couldn't imagine my mother saying such a thing.

However, Janice did look stunned for a moment and more embarrassed than she had hoped *I'd* be.

"Well, everyone's talking about it," she moaned in self-defense.

"Thanks to people like you," Phoebe said, "who have nothing better to do with their lives and probably never will."

"Stuff yourself," Janice replied, and turned quickly.

Both Jared and Phoebe surprised me by laughing. They had both met my mother a few times. I knew they were impressed with her, and not only with her looks. Jared had called her stately, eloquent. He'd said my father was very lucky.

"Perhaps it's just a temporary glitch in your family life," Phoebe offered now. She didn't hug me, but she touched my hand and smiled warmly, hopefully.

I started to look down, my body trembling.

Jared put his hand over mine, too. "Don't let an idiot like that get to you," he said. "She's not worth a second of your attention, much less an iota of thought."

"Just tell everyone it's personal," Phoebe suggested. She looked at the girls clacking away around Janice. "Not that much is anymore. We all might as well live in glass houses thanks to Facebook and other Internet confession booths.

"I went to the bathroom twice today," Phoebe joked.

"My father has a pimple on his nose," Jared added. They both laughed.

I couldn't help but smile. "I'm sorry I didn't tell you guys," I said.

"Hey. Didn't you just hear me?" Phoebe replied. "It's personal."

I looked across the cafeteria at Janice, who had regained her composure and was now complaining and stoking the fire in the others. She'd have everyone in our class knowing about my mother before the school day ended. Visions of revenge began to stream into my mind. I thought Phoebe could see it in my face.

"Whatever you're thinking, she's not worth it, Scarletta," she said. "Concentrate on helping your father."

Yes, I thought. *She's right.*

I didn't want to lose him, too.

"Thanks," I told them.

Neither said, "You're welcome," or asked a question to continue the topic. Instead, they began to talk about the subjects for our upcoming term papers. It was as if the real world was merely an inconvenience.

Maybe they were right.

Later, I did far better than I had expected I would at track practice, even though I could feel the curious eyes of my teammates practically glued to my every move. They were probably anticipating my emotional breakdown. I channeled my anger into my physical efforts and ran faster and jumped higher than I had all season. Mrs. Ward, the coach, gave me some terrific compliments. I knew they were born not out of sympathy but out of true appreciation. She was very unforgiving and stingy when it came to praise. A grade of B from her in our health education class was like an A from any other teacher.

Afterward, although I could feel so many eyes on me on the school bus home, I sat stoically and pushed aside all feelings of self-pity. I even smiled to myself, pleased with how I had gotten through the day. It was as if what my mother had done had changed me. Like a snake, I had shed old skin. Perhaps it was weird, but I felt older, wiser, and more equipped to face a world of competition. My mother's behavior had opened the door to the real world, a world reserved for adults. My childhood faiths were falling like autumn leaves. Everything about my teenage world that had worried me was suddenly silly and meaningless. I had new eyes, new ears. When the bus reached my stop, I rose slowly. I thanked Mr. Tooey, our driver, who looked up, surprised.

And I didn't leap off the bus the way I often did. I stepped down carefully, slowly, the way my mother would, and then walked with her confidence, not looking behind me or around me to see how anyone was reacting. I felt good not caring. When I reached our walkway, I paused. Water sparkled as it gushed from my mother's statue of a cherub. Flowers were blooming with their rich reds and yellows. The house grew in stature and looked like a prime candidate for a historical site designation. Yes, very important people really did live here. It was sinful and dangerous to make them the subject of gossip.

This resurgence of confidence gave me the feeling that maybe, just maybe, my mother had returned. I walked to the steps and gingerly, deliberately, went up the short stairway, pausing as usual at the front door to be sure I looked as perfect as I could. My first words would simply be "Hello, Mother." She'd be shocked, of course, at how undisturbed I'd be about her little fling yet quite proud of how I was carrying myself through the crisis she had created.

Of course, she would take credit. She had made me strong enough to deal with almost any emergency life could toss at me. In fact, this had all been a plan she had concocted and forced my father to participate in as well, just to teach me and make me grow up even faster. "The teenage years are overestimated."

But the house was deadly quiet when I entered. I stood in the entryway for a few moments, listening hopefully for some sounds of her. The silence was terribly depressing. It fell around me like dark, cold drops of rain. I walked up the stairs slowly, weakening inside. If she was gone, really gone, could I put on my new skin again tomorrow? Had my strength come from foolish hope, which would fade? Or had I really grown years in hours? I didn't want to think about it. I'd do as much of my homework as I could before Daddy took me to dinner. *Keep busy*, I told myself. *Keep so busy that you don't think.*

I really believed I could do that and get through the rest of the day and even the night. However, when I entered my bedroom, all that hope fizzled and sank to the floor.

There, lying on my bed, was the blue dress my father had bought my mother last year. The matching shoes were at the foot of the bed, too. He must have come home at lunchtime, gone into her closet, and put it here.

I should have thought that all he wanted was to help me look pretty. I should have thought that he imagined I had always wanted to wear this dress, and now that my mother was gone, there was nothing stopping me. I should have thought that all he was trying to do was find a way for us to be happy, even for a little while.

He wanted us to have hope and be strong.

That's what I should have thought.

But I couldn't. Something I was yet unable to identify was filling the air with static and pressing into my heart, replacing sadness with cold, sharp fear.

I couldn't explain it, but I couldn't make him unhappy, not now.

"Concentrate on helping your father," Phoebe had advised, and after all, she was brilliant.

As if my father was here, filling my ear with new suggestions, I threw down my schoolbooks and went to take a shower. I would fix my hair, and I would put on makeup.

And I would do it at my mother's vanity table, using her cosmetics.

Pru

I AWOKE IN my bed, naked, with only the string of
pearls around my neck and resting between my breasts.
I was lying on my blanket. My nurse's uniform was on
a hanger attached to the top of my bedroom door. It
looked washed and pressed. My shoes and socks neatly
below it. For a few moments, I was completely confused.

Sitting up slowly, I glanced around my room. I felt
like one of those people who have a strange reaction to
Ambien. Things had been done in my room that I had no
recollection doing. Everything on my small vanity table
was organized, the small trash bin beside it that I knew
had been nearly filled was completely empty; it even
looked washed. There was nothing on the wood floor and
area rug, both looking just vacuumed. The door of my
closet was closed. I usually leave it open, something my
mother often chastised me for doing. It added to the slop-
piness of my room, for my room was always untidy to her.

I rose slowly, stepped out of the bed, and went to the closet. When I opened it, I saw that all my clothing was better organized and my shoes were much more neatly stacked on the shoe case on the side. My mother would have fainted with shock at such a sight. Usually, this was something she had to do for me, even when I was in high school. I'd come home from school and find my room put back together as it should be.

What was happening? What did happen? I listened for the sound of someone else in my apartment, but I heard nothing except for the ambient noise outside my windows facing Santa Monica Boulevard, car horns, music spilling out of windows and convertibles, and occasional shouts.

I closed the closet door, my heart beating harder as I turned to look at myself in the full-length mirror. I saw no trauma, not even redness anywhere. I looked untouched, as clean as I would coming from a fresh bath. The back of my head did feel a little damp. My mind reeled with the possibilities. Could it be that I had been bathed like a baby? I hurried to the bathroom to see if there was anything that pointed to such a bizarre thing, noting that all the dirty laundry in the hamper was gone.

The bathroom was also very neat, towels folded as well as the washcloths, not something I did so well or at least as well as Chandler. The tub looked clean but not recently used. That gave me relief, but when I turned and looked at the toilet, my heart did feel like it had stopped and started. There, floating in the water, was a used condom. I gasped and clutched myself. I felt no pain, no ache, and of course, I had no memory of being sexually violated. Nevertheless, had I been?

The only way to confirm it was to do a rape-kit exam. I studied myself in the mirror, looking for hair on my body that I knew wasn't mine. I was spotless, as spotless as I could be if someone had taken a washcloth and a fine-tooth comb to my pubic hair. Without any sperm inside me, I probably wouldn't have any DNA evidence to collect. And then again, what if I hadn't actually been violated? That condom floating in the toilet didn't have to have been used inside me. Still, I didn't flush the toilet or fish it out. *Keep your options open*, I told myself. *Think, think.*

Confused and indecisive, I walked into the kitchen. When I had come home, there had been a lot to clean up, but there was nothing there now. Everything was spick-and-span, and all dishes, glasses, and silverware had been put away. The counter looked wiped clean, as did the kitchen table, and the floor looked washed. The tile gleamed.

Nothing was out of place in the living room, either. I suspected it, too, had been vacuumed. Even the windows were washed. Was this all done to ensure there was no evidence left behind? The champagne bottle was gone, and there was nothing in the trash bins in the living room. I returned to the kitchen. The garbage disposal in the kitchen was empty. I saw that the garbage bag had been removed and replaced with a fresh one. I could dress and go downstairs to the large bin and start searching through it to find something to present as evidence later, but a vision of myself sifting through discarded food, plastics, paper, and other assorted refuse was the vision of someone who had gone completely bonkers.

I debated calling Chandler. He should know what had happened, I thought, and then I thought about what exactly I would tell him. How was I going to explain this? I had let Douglas Thomas into my apartment with a bottle of champagne, had worn the pearls for him so he could take a picture, and he had performed a toast. He had obviously put some powerful sedative in my glass of champagne when I had gone to get the pearls. I now remembered all that. *Better also think about Chandler's reaction*, I told myself.

I sat on the sofa, fingering the pearls and thinking. Perhaps it had been gamma-hydroxybutyric acid, or GHB, commonly known as Liquid Ecstasy. A particularly strong dose of that would have done me in. I could hurry down to the ER and get a toxicological analysis. Often it is only rarely detectable in blood for up to eight hours or in urine for twelve. I imagined I fit into the time limits, but then what? I had to prove he was there. From the looks of what he had done to my apartment, that might not be so easy. Of course, someone might have seen him come into my building or go out. Another tenant could recall buzzing someone in about that time. But usually someone who had done something that stupid wouldn't want to reveal it. A full-blown investigation would have to be started, and people, especially nowadays, weren't eager to be witnesses.

Besides, every other woman in this building would become paranoid and blame me. They'd all want to know what I had done wrong. How did I permit this to happen to me, a nurse, someone who was supposed to be more intelligent? What should they avoid? Should we form a neighborhood watch, strengthen the building security, and finally install those cameras that were suggested despite the additional homeowners' association dues?

What would Chandler think? I asked myself again. What did I think? I should be in more of a rage than I was and surely be at least a little hysterical. Even if there was no penetration, my body had still been violated. Surely he had taken pictures of me naked with these pearls lying above my breasts? What if they started to appear on the Internet, despite what he had promised? What if everyone on my staff saw them? Maybe Annie Sanders would print them out. Of course, I should be panicking.

Surprisingly, I wasn't. I was quite calm, actually, but

maybe that was because I was still in the throes of the drugs. The full impact of all this continued circling me like angry hummingbirds. And of course, I was trained to confront crises professionally, trained to handle trauma with composure. The worst thing was showing your panic and terrifying the critical patient even more.

But this time, I was the critical patient. Shouldn't I be raging with anger, calling the police, and going after him?

I returned to my bedroom and sat on the bed. If I did that—called the police even if no pictures of me appeared on the Internet—how would I escape derision once what happened was public knowledge? The man for whom I had alienated most of the people I worked with had drugged and violated me after I willingly let him into my apartment and drank champagne with him while wearing his gift of expensive pearls. Oh, yeah, they would all feel so sorry for me. Fat chance. Some would whisper I had probably agreed to everything and then, when I regretted it, claimed I was violated. The smug smiles and laughter would drive me to jump out the window.

But here I was, like so many sexually abused and violated women, looking for a way to avoid reporting it. I rose, determined not to be that kind of a woman. *I won't let myself be a victim without a voice. I can't take the chance of destroying some DNA evidence that might still be on my body or on my bed*, I thought. Anger replaced self-pity. I turned and looked at the sheets and pillowcases. A forensic expert could find something. But then my heart sank again.

It immediately struck me. They had been changed, too. I hurried out to the washing machine and dryer. The previous sheets and pillowcases were already in the dryer, waiting for me to take them out. Frantically, my mind went from one idea to the next. What would I suggest be examined for evidence? I was back to only the condom. Why, if he was so meticulous about everything else, did he leave that behind, almost taunting me with it? Why hadn't he flushed it away? Perhaps for that very reason, the taunting.

Maybe there was nothing he wished for more than my accusing him and then having to support the accusation. Sex was committed here, but what proved it was unwanted? Who knew what fabrications he would create? The man didn't live in this world. He moved in and out of an alternative reality, for sure. He'd claim I had wooed him while he was my patient. I would fill his ordinarily boring life with some excitement. He'd be bragging about it at work. *He wants me to make that call. He's practically praying I do.*

I could easily imagine the expression on the skeptical detective's face, even if it was a woman. "You sure you didn't encourage him?"

If nothing definitive could be discovered in a toxicological test, there would be that he said, she said argument even if I scooped out the condom and had the contents analyzed to prove Douglas Thomas had been here. The skeptical detective would be right. I took his pearls, didn't I? I willingly was drinking champagne with him. Why couldn't his version of events be true? Why couldn't any sexual encounter have been consensual? Want to get into the depositions and the courtroom? Belinda Spoon would probably fix her schedule so she could attend, among others from the hospital staff. She might even be willing to testify and claim I encouraged him.

"There was somethin' goin' on between her and Mr. Douglas, fer sure. I ain't seen any other patient give a nurse somethin' so valuable. I think they was puttin' on an act for me. That's what I think."

Would I shrink in my seat?

More frustrated and still quite angry, I wandered into the living room and stood there for a moment trying to recall every detail of what had occurred, hoping for something to prove definitively that I had been abused. I heard my mobile ring.

That had to be Chandler, I thought. I had to be careful about how I sounded. He was too good at hearing my feelings.

"Hello," I said.

"Didn't you get my earlier message?"

"Oh, I haven't looked at my mobile. I see I still have it on vibrate. Sorry."

"Where have you been?"

"I went shopping after work and then lay down to take a short rest and drifted off. I guess I was more tired than I thought."

"Yeah, you sound like you just woke up. You all right?"

"Sure."

"I'm coming home tomorrow. Got to go over things with the partners. I've made plans for us to go to dinner. Expensive, the Lighthouse, but that's what I'd like. Reservations made for seven. Hope that's fine with you."

"It's fine."

"Sure you're okay?"

This is it, I thought. *Tell him everything or keep it forever a secret.*

Rationalization came pouring in from under the door, through the windows, everywhere, being pulled up and out of the well of excuses and avoidance from which most violated women unfortunately drank.

Apparently, no serious physical harm was done to you, Pru Dunning, I heard another voice inside me say. *Get over it. You made a mistake, but from the looks of it all, what suffered the most was your ego. There is even a silver lining: your apartment is the cleanest it has been in a long time.* I almost laughed.

"Sure. I'm actually very hungry now."

"Good. I'll call you when I arrive. Really looking forward to seeing you, Pru."

"Ditto," I said.

He laughed. "We're okay with going to dinner tomorrow night, right? You haven't taken on someone else's shift again or anything?" he asked, to double his confirmation.

"I'm fine. I'll try to be expensive."

He laughed again. "It's all going much better," he said. "You'd probably take one look at me and know the truth anyway," he added.

"Oh?"

"You know how we can read each other. You were right to suspect they'd offer me the office and a partnership."

"And?"

"I gave them the answer I told you I would. They were suspicious and had good questions."

"About what?"

"Us," he said.

I held my breath a moment. "What exactly?"

"Cliff Barnes asked if I was so involved with you this long, why haven't they heard we were engaged or anything?"

"We qualify for 'anything,'" I said. He laughed but then was silent. "So how did you reply to that?"

"I said there's something on the horizon. Cryptic but satisfying enough to stop the inquisition. They were also suspicious of my taking another position at another firm."

"No one trusts anyone anymore," I said.

I was really thinking of Douglas Thomas. Was this a way to ease into it? He couldn't see me shake my head, of course, but I did, as if there was someone else sitting there with me, urging me to tell him.

"I trust you," he said. "Is there something on our horizon?"

"As long as it's there for us and not to satisfy some lawyers at your firm," I said.

He laughed, but he didn't sound as confident. "We'll explore that when I come home, okay?"

"Yes," I said.

I wasn't really thinking about what he was saying. My voice was weakening. I could feel the onslaught of tears. A mixture of insecurity, deeper fears, and guilt was rising up in my throat. Scenes of old nightmares flashed, and I was on the verge of telling him exactly what had occurred. I knew my voice would crack and I'd start to cry. It would be like small explosions all around me.

"Pru?"

"I . . . can't wait to see you," I blurted out, and he voiced the same thought.

"I'll call you as soon as I land tomorrow," he promised. "Love you, Pru. Really do."

"Likewise," I said. It wasn't a very romantic or convincing thing to reply. "And miss you," I added, like some spice to enhance the mediocre word.

He hung up first.

I sat there, staring at the wall.

Suddenly, I thought I had to get out for a while. Visions of Douglas Thomas were flashing all around me. I had a chill like you'd have when you realized someone was watching you. It was as if he would be standing there when I turned and looked toward the living room. Maybe he never had left. He had been in the closet by the entrance the whole time, enjoying my surprise and confusion. He was crazy enough to do something like that, wasn't he?

The fear was so palpable that I took out a bread knife and started into the living room slowly. Could I stab him if he popped out of the closet? The irony of the nurse who stopped the patient from taking the wrong medicine now being the one to kill him didn't escape me. How delicious it would be for Annie Sanders.

But how dare he drug me? How dare he undress me? How dare he do something sexual either to me or on me, even near me? *I will not be violated.* I moved forward with more assurance. When I reached the closet door, I paused and lifted the knife high. There would be no hesitation. Slowly, I reached for the doorknob, turned it, and then thrust the door open.

For a moment, he was there, and then I realized he wasn't. The closet had nothing in it but some jackets, one of them Chandler's, an umbrella, and two hats. I closed the door and hurried back to the kitchen, still trembling. I needed fresh air for sure. After I put the knife away, I put on fresh panties, some jeans, a bra, a blouse, and a light sweater. I slipped on my running shoes and then stood in the hallway for a few moments deciding.

This is how I'll handle it, I thought, *myself*. Where the confidence came from, I couldn't say, but it came. With determined steps, I went to the bathroom, gazed into the toilet, and then flushed it. I watched my only evidence go down into oblivion. It didn't frighten me. I would handle this. I was caught unaware, but that would never happen again.

As soon as I stepped out of my apartment, I hesitated in my hallway and listened. I listened so hard that I could hear someone breathing. He wasn't here. I descended the stairs slowly, pausing between steps to listen for someone possibly following. There was silence.

When I reached the entryway, I paused. Fortunately, there was no one else from the building coming in or going out. I was afraid of small talk, afraid anyone could look at my face and say, "You were sexually violated, weren't you? It's all right to talk about it."

I stepped out and took a deep breath. The traffic was heavy as usual for this time of the day. There weren't that many people walking, but those who were going somewhere on foot were not rushing the way people do in other cities like New York. Maybe it was the warm weather and the frequent sunshine, but people here were just more laid-back. When they walked, it was closer to strolling, and when I saw people casually moving along, crossing streets, talking quietly, I slowed down, too.

I walked with my arms folded across my breasts and avoided looking at anyone. I paused at a boutique clothing store and looked at the clothes. Nothing excited me, and it was closed by now anyway. I walked on. When I reached the corner, I turned. It would take me around the block, past residences and not stores.

Something caused me to look back just before I made the turn. I was sure I caught sight of a woman wearing a wide-brimmed black hat as she turned to avoid looking my way and oddly just stood there with her back to me. She was under a streetlight.

Could that be her? Scarletta?

A new fear chased me. When I started to walk again, I was no longer strolling. Now I was practically running. After I had made the full circle, never looking back once, I paused and looked down the sidewalk that passed my entryway. Maybe she was there waiting inside, finally willing to confront me? I was shaken by all I had just gone through, but I was ready for her, I thought.

I clenched my hands and took firm strides toward the building. When I was in front of it, I hesitated and studied the entryway. There was no one waiting there, but that didn't mean she hadn't gotten in somehow. She could easily be on the stairs, or, like Douglas Thomas, she could be right in front of my apartment door, waiting.

But how would she have gotten in? I wondered. Did she do what Douglas Thomas must have done, pressed a button ringing some other tenant? Maybe she claimed to be a relative who had just flown in. People, especially if it was a man who answered, tended to believe women. Women weren't as threatening anyway. "She sounded so sweet and innocent." "Please help." He'd probably have an orgasm over the phone. Besides, how many lone women break into apartments to steal or kill?

A few? She could very well be one.

Forget it, I told myself. *I can't stand out here forever, can I?* I entered but started up the stairs gingerly, pausing to listen. There was a turn for the second floor. I held my breath when I made it. Maybe I'd rush her, grab her, and throw her down the damn stairs, I thought, and started up again.

There was no one around the corner, and when I emerged on the second floor, there was no one waiting at my door, either. I was actually disappointed. In the state of mind I was in, I looked forward to a confrontation. It would be easy to redirect my rage at Douglas Thomas toward her and come at her with such a threat of violence on my face that she'd shrink and then flee forever. If she was one of the hospital staff, she'd resign rather than face me again. She had come here anticipating my weakness, ready to enjoy my plea, begging her to leave me alone.

None of that had happened. I opened the door and entered the apartment. The machine was blinking. For a fleeting moment, I thought it might be Douglas Thomas thanking me for permitting him to celebrate with me. He could be that nuts.

My hand trembling, I brought my right forefinger to the machine and pressed Play Messages.

You can run, she said, *but you can't hide.*

Scarletta

FOR OUR DINNER out, Daddy bought me a wrist corsage of white orchids, my mother's favorite flower. When I heard him come home, I started down the stairs in the manner my mother had taught me almost from the time I could walk: holding my head high, my back straight, walking down slowly, each step firm, and keeping my right hand sliding along the smooth mahogany banister for balance but not looking like I was clinging to it.

"That's the way your grandmother would walk down stairs, descending and clutching that banister as if she could tumble at any moment. She was always just looking for attention," she told me when she caught me once last year not thinking about how I was descending. "She wanted everyone to hold his breath as if she was created out of fine china when she was really made of hard brick."

Right now, Daddy paused in the entryway to look up

at me, an amazed, even a bit shocked, expression on his face. As I drew closer, I thought he was a little pale, which worried me. Had he been suffering all day, keeping his pain bottled up? But then he smiled with such delight it rushed the color back into his cheeks.

"In that dress, with your hair done in that sleek knot, I thought I was looking at your mother twenty years ago," he said, his voice so low it was more of a loud whisper. His smile widened even more, his eyes brightening just the way they would whenever my mother entered a room or descended these very stairs. "I'm so happy you decided to wear the dress, Scarletta. It's a perfect fit. And look at what I bought for you on the way home today."

He revealed the wrist corsage he had been holding behind his back. I had never worn one, although my mother let me try on one my father had bought her before they went to a charity ball a little more than a year ago. It looked like a replica of that corsage.

I stepped off the stairway, my eyes fixed on the flower as I approached him.

"Hold out your arm," he said. He fastened the corsage to my wrist. His ruby-blue eyes dazzled with excitement when I held it up and looked at it as if it really was a diamond bracelet. Jewelry was always more important than flowers for my mother. "Flowers die; a diamond is forever," she had said, and then laughed and added, "Buy me a bouquet of them, Raymond, dear."

"Thank you, Daddy. It's beautiful," I said now.

"It is on you," he replied.

I couldn't recall putting that much delight into his face, even when I did things he thought were wonderful and beyond my age for a child.

He stared at me a moment, and then suddenly, he took my hands into his and, holding my arms apart, stepped back to look me over.

"You did your makeup just the way she would, too," he said.

I had done some eye shadow and chosen one of her lipsticks because the color worked well for both of us. We had similar complexions.

"Is it all right?"

"Of course," he said. "You're beautiful. You need just one other thing to complete this picture. After I shower, shave, and change, I'll bring it down with me. I can't believe how perfectly you did your hair."

"I watched Mother do it many times."

"Yes, I bet she made sure of that," he said, the bitterness seeping into his voice. But his smile instantly returned. "This is so good for us, Scarletta. When two people have been so deeply wounded in their hearts, they need to steal a few moments of pure joy from whatever they've been promised and whatever is waiting for them in this world, even if it's short-lived. It will help us find the strength to go on."

He released my hands, kissed me on the cheek, and then hurried to the stairway. I looked from the corsage to him charging up the stairs like a teenager. He had left the house looking twenty years older, and now he looked twenty years younger. After my tense day at school, I couldn't deny or in any way refuse to accept the moments of happiness we were stealing. If my mother had hoped we'd be in mourning tonight, she'd be terribly disappointed.

My glee is a good thing, I thought. *Isn't it?* Apparently, she could casually drop me out of her life as easily as she could discard a gum wrapper. Where was our intimate mother-daughter relationship in all this? Although she was disdainful of the way other women her age related to their daughters, trying to be as young, she never heard my friends describe how they got along with their mothers. I envied them for having best friends in their mothers, too.

My mother had never confided in me about her new love. There was never even a hint. Was she afraid I'd run to my father with her secret, betray her instantly? All right, maybe that was it, but why couldn't she have at least said a proper good-bye, held me, and promised someday soon to see me? What more could I have done to show my love for her than obey her every command? Was there another daughter who was as obedient, who even took her mother's side in just about any disagreement she might have with her father, whether she believed she was right or not? Even if I felt sorry for him, I tried to hide it from her.

So here I was, the day after she had come out of her room, suitcase in hand filled with whatever of her things she had wanted to take. She had walked right by my room, maybe without a glance into it, down those steps, and out our front door, closing it behind her probably with little or no hesitation.

Here I was left with no other explanation than what my father had read to me from a printed-out note. Why couldn't I drop her with the same indifference? At least for right now, it was okay for me to be more angry than sad. As time passed and she was still gone, I'd be both, for sure, and surely sadder eventually, but at this moment, anger kept me from crying. I welcomed it.

I couldn't imagine forgiving her should she call me to explain. What would I say? *It's all right for you to care only about yourself, Mother? Go enjoy your new life with your new lover? See the world and pretend you don't have a daughter?*

A mother's love for her child should be stronger than her love for a man, even her husband. I remembered her telling my father that once. Was she just talking, mouthing words she wasn't going to follow? I swore to myself back then that what she had claimed was how it would be for me when I got married and had children. I would never do what she had now done to her family. It was rare for me to think something this terrible about her. However she had displeased me or Daddy in the past, she always seemed to have good reasons, even if they were reasons I wished didn't exist. No matter what she did or said, although I didn't have the power to do it, I excused her. I forced myself to see everything the way she did. I was so proud of her and admired her so.

Actually, nothing was different about that now. Despite the pain I saw in Daddy's face and the pain I had in my own heart, my hating her for what she had done was like trying to put on shoes the wrong size. I could be angry at her, but I couldn't despise her, not like Daddy did. Was she confident of that? Did she believe I'd welcome her back no matter how long she had been away and how coldly she had left me?

I went into the living room to wait for Daddy and think more about it all. What we were living right now wasn't exactly a nightmare. Nightmares came and went. They might be remembered for a little while, but I couldn't recall all the nightmares I had as a child, and besides, time made them less threatening, even silly. How could time change this? Would I forget my mother a year from now or two years from now? Could I ever forget her? Was her love for this other man really so strong that she would forget me? What would she do on my birthday? Would she be on some island somewhere or in some other country, as Daddy believed, and deliberately do something to keep herself from thinking about it?

This wasn't the first time I wondered about such emotionally challenging family tragedies, but it was always something involving someone else. Now one was touching me, too. I had classmates whose parents had divorced, some with fathers who had moved far away. I listened to them talk about receiving gifts or phone calls, but as well as they were hiding the pain, I could still see it swimming in their eyes, floating under their words, and hiding behind their smiles, smiles that would freeze on their faces when their friends mentioned something their own fathers had said or done recently. Those who lost theirs were surely remembering something similar before their world was shattered. Was it painful for them to think of their fathers now? Did their hearts ache every single day? Would mine fold into itself like a poked caterpillar every time I thought of my mother?

Now I, too, would be wearing the same dumb smile the children of divorced parents wore when children from happy families talked about something their families had done together. I would surely resemble someone who had been struck in the head, someone who was thinking the same dark thoughts about her own life and people she loved. As a child, whom did you believe in more than your parents? After they broke their promises and vows to each other, what could you believe about the vows and promises they made to you?

How would it all show in my face? Would my eyes grow darker, my smile become as thin as cellophane? Would the corners of my mouth weaken and settle into an obvious habitual smirk? Would the color in my cheeks fade so that I resembled a flower pressed in a book of memories, the color diminished and the aroma gone? My "frame" would splinter, and the eyes of others, boys especially, would pass over me as if I wasn't there. Most of the time, I wouldn't feel like I was there, either.

People died for you in different ways, especially a parent lost in a divorce. Distance killed them a little. Time smothered their faces. Their voices thinned out over the telephone. Their images faded or blinked off on computer screens after Skyping or FaceTime. "Good-byes" cut deeper and deeper, until one day, you realized your father or your mother had become almost a total stranger. You could even imagine having to be re-introduced decades later. "You remember your mother, I think, don't you?" "Oh, yes. How have you been?"

After all, the parents who left you lived completely different lives with different experiences and memories gathering during the time they were gone. The shared DNA wasn't enough. There were fewer and fewer "remember whens." Pages of albums would be blank. Occasions were missed, moments lost. Part of your life was evaporating.

But wouldn't there be that moment, that terrible, heart-wrenching moment, when your father or your mother looked at you and thought about all that he or she had missed when you were growing up, memories lost forever to them, too? Wouldn't they feel regretful and realize how selfish they'd been? Wouldn't they look for you to forgive them? How would you forgive them if time lost could never be regained? You wouldn't forgive; you'd forget or, really, just force it all out of your mind, like squeezing a balloon full of water until it was only wrinkles.

Do birds ever see their babies fly by and remember who they are? It doesn't look like it. Are we really like them, flying by each other with indifference?

These thoughts rushed over and through me. I had done most of my homework before I had come downstairs. It had helped me to avoid thinking, but I couldn't do that now. Silence drew the painful thoughts from the deepest, darkest places of my mind. Daddy's excitement was barely a Band-Aid.

When I had first gotten off the bus and started for home today, I wasn't really looking forward to us going to this restaurant. I even played with the idea of suggesting we go somewhere else, but now, when I looked at my corsage, I thought it might just be perfect, if not for me, then for Daddy. He needed me to help keep him from suffering, and when he didn't suffer, I suffered less. I leaned back, confident we were doing the right thing. Staying home and staring at my mother's empty dining-room chair would have made it all more painful than it was.

I suddenly realized I had chosen to sit in the corner of the Chesterfield sofa where my mother was always sitting comfortably. Did I do that deliberately so that I wouldn't look at the empty seat? It was funny how certain places in our home, maybe everyone's home, got identified with one person or another. The heavy matching Churchill chair across from me was Daddy's. Neither Mother nor I ever sat in it. The seat of it looked worn to his size. I could easily imagine the chair squirming and moaning if someone else sat on it. On the dark cherrywood table beside it was Daddy's pile of business magazines. Seeing it now brought back memories.

"You don't relax by reading what returns you to work," my mother once told him when he had begun reading one. In the early evening, she often would sit with her legs crossed, sipping an after-dinner drink, and gaze at him judgmentally with her eyelids narrowed.

"You are what you do," Daddy said, smiling.

She laughed, but not because she thought he was funny. It was an "aha" laugh. To me, even at my age, sitting and doing my math workbook assignment that day, it seemed Daddy had fallen into her trap.

"Exactly, Raymond," she said. "You often look like a stick of furniture."

"Ha-ha," Daddy said. But I saw something beneath his smile. There was a layer of anger he kept so well hidden that my mother either didn't see it or didn't care. It frightened me even though it was only a flash.

"I want to change this rug," she said. "It's not wearing as well as I thought it would. There's always a reason something's a bargain."

She looked at me.

"Remember that, Scarletta," she said. She threw her wisdom out like someone throwing peanuts to pigeons. "You get what you pay for in this world."

"This wasn't meant to be a bargain, Doreen," Daddy said. "I squeezed the Fullers to get that price. They wanted to be part of a bigger deal that I was doing."

"Whatever," she said. She'd wave off any disagreement with a backhand slap of an invisible, annoying fly. "I still want to replace it."

"Sure," Daddy said. He returned to his magazine, holding it in front of his face more like a shield than anything.

That was about the time I began to wonder whether we fit the definition of a happy family, one of those families I especially saw on television commercials around Christmas. It looked like smiles floated through those homes like bubbles. And there was always so much laughter. How often did we laugh? How often did I see bubbling smiles? Mother was always too busy teaching me things to make small talk or joke. I imagined a blackboard on wheels rolling behind me through every room.

"Do it this way" and "Say it this way" were like chants echoing everywhere, even outside. I heard them when I played in the backyard or when I rode my bike. They followed me to school. "Don't hike your skirt up so high." "Don't sit with your legs apart like that." "You bring your cup to your mouth, not your mouth to your cup." "Elbows," she would sing at dinner, and I would take them off so fast that someone sitting there would think the table was on fire.

I could hear all of it now as I sat quietly waiting for Daddy to come down. It occurred to me that my mother never could completely leave this house, even if she had run off with someone else. The walls had absorbed all her lessons, warnings, and threats. Every once in a while, one spilled out at my feet, and I could hear her saying it.

What a strange feeling it was to sense my mother still here, but I was far from used to the idea of her being away. Maybe I never would be. Right now, I half expected to see her come in or hurry around a corner the way she often did. I would look up. She would surely appear surprised and a little angry. "What's this about my running off with a lover?"

Was that the sound of her stiletto shoes on the floor above me? My mother's presence was always so strong that I could sense her even if she was in another room.

Her image preceded her. It was as if her silhouette could take off on its own and she would have to follow it instead of vice versa.

The ringing of the phone seemed to climb up my spine to my ears. I jumped and waited to see if Daddy would pick up. He didn't. I imagined he was still in the shower, so I lifted the receiver on the fourth ring. My mother's instructions for answering the phone accompanied the smooth, calm way I brought the receiver to my ear. After all, this might very well be her, calling to say she was on her way back. I wouldn't want her to begin by chastising me for not following her instructions.

"Barnaby residence," I said. "Scarletta Barnaby. With whom would you wish to speak?"

"Jesus," Jackie Hansford said. "Is this the White House or something?"

"Something," I said dryly.

"I just say hello when I answer the phone."

"How can I help you, Jackie?" I asked. My patience, like an old spiderweb, was quickly drying and coming apart. Of course, I thought her call might be about homework. I wasn't usually her first call for anything anymore. What else could it be?

"Help me? I think it's more me helping you. I'm having a TGIF party this weekend, and Chet Palmer says he won't come if you're not invited. If he doesn't come, Sean Connor won't come. They're like attached at the waist, and I have this thing for Sean. I told you, remember?"

I didn't. So much of her conversation and the conversation of girls like her in my class went by me like road signs when we were traveling fast on a major highway. All of it a blur, one merging into another.

"What's TGIF?"

"Are you kidding? Thank God It's Friday. What world are you in? It's an excuse for a party, Scarletta. My parents are leaving for the night, a sort of second honeymoon thing, and I'm left watching my brother Stuart. We'll drug him about seven," she said. I wasn't sure she was kidding.

"What's this about Chet?"

"Apparently, Miss Oblivious, he's got this serious crush on you. You don't have to dress formally for my party," she quickly added before I could respond. "Wear jeans and a blouse and sneakers. None of those expensive fancy shoes. No one's going to wear a dress. Come over about six, and we'll plot how to separate the two joined at the hip. You'll take my room, and I'll take my parents' when we do, okay?"

What was she suggesting? Good-bye to virginity? Some of them acted like it was a cannonball chained to their ankles. You'd think they breathed through a vagina.

"I don't know if I can attend."

"Attend? Well, now. Look, if you're worried about it, I'm not inviting you because we all feel sorry for you because of what your mother has done. It's a party, not a pity. We're going to have fun, and someone very good-looking is interested in you. This isn't brain surgery. Don't call Jared or Phoebe for advice. Okay?"

"I'll ask my father," I said.

"How is he doing?"

I knew she was asking more for her parents than herself. She hardly had spoken to him the two times she was here, and where else would she have seen him or had a chance to get to know him?

"We're fine. We're going out to dinner," I said.

"Sounds like you're celebrating. Whatever," she said. "Let me know as soon as you can. I'm depending on you. And you should be very excited. Just about every girl I know would like Chet to be after her booty."

I heard my father start down the stairs.

"Got to go," I said. "I'll call you later or let you know tomorrow."

"Call me later!" she practically screamed. "I have to make plans. Don't ruin it for me!"

I hung up the phone and sat back. Chet Palmer? Why hadn't I noticed he was interested in me? Was I really Miss Oblivious? Nevertheless, the invitation really seemed odd. Didn't Jackie think I might not be in the mood for a party since my mother had left us? Were parents breaking up and families splintering as important as a yawn to her and some of my other classmates?

"Hey," Daddy said, smiling from ear to ear. He was wearing his blue sports jacket and dark blue slacks with a sporty pair of blue and black loafers. He was also wearing a dark blue tie with his light blue shirt. My mother had told him blue was his best color, and he often went out of his way to find something blue to buy.

He held up my mother's best pearl necklace. In his other hand, he had her matching earrings. I stared, amazed. Those were the pearls she wore in her portrait. I glanced up at it. She seemed to be glaring down at me angrily.

"Mommy left those?"

"Yes, in her haste, she forgot she had them hidden in a drawer. She was paranoid, remember? She never kept her best things in her jewelry box. Too obvious and easy for a burglar. I was surprised it was there myself. I saw it last night and thought someday it would be yours anyway. Well, tonight it is," he said.

I rose slowly. First he gave me her dress, and now her pearls. My inheritance had been sped up. Was that the silver lining? Would it ever compensate? Instinctively, I glanced back at the sofa as if I thought my mother was sitting there, watching. I would always look for her approval, probably until the day I died, whether she had left us for good or not.

Daddy put the pearl necklace around my neck and fastened it. Then he handed me the earrings.

"Go in the powder room and put them on," he said.

I took them, gazed at them in my palm, and then went to do what he had asked. When I looked at myself in the mirror, having put on her dress, fixing my makeup like she would fix hers, wearing her pearl necklace and earrings, with my hair done like her hair, my heart began to pound. I didn't want to look good in her things, I didn't want to be happy wearing them, but I couldn't help feeling that yes, I could be as beautiful as she was. Nevertheless, it made me feel mean. There was a part of me that either I had ignored or that had just been born, the part that was willing to be happy she was gone, even if that was only for tonight.

"Truly beautiful. The jewelry looks like it was made for you," Daddy said when I stepped out. He held out his hand. "Let's go enjoy a wonderful meal and talk only about you."

I took his hand, and we went to the door to the garage. He hurried around to do something he only did for my mother, opening her door. After he got in and backed out, he looked at me and smiled. Was he acting this way for me? He was happy or really doing a good job pretending.

"So really, how was your day at school?" he asked as we drove off.

He nodded as I described it, even including the nasty way Janice Lyn had come over to me to ask about my mother. Once again, he found that deep expression of rage.

"It's one thing to disregard *my* feelings," he said, "but to do something like this to *you*, knowing how hard it was going to be, is unforgivable. Scarletta, I swear, I wouldn't take her back if she came begging at the door."

I didn't want to say I wouldn't, either, because I would. It would be like an Etch A Sketch. I'd lift the sad and ugly days away and start another as if nothing ugly and sad had happened. Everything would be as it was. Daddy wouldn't even mention it, either, because he'd want us to be happy together. How could any man love his wife more than Daddy did? He'd get over his rage quickly, just the way he often did. Those flashes of anger would see that they had no place in his heart and flutter off like unwelcome birds.

We parked at the restaurant, and Daddy came around the car as I stepped out. He took my hand, but not like he had when I was a little girl. This time, he wanted to draw me closer and walk like he had with my mother.

"Come here," he said, first putting his arm around my shoulders and then taking my hand. "I'm not going to let a woman as pretty as this trail along as if she didn't belong to me."

Was I really as pretty as he was saying, or was he telling himself all this to keep himself from crying again? My father was always proud to be with my mother. More times than I could count, he would tell people, "She makes me look good."

When we entered the restaurant, I did feel everyone's eyes on us. I could also sense I was blushing under their scrutinizing gazes, some of the men smiling conspiratorially as if Daddy had walked in with his secret lover. My mother would say that was something they wished they could do.

"Looking at some of their wives, who'd blame them?" she'd mutter loud enough for me to hear.

Daddy knew the maître d', Sergio, who, if he could fly over to us, would have. He cut short his conversation with another couple and rushed across the room to greet us.

"Mr. Barnaby, welcome. I have your favorite table."

"Thank you, Sergio. You remember my daughter, Scarletta?"

"Oh, yes, but to see her now so grown-up and beautiful, I thought for a moment she was your wife."

"Not an unexplainable mistake," Daddy said proudly.

Sergio led us to the table in the right corner that was just up enough on a small rise to give it the look of someplace special. It was visible from every angle in the rest of the room, and most of the other people were looking at us. I wondered how many Daddy knew and how many knew about my mother's leaving. I saw no one from my school. Actually, I never heard any of my classmates talk about Dante's. Either their parents never took them here or they went here only by themselves or with adult friends.

I wondered why Sergio hadn't asked after my mother after he had referred to her. Had the news spread so quickly far and wide? What news compared in speed to bad news? Some headline about an international incident didn't have a chance against local gossip.

"A martini, Sergio, and then a bottle of our favorite chianti, please," Daddy said. "And one glass, of course."

"I'll see to it," Sergio said, handing us the menus.

Daddy didn't open his. "Long ago memorized," he said, tapping it. "I'm pretty sure you liked the veal scampi. When you were younger, you shared it with your mother. Remember?"

That was only earlier this year, I thought. What did he mean by "When you were younger"? I nodded, remembering to sit up straight and not look around the room like some "curious busybody." I could feel Mother sitting beside me, telling me that you let people come to you in places like this. "You don't go running about as if you are desperate for friends. It diminishes you, Scarletta."

My father, however, was usually not like that. He would tell her that it was important for his business to network with people. "Many a good sale came from a casual conversation," he told her, actually the last time we were here. He had gotten up to go to someone else's table.

"How desperate you look," my mother remarked when he returned, but he smiled as if she simply didn't understand the world of commerce.

"I stamp my personality on everything I do," he said.

She looked at me, raised her eyes toward the ceiling, and shook her head.

Daddy smiled at other people now. He would show no one an iota of sadness.

"When something terrible happens to you," he said, more like he was convincing himself than me, because he wasn't looking at me as he spoke, "especially something personal like family disappointments, it's better to get out in public as soon as possible and illustrate to the world that you are still standing. We're still standing, I mean," he added, turning to me.

The waiter brought Daddy his martini.

"Would you like a Sprite or something, Scarletta?" Daddy asked.

"Water's fine," I said.

Daddy raised his eyebrows and looked at the waiter, a dark-haired young man who was staring at me, trying, I imagined, to determine my age.

"Women. Always thinking of their figures," Daddy said. "That is, pretty women."

"Absolutely, sir," the waiter said. He poured me a glass of water.

"Give us a moment," Daddy told him.

After he walked away, Daddy lifted his martini. "Let's toast, Scarletta, to us, to survivors," he said.

I didn't like to think of myself that way or him, either, for that matter. It made it sound like we had gone through a war or a shipwreck. But maybe it was accurate to describe our ship as being badly damaged. We were both in a lifeboat together now. Where it would take us I did not know, but I tapped my water glass against his martini, and he drank it all in one long swallow. The surprise on my face brought a smile to his.

"Your toast means more if you drink it all in one gulp," he said. "A friend of my father's told me that. He was from Hungary, a good businessman. But don't you ever drink like that," he warned.

"I'm like Mother. I'm not fond of hard liquor, Daddy. Not that I'm any sort of expert about it."

"Some stupidity is good," he muttered.

I didn't think he liked my saying "I'm like Mother." He had winced when I said it.

He signaled the waiter, who came instantly.

"We'll share a Dante's salad and both have the veal scampi," Daddy said.

"Very good, sir."

"You can bring the wine with our salad, but in the meantime, another one of these," he said, giving him his empty martini glass.

"Very good, sir."

"I really can't believe how grown-up you look, Scar-letta. I feel like I've been away or something. Funny how things in life get you to look harder at what you look at every day."

"I don't get dressed up like this often, Daddy."

"No, I guess not," he said sadly. Then he smiled again. "Maybe you will now, more often."

I wasn't sure why I would, but I nodded.

The waiter brought my father his second martini. He drank it almost as fast as the first.

Just as he finished, the waiter brought the wine Daddy had ordered and opened it, pouring a little in the wine-glass for my father to taste. Whenever I was with my mother and him and they ordered wine, he usually had her taste it. She was more particular, I thought, and he was always concerned about her being pleased with what they had ordered.

"Good," he said, and the waiter poured him a glass.

"Let's toast each other again, Scarletta," he said, rais-ing his glass. "One of my favorite quotes is quite apt. 'What doesn't destroy us makes us stronger.' You and I will get stronger. I promise."

I didn't smile this time, but I tapped his glass with mine again. To me, he was making it worse for us by continually referring to what had happened and what would have to happen now. Although I wouldn't pretend my mother hadn't deserted us, there was still a little hope that she would realize what she had done and return. Surely if she did, Daddy wouldn't want me to mention any of his quotes and toasts.

I could almost feel other people watching us, wondering what we were celebrating. Daddy was surely trying to show them very clearly that he wasn't destroyed. I imagined some of the women were already thinking of someone to introduce him to at some social event or another. His cheerfulness wasn't unexpected. How could a man so handsome and successful be destroyed by one woman? He could snap his fingers and get half the eligible women in this community coming after him.

During dinner, Daddy didn't ask me another question about school, the track team, or any of my classmates. Even his tone was different. He talked to me as if he was truly out with my mother, telling me about some business decisions he had made and his plans for expanding the factory. He talked constantly and drank the wine quickly, ordering another martini after he had finished the bottle. He was finishing his food quickly, too.

"Are you going to change anything in our house?" I asked, really to bring us both back to reality.

"What? No. Why would I change anything?" He studied me a moment. "Is there something you'd like to change?"

How confusing, I thought. He acted like he believed my mother would never return, but he wanted to keep everything she had done.

I was tempted to talk about my room, but seeing how he wasn't changing anything and the way he had reacted to the suggestion, I thought perhaps he didn't want to admit or show me that he still believed my mother would return.

"No, nothing."

He smiled, looking relieved. Then he looked around and nodded at someone. People leaving did stop by to say hello to him. He introduced me as Scarletta and never added "my daughter." I think he wanted me to feel more grown-up. One man, Preston Forest, a business attorney who had done work for Daddy, held his incredulous smile and asked, "Isn't this your daughter?"

"Is it?" Daddy joked. "I thought she looked familiar."

"I'm not surprised she's become so beautiful," Preston said.

"She's mature for her age, in every way," Daddy practically snapped back at him.

"Right. I'll call you on Tuesday about the Farmington deal. They are very interested," he said, turned back to me, and told me how pleased he was to have met me.

I gave him my hand the way Mother had taught me. "Not like a man about to shake," she had warned. "Keep your hand dainty, feminine. Don't squeeze his fingers. You're permitting him to touch you. That's all."

Preston smiled even more brightly, glanced at Daddy, gave him a little nod, and then left us to join two other men with whom he had been eating. Whatever he told them got them to look our way and smile to each other the way boys do when they're whispering something X-rated.

Daddy didn't notice.

"Farmington wants to furnish all their offices with my furniture," he said, leaning toward me. "Custom made. *Mucho dinero*. We'll build that pool in the back I was thinking about last year. And fill it with money," he added.

My mother would tell him not to sound so coarse about money. I just nodded. Maybe it was because of how much he had drunk, but he was even more animated than when we had first arrived at the restaurant and was intent on proving we were just fine.

I never thought we weren't rich. We bought or didn't buy things based on what my mother wanted or didn't want. Never once did I ever hear Daddy say, "We can't afford that now," or, "You're spending money too fast, faster than I can make it."

I hadn't noticed, but whether it was assumed or not, the waiter brought my father a glass of sambuca. It had the coffee beans in it. It was actually more my mother's favorite after-dinner drink than his. He sipped it immediately and leaned toward me again like someone about to whisper.

"I think we can do this," he said. "We have a right to

celebrate a bit despite what's happened, meaning you, too, should taste a bit of success. I'm already planning for the car I'm going to buy you when you get your driver's license."

He poured a tiny bit of his sambuca into my empty water glass.

"I know you like this, too."

I drank it, but I didn't like it and had never told him I did. If anyone from the restaurant saw him give some of his sambuca to me, he didn't complain. Daddy seemed to grow happier by the minute, and truthfully, I wasn't feeling as sad as I had before we had left the house. I had come with him expecting to feel guilty when I enjoyed myself, but those feelings had quickly faded. Also, I sensed that one sad or gloomy expression would ruin it all for him, so whether my smiles looked artificial or not, I kept them going.

We had tiramisu for dessert. Daddy ordered an espresso with vodka, drank it quickly, and then ordered another. He let me taste it, and I did think it was good. I might tell some of my friends, I thought, just to show them I was sophisticated. I was sure few, if any, even Jackie, had ever drunk one.

Daddy flagged the waiter for our check. Without even looking at what we had spent, he gave the waiter his credit card. My mother would have snapped at him. "At least pretend to care," she would say.

When we started out, practically everyone working there made a point of nodding or saying good night. Funny, I thought, how a really sad thing had suddenly turned us into celebrities. It was as if they all were hoping we'd say something they could spread like inside news, a scoop of local gossip that would make them seem more important.

Outside, Daddy held my hand tighter and quickly opened the car door. He was strangely silent now. Again, I thought it was probably the effect of all that alcohol. Actually, I was afraid we'd be stopped. If it was a local policeman, he might feel sorry for us. Still, pity would be pouring gasoline on a fire.

He drove out, not looking at me. I couldn't tell if he was content because we had enjoyed our dinner and dealt with the curiosity of strangers or if he was raging with anger inside. Finally, he gave me a compliment, a reluctant compliment.

"Your mother brought you up well, Scarletta. I meant what I told Preston. You're heads and shoulders above girls your age, thanks to her. Everyone in the restaurant was impressed with you. I could see it on their faces. You must be frustrated with how immature your friends are."

"Sometimes," I confessed. And then I thought about Jackie. "I was invited to a party Friday at Jackie Hansford's house."

He spun around so abruptly that I thought we'd go off the road.

"Someone invited you to a party now?" Before I could reply, he calmed and added, "They probably feel sorry for you. You don't let them pity you, Scarletta. I won't have it. Stay home instead."

"No, that's not the reason I was invited, Daddy. There's a senior boy who likes me, and Jackie likes a boy he's friends with. She's plotting, but that doesn't mean I'll be part of it. If you don't want me to go now . . ."

He stared ahead without talking. Almost a full minute went by.

"When I was your age, girls from broken homes were thought to be easy."

"Easy? What do you mean?"

"One or the other of their parents had committed adultery or was a hopeless alcoholic or drug addict, so it was just assumed their children, especially a daughter, would have less morals. Easy," he said.

I was stunned for a moment. Jackie had said we were going to split up bedrooms. Now that Daddy had mentioned "easy," I thought Jackie was making quite an assumption about me. I reviewed what she had told me. I should be grateful Chet Palmer wanted to make love to me, grateful and clearly willing. Until this moment, I didn't see anything wrong with being curious about myself. How far would I go at this party if I went into the bedroom with Chet? Wasn't it normal, natural, for a girl to wonder?

I really hadn't thought deeply about why Chet Palmer suddenly seemed so interested in me. I was just surprised and blamed it on what she had called me, "Miss Oblivious." Was my father right? Was I really a simple, naive girl about to be exploited?

"It's all right. It's not very important to me," I said. "If you think it's wrong for me to socialize right now, I . . ."

"I'm not saying that," he said sharply. "That's exactly what she would expect me to say."

I was silent. Would my mother really want him to say that? We had gone to dinner in her favorite restaurant, almost as if we had intended to throw what she had done back into her face. It was important to my father to prove to everyone that he was not devastated. Was it supposed to be that important to me as well? Otherwise, what would become of me? For the rest of my high school life, I would be an object of pity. *There's that girl whose mother left her without so much as a good-bye. Imagine. Now you know why she's such a slut.*

"Actually," Daddy said, "now that I really think about it, if you don't socialize, they'll believe you're suffering or I'm suffering and you have to babysit me. I won't give her that satisfaction. Ever."

He sounded brave, defiant, but no matter how much we had enjoyed our dinner, we were suffering. I wouldn't dare say that while he was feeling so confident, but unless he went around the house wearing blinders, he would realize it.

"Okay. I'll do what you say, Daddy."

"It's all right to go, but I'll pick you up at eleven thirty. I think considering your age, that's when your mother would want me to do so."

"Fine," I said, but clearly not with great enthusiasm. Knowing the others, no one else would have as early a curfew, if any.

He smiled at me. "Don't dare punish yourself for what your mother has done to us," he said. "I won't hear of it."

I nodded but said no more. The revelation and conversation seemed to have sobered him quickly. Daddy and I were both silent, lost in our own thoughts, as if we were alone in the world during the last minute or so of our trip home. I was sure we were both thinking so hard about my mother that it was truly as though she was sitting in the rear listening to our thoughts and either grimacing with pain or condemning our conclusions the way she could with an icy glaze over her eyes and her lips pressed together so hard they formed little white pockets in the corners of her mouth.

"We're here," Daddy muttered as we pulled into our driveway.

He sounded like we had traveled half the universe in a rocket and were never sure we would arrive safely. Was this going to be the way it would always be for him whenever he came home, driving in with the realization that she was gone pounding harder and louder? After all, if a house could have a soul, an essence, ours had come from my mother.

Truthfully, when we entered it, our house had never felt as empty. Mother was usually already there by the time we had arrived after Daddy picked me up after school for one reason or another, or anywhere I was, for that matter. It wasn't only the whiffs of her pungent perfume that greeted us. We could feel her presence. If the house breathed, it was her breath. Whether it was the sounds from the kitchen or hearing her moving about in the living room or descending the stairway, the house was revealing her to us.

Daddy might announce, "We're back," as if he was warning her or reassuring her. I was never quite sure.

She was the one who took me to see our doctor if I needed some medical attention for a cold or flu. It mostly fell to Daddy to take me to and from the dentist whenever possible. Mother hated waiting anywhere. She was not a magazine reader and detested small talk.

"People," she said, "are simply too nosy. However the chitchat begins, it always turns on a personal question. Women today will tell you if they have a vaginal infection, even if they just met you. And then they'll wait to see if you will offer something personal, too. I hope they always feel like fools. You can see it on their faces: 'I told you a secret. Now you have to tell me one.'"

Tonight the echoes of silence reinforced the emptiness I had felt since she left us. I was tired from riding the roller coaster of emotions all day and evening. I practically dragged myself up the stairway.

As soon as I had stepped into my room, I called Jackie to let her know. I was interested in what she might say and looking for something that might give me more insight into why she and Chet actually wanted me at the party so much.

"Good," she said. "We'll talk more about it at school tomorrow. Don't go sit with the brains at lunchtime. They'd probably tell you a party is a savage custom or something equally stupid. Think only about Chet," she said. "Dream about his fingers."

"His fingers?"

"On your nipples. You have them, don't you?" she asked, and laughed. "Nighty-night."

I felt the heat rise to my face, hung up, and got undressed. I was really worrying about it now. Maybe I shouldn't go, but I knew I had to find a way to prove to my father that it wasn't because of what my mother had done to us. Perhaps I would make it up, tell him I overheard the boys say I was easy. He'd believe that. On the other hand, what if I was wrong? What would I look like then? What kind of a life loomed ahead for me in my school, in this community?

I was almost dizzy with the confusion and now

eager to just go to sleep and think about it all in the morning.

But when I opened my closet to take out my nightgown, I froze.

Hanging there on the door was my mother's pink lace and chiffon nightgown.

And her slippers were on the floor.

Pru

CHANDLER STEPPED IN the moment I opened the door, put his arms around me, and kissed me as if he had crossed the ocean to meet me. He often kissed me with such passion that he swept me off my feet, especially now that we were apart longer. But there was something about this kiss that was different. It was a kiss that was searching for confirmation, examining and testing. He held his lips just off mine, waiting for me to kiss him again. Would I? I knew that feeling of uncertainty he was experiencing. Doubt, especially when it came to romance, was an old acquaintance.

"You all right?" he asked suspiciously after I gave him a short second kiss, my lips snapping on his with the click of a match being struck. "You sounded upset when I called you from the airport. Something happen at work?"

His eyes were two microscope lenses searching my face for clues.

"No," I said, turning away from him quickly. I didn't trust my normally inscrutable face under such scrutiny. In a moment, he would know all.

But I understood why he had questions and concerns. No doubt I had sounded troubled when he called. Practically the entire time I was getting ready and dressed to go to our fancy dinner, my hands had been trembling. At one point, I had to stop and rub them together vigorously because they were numb. It felt like blood wasn't getting to my fingers. The tips looked white. I was beginning to disappear. The strength, determination, and courage I prided myself on having as an independent woman seemed to be crumbling. Little parts of me like late autumn leaves were breaking off and floating down.

Now I wondered what Chandler would realize. Would he take one look at me and know what Douglas Thomas had done? I really was afraid of that happening no matter how I tried to disguise myself. I had seen victims of rape in the ER waiting to be examined. Their faces looked frozen in shock, but the explosion of emotion, horror, and violation was imminent. They were time bombs ticking away. Some had difficulty breathing, others couldn't stop crying, and then there were those who decided they couldn't go through with the exam and confirmation. They would live with the pain. Of course, they never would. It was forever part of their essence, printed on their bones. They would take it to their graves and wait for it to fade into dust.

What would I do now?

Which face would Chandler see? Perhaps my reaction to what Douglas Thomas had done was buried under my second emotional trauma in less than forty-eight hours. Ironically, I should be grateful to Scarletta. At the moment, the shock and distress she had caused had risen to the surface and forced everything else beneath it. Of all the messages Scarletta had left, this last one struck the center of my heart of fears: I could run, but I couldn't hide? Nothing she previously had said was as clearly colored with her determination to do me some harm. She was out there. One way or another, she would not rest until she had destroyed me, destroyed Pru Dunning.

And the thing about it was I really didn't know why. If I was pressed for possible motives, I wouldn't show confidence in my theories.

Should I tell it all to him now, reveal it like a confession? *Yes, I have kept things from you. Yes, I have not been honest, and I know people who are in love have to be honest with each other above all else. One simple deceit destroys trust, and then love itself crumbles.*

I could begin calmly with *This is what happened since you've been gone.*

How strong was Chandler's love for me? Would he survive the flood of such revelations? Could he believe in or care for a woman who had kept these things secret from him, treating him more like a stranger? What about her faith in him? Why wouldn't I have told him immediately? At this moment, I felt doomed if I did and doomed if I didn't.

"Something's definitely bothering you, Pru," Chandler said. "No sense denying it. Remember? We can read each other like Google reads a map."

Of course, he was right. Nevertheless, I stood there, still deciding. I realized he was probably wondering if there was something wrong between us, if I was trying to find a way to tell him that I wanted to break up. After all, what other suspicion would he have? I had been avoiding a long-term commitment. No matter what I said, he couldn't help but think I wasn't quite sure I was in love with him. His patience was thinning. Perhaps at least some of the truth was the only way to keep his faith in us. Dose it out like distasteful medicine to a patient, a spoonful at a time but quickly, I told myself.

"Pru?"

He put his hand on my shoulder. I was still turned away, looking down. Finally, it came up and out of my lips like sour milk.

"Someone's stalking me," I said, without turning back to him. *Stick with this first*, I thought. *Get his sympathy, and he'll blame you less for not telling him what Douglas Thomas did. After all, look at what you've been going through.*

"What? When? After work? Following you home?"

"It began on the phone, only leaving messages until now, messages designed to upset me."

"How long has this been going on?"

"A while," I said. "On and off. Sometimes weeks would go by with no calls, and then sometimes twice or three times the same week."

"Weeks? Why haven't you told me this? Have you told anyone? Gone to the police? What?"

"No, I've told no one."

"I don't understand. Why not? Why not tell me?"

"I thought I could deal with it myself," I said, turning to face him fully now. My confidence had returned. "Crank calls." I shrugged. "Who doesn't get some?"

"But what did you mean just now when you said 'only leaving messages until now'? What's changed?"

I did blurt that out, didn't I? I thought. Why didn't I just leave it at phone messages? That would have been easy. My father's toothpaste analogy returned. There was no Delete button.

"I suspected someone was following me yesterday when I went out for a walk around the block. 'Suspected' is the key word."

"What did he look like? Was it someone recognizable, from work, a former patient?"

"It's not a man."

"A woman is stalking you?"

"She calls herself Scarletta, but I suspect that's not her real name."

"Scarletta? Who could that be?"

"I thought it might be someone at the hospital trying to torment me, but I didn't recognize this woman's voice. Not that I know everyone who works at Cedars, of course."

"It's a woman?" He thought a moment. "But why would someone at the hospital be doing this to you?"

"Jealousy, maybe. It's become a little more intense lately."

"Why?"

"I told you how upset they were after I told my patient he was given the wrong medicine, the exact opposite of what he should have been given. I was praised for being alert and stopping it, but it didn't fly well with most of the others."

"But you said this harassment has been going on for a while. Before that incident?"

"Yes."

He looked at my answering machine and said, "So that's why you changed your number?"

"Yes."

"But you did that shortly after we started dating, Pru. It's been months, then, not weeks. I can't believe you kept it to yourself and didn't tell me the real reason for the change. Not even a hint."

"Sorry. I didn't want you worrying," I added. "And especially now, with you being away and all. I didn't think it would go on this long. Like I said, everyone gets annoying calls." I pulled my shoulders back. "I'm not, nor will I ever be, the sort of woman who runs to her man for everyday little problems."

"But this doesn't sound like your everyday little problem. Now someone may be following you? What sorts of things has she been saying? What does she want? Is she threatening you? That's a reason to go to the police and get the phone tapped."

I sat on the sofa. Time to walk it back a bit, I thought. He was getting red in the face from both frustration and sincere fear for my safety.

"They're not threats, exactly, Chandler. Mostly annoying, teasing things. In a recent message, she knew about the pearls my patient had given me. That's the main reason why I now feel certain it's someone at the hospital."

"What did she say about the pearls?"

"She said if she were me, she'd get rid of them, flush them down a toilet."

"Flush . . . why?"

"She said you'd be jealous."

"So she knows about us, too, then?"

"Yes."

"You told me you didn't talk about your personal life at work."

"Very little and very generally, especially with patients."

"But you're sure you didn't mention me? You once told me that you made it a point not to talk about us at work in particular, Pru. You seemed adamant about that."

"Not because I'm ashamed of you. I don't like the busybodies X-raying my social life. You'd be surprised at how much hospital employees gossip about each other, especially when it comes to tidbits about doctors and especially about those nurses who flirt with them. You'd think they're all back in high school or something. What's going on medically is almost a distraction. I refused to be a part of that."

I saw that I had calmed him a little.

"Maybe that's why they distrust me, dislike me," I said. "It happened the same way in high school. You'd think people with that much authority and importance would be mature."

"Well, I'm not really jealous about the pearls. As I said, I'm worried about improprieties. Where are they?"

"In my bedroom. The pearls aren't the important thing now, Chandler. A woman was following me yesterday. Maybe it was the same woman. She's been making sexual comments lately, too," I added. I wasn't sure if that made it sound more or less troubling.

"Sexual? Like what?"

"Admiring my body, my walk, talking about fucking me, drawing it out with salacious details, practically having an orgasm over the phone."

"Really? So . . . she's an admirer of sorts, a lesbian?"

"Maybe. It seems like these days, you can't be sure about anyone. You're afraid to open closets."

He nodded, thinking. "Are you sure it's not someone else, someone from the past? Scarletta doesn't sound familiar?"

"Meaning what? You think I might have had a gay lover in college or something?"

"Maybe she just wants to hurt our relationship," he said, instead of replying.

"Good luck with that," I said.

That pleased him for a moment, but he lost the smile quickly. "So you have no real idea who it is, no clues?"

"I now suspect the nurse who gave the patient the wrong medication has something to do with it. She was always jealous of the compliments I received, even before the incident."

"Well, does it sound like her on the phone?"

"No, but she could be getting someone else to do it, maybe one of the other aides that I don't know. I think she's capable of that."

"Pretty juvenile behavior," he said. He turned to the answering machine. "Play some back," he said.

"I erased them," I said.

"What? Why? That's evidence, Pru. We might need it later."

"I couldn't stand hearing them, especially after the last one. It was irrational, I know, but it was creepy to me to have her voice stored in there. It was like she was here all the time."

"What exactly was the last one? Why was that so much more disturbing?"

"She told me 'you can run, but you can't hide.' That was there after I had seen the woman I think was following me. I lost her when I made some turns and sped up. I actually hid for a few minutes in another building's entryway so I could pounce on her when she appeared. She didn't follow, and she wasn't at my entry when I returned. So maybe she wasn't following me."

"But this last message was left before you returned to the apartment? It was waiting for you?"

"Yes."

"So it probably was her. She was out there wanting to confront you in some way, and for some reason, she might have changed her mind. Now I'm really sorry you didn't tell me earlier. It does sound dangerous."

He thought a moment. I could see his mind was twirling with the possibilities. He was going to insist I call the police. Why didn't I kiss him the way I always did? Why didn't I just keep all this to myself and deal with it myself?

"This is a lot more serious than it might seem, Pru. You shouldn't have let it go on this long. I'm very concerned. It's all too weird, especially if it involves another nurse at your hospital. Who knows what else she is capable of doing? She could deliberately hurt one of your patients. She could—"

"I knew you would say things like that. That was why I didn't want to talk about it."

"But she's gotten to you now, and she knows where you live, and—"

I stood up. "I don't want to go to the police and start a whole big thing, Chandler. It's what she wants, I'm sure."

"Stalkers can be dangerous. Who takes the time out to make all these calls for so long and then follows you? She's intimidating you with the sex talk, too, and we're not sure for what purpose now or when it will end."

"I'll end it," I said, and went over to the answering machine. I detached it and took it to the garbage can in the kitchen.

"That doesn't solve the problem," he said when I dropped it into the can.

"I'm disconnecting my landline, too. I'll inform the hospital I'm on mobile only."

"What if she gets that number? Nothing's sacred anymore."

"I'll change it."

He shook his head. "You could just be driving her to

make new contact with you, more direct contact. Besides, from what you've described, she's already gone beyond making nuisance calls, Pru. I don't think it's merely some infatuation, something sexual, either. She'd have made it possible for you to contact her by now." He shook his head. "No. This is more serious. She might come at you before you could defend yourself or something. I don't like not telling the police. Later we might regret it, and that will be the first question they'll ask. 'Why didn't you call for help?'"

"Let's wait a little longer," I said as firmly as I could. He was getting me to doubt myself. "Maybe if she can't get to me, realizes I'm not going to respond, she'll stop bothering me."

"But considering the message she left last . . . and what she's already done . . ." He shook his head. "This is a lot more than just bugging people on the phone for gags." He nodded. "I think you might be right thinking it's someone at the hospital. If it's become revenge now, it sounds pretty sick."

"I'm a nurse. I can handle sick."

"Don't joke about it, Pru. Damn. I wish you had told me when it first began. If the police didn't take it seriously enough, I'd have used our private detective service."

"Let's stop talking about her. I'm sorry I brought it up. It was a mistake to upset you."

"What? What are you saying? I'm glad you did, Pru.

What happens to you is important to me, and I would hope vice versa."

"I know. I'm not trying to diminish your concern for me. Of course you would care. I just don't like her coming between us."

"You talk about her like you really do know her," he said suspiciously.

"I don't. I swear."

He nodded. "Nevertheless, we have to recognize that we live in a world where people just decide one day to shoot innocent strangers. We can't ignore things like this. I want you to at least tell me anything else that occurs as soon as it does, okay? And if that name suggests someone, anything that comes to you, let me know."

"Yeah, well, I'm sorry I ran from her. Next time, I'll confront her."

"Have you accused this other nurse, the one who made the medicine mistake, said anything that might get her to believe you suspect her of doing this now?"

"No. She'd really like that, having me make a scene at work. Please. Stop thinking about it. You're whittling away at my courage. I don't need more help gathering nightmares."

"Okay, okay. We'll talk about it later and make a better plan. Let's go to dinner," he said. "I wanted this to be a special night for us," he added, practically under his breath.

"We won't let her ruin it, then," I said, even though I couldn't imagine it would be the beautiful evening he had planned.

When he opened the door, he paused. "Can you describe the woman you saw, the woman you think was out there waiting for you?"

"Chandler . . . we just agreed . . ."

"Four eyes are better than two out there."

I sighed. Now I was working harder at calming him down than I was at calming myself.

"She was about my height, I think, wearing jeans and the layered look, a light blue sweater over a blue and white blouse. Dark brown hair, I think."

"You think?"

"I caught her under a streetlight. It might have been closer to black."

"Fat, thin?"

"No, a nice figure. Oh, she had blue running shoes, but I didn't see any socks."

"So she was that close to you?"

I shrugged. "A half block or so. I do have good eyesight, Chandler."

"Well, did she look like that nurse?"

"No, but as I said, it might be someone she put up to it. That makes sense to me, because if she did it herself and I saw her, I'd know this was all her, and I certainly wouldn't have tried to lose her. I'd confront her. She doesn't live in this part of LA, so she'd have no excuse for being here."

"It's thin, someone doing all this for so long out of professional jealousy and raising the intensity because you caught her medicine mistake? Someone that obsessed would attract more attention. We might be dealing with something completely unknown, Pru."

"I have no reason to suspect anyone else. There's no one from the past who would suddenly appear and go after me. Please. Stop thinking about it. I'll find a way to end it."

"I don't know. Something's not right about this."

"No kidding."

"Okay. When we step out, we'll pause so you can look around carefully."

"If we behave like paranoids, she's won," I said, but when we stepped out, I did pause to look up and down the street. He waited for me to say something. I shook my head, and we walked to his car. As he opened the door for me, I watched him scrutinizing every woman walking on the sidewalk and crossing the street.

"You look like a Secret Service agent, Chandler, a pretty obvious one. You'll make her happy we're spooked."

He nodded, closed the door, and went around to get in.

"Maybe if she sees I'm around, she'll get more discouraged," he said after he got in.

"Please, please. Let's not talk about this anymore," I said. "Tell me about San Francisco and what you've done and have left to do."

He started the car and began to describe his work as we headed for the restaurant.

I listened, but I barely heard a word.

At dinner, Chandler did try to make the evening special, but every smile, every laugh, seemed to struggle under the weight of what I had revealed. He constantly gazed around the restaurant as if he was afraid someone was near us, watching us, waiting for an opportunity to stab me or something. When I rose to go to the bathroom, he looked like he was going to follow me to the door.

"It's all right," I said, smiling. "I have a derringer in my purse."

"What?"

"Joke," I said, and left him.

I kept chastising myself for telling him anything. What made me do it?

"You keep secrets," my mother once told me, "to avoid hurting someone."

When I returned, I saw him watching me with the eyes of an Israeli Mossad agent. He had finished our bottle of wine and replaced it with a bottle of champagne chilling in a pail. It wasn't opened. I froze. It was Dom Pérignon, the same champagne Douglas Thomas had brought me.

"You all right?" Chandler asked. "You look a little pale."

"No, I'm fine."

He rose quickly to pull out my chair and then sat.

"I don't think I can drink much more, Chandler," I said, nodding at the champagne.

For a moment, it was Douglas Thomas sitting across from me, smiling. I might have gasped. Chandler reached across the table for my hand, but I saw Douglas Thomas's bony, prehensile fingers. I pulled my hand back.

"What's wrong?" Chandler asked. "Pru!"

I looked at him. Douglas Thomas faded back into Chandler, and I breathed again.

"I'm sorry. I know I told you we should forget what's been happening to me, but despite how I was before, thinking about it now angers me so much."

"Exactly," he said. "We've got to put an end to it."

I smiled and reached for his hand. "I do love you for the way you love me, Chandler, but can we postpone that champagne?"

Disappointment flooded his face. I suspected the reason he had asked the waiter to bring it, but even he realized the timing was off now.

"Sure. Let's just go back to your apartment. I'm not leaving you tonight," he said, and signaled the waiter. He explained that we were not doing the champagne this time and asked for the check.

"I'm sorry, Chandler."

"It's all right," he said, but I knew it wasn't. He probably had been thinking all week of that champagne and what he was going to say. In a real way, Scarletta was ruining my life.

We were silent almost all the way back to my place. After we parked, he just sat there looking out at the street and the traffic. I did, too. He turned to me, his eyes questioning.

"I don't see her, Chandler."

"It can't go on. I want to get our detective on this," he said. "He won't bother you, and no one will know anything. Also, I'd like you to put the answering machine back and not change your number. We want to catch her, give her a chance to make a mistake."

I started to shake my head.

"We won't involve the police. I promise. My guy is just an added layer of protection. We'll bring it to an end. Okay?"

"I suspect you would do it if I agreed or not," I said.

"Yes, but it will be a lot easier with your help."

"Okay, but I don't want him coming around the hospital asking anyone questions. Promise that."

"I promise. He's pretty good. If he did, neither of us would know anyway."

"I'd know, and I would be very upset," I said. "Will I meet him?"

"No. It's better if you don't look for him or look at him and that way warn your stalker."

"Okay," I said.

He pressed his hand on mine. "We'll work this out, Pru. I promise."

"I know."

"You still have that port I brought back from New York?"

"It doesn't work as shampoo, so yes."

"Very funny," he said, opening the car door.

Even though he tried not to make it obvious, he was looking everywhere as we headed for the building's entrance. It was misty now, some low cloud cover. Traffic was just as heavy as ever. It seemed like no one stayed home in Los Angeles. There weren't many pedestrians, but those who were near us seemed totally involved in themselves. Chandler held the door open for me but continued to look up and down the street. I had to wait for him to enter behind me.

Still in his protective mode, he walked up the stairs just a little ahead of me. When we reached the second floor, he paused, stopped abruptly, actually. I caught up with him, and we both looked at my door. I felt the chill move up my legs to my heart.

There was a bouquet of long-stemmed red roses lying there, the bottom wrapped in blue tissue paper. Chandler looked at me, and I shook my head and shrugged. We both approached it as if it was a land mine. He knelt and picked up the roses. There was no card, just the roses. They were fresh.

"This is really sick," he said. "She came to your door and left this?"

It was on the tip of my tongue to say it probably wasn't my stalker.

But then I thought it probably was.

After all, I had two.

Scarletta

I WASN'T GOING to put on my mother's nightgown, but like a child years younger, I did, because it made me feel closer to her. The sheer nightgown was perfumed with her lavender scent, a scent she claimed helped her fall asleep. I imagined how content my father was having it float to his nostrils, twirling into his mind to bring him a restful sleep while he lay there beside her, never dreaming of what would happen.

The gown was so light, so much lighter than my own, that I felt like I could float in it. My body tingled under the airy material. I turned and skipped like Peter Pan into the bathroom to prepare for bed.

When I paused and stepped back to look at myself in the mirror after brushing my teeth, I felt a very warm excitement at the sight of my perky breasts, my narrow waist, the small of my stomach, and my patch of pubic hair. No boy had yet seen me naked. I was even bashful in the locker room with my teammates.

Once again, I wondered. What would I do with Chet Palmer this Friday? What had Jackie really told him about me? Did she convince him that I was close enough of a friend to tell her intimate things about myself? I had never shared any with any other girl in school, not that my classmates, even my teammates, were dying to know things about me, especially my love life. Anyone could see that Jackie and many of my classmates made me feel so immature sometimes.

Being touched everywhere on your body, having a boy's lips on your most private places, masturbating, experimenting with drugs and sex, alcohol and sex, all of it swirled around me daily at school, dressed in giggles, whispers, and smiles. On the one hand, the most popular girls openly bragged about their sexual relations, hooking up in the backseats of cars or in a girlfriend's house, while other girls either listened in awe or fled. Was I one who fled? I did avoid hearing about these things. But was that because the girls made them more tempting or more frightening?

My mother had once told me that rare things have greater value and there was nothing as important and as valuable as your own body. How long could I continue to treat my body like a holy chalice before the emerging woman in me would lose patience? I couldn't be a pretty little girl forever and ever, a girl people admired like some precious doll made to be on a shelf, touched gently and certainly with no sign of sexuality. *Grow up*, I told my image in the mirror. *If you put yourself too high up on that pedestal, no boy will even notice you, much less reach for you.* Was I ready to come off the shelf?

Maybe I should look forward to this party Friday night, I thought, and be as excited about it as Jackie was. I knew she wasn't particularly interested in my being happy. She was quite clear about her selfish motives for inviting me. She didn't have to tell me she didn't pity me. She was using me, but maybe I could use her, too. Daddy had his work to distract him from facing our new tragic reality. The family was wounded, perhaps fatally. Only time would tell if we could manage any recuperation that permitted smiles and laughter, hope and pleasure again. I needed something to give me some relief, too.

I went to bed, practically forcing myself to dream about the party, imagining myself drinking forbidden things, dancing very closely with Chet, and eventually doing what Jackie had predicted and retreating to her bedroom. "Time to cross the Rubicon," my mother would say whenever she wanted me to do something on my own. I had no doubt she didn't mean it for something like what I was contemplating doing with Chet, but I was totally lost in the fantasy. I was going to enter that bedroom an almost asexual American Girl doll and emerge as a sophisticated, sexy Barbie doll.

Surely afterward there would be a different look in my eyes, the look of someone who had been there and knew the deepest secrets of being a woman. Would I walk differently, walk without hesitation, never again be intimidated by any boy's gaze exploring my body in his imagination? I did like the idea that I could stare him down, make him blush for a change. His friends would laugh at him and ask him if he was playing with himself. I'd strut off like a conqueror.

Or was that really just a fantasy, a rationalization for doing something just to prove myself to people whose respect I really didn't cherish deep inside? It was possible to be a victim of yourself. I think my mother was trying to teach me that. "Don't let other people decide who you are, Scarletta."

My dreams came and went quickly. I knew that, because not long after I fell asleep, I was woken by sensing someone beside me. The dim light from the hallway came through the now-opened bedroom door. I remembered that I had left it almost completely closed. It was the way I had my bedroom door before I went to sleep from the age of eight on, mainly because of my mother explaining that a woman should get used to her privacy as soon as she can.

"Because you are still a child, it's permissible for you to have it slightly open if it makes you feel safer. Just know that you're old enough now to deal with your nightmares and bad dreams. You'll have to come to our closed door if you can't. By now, I hope you can."

Whether I could or not, I provided myself just a narrow slip of opening, my reassurance. It took only a moment to realize this light and silhouette wasn't part of some dream.

Wearing only the bottoms of his pajamas, Daddy was standing there at the foot of my bed gazing at me. The slight smile on his face gave me a chill. During my short sleep, I must have pulled my blanket off. How long had he been standing there staring at me? Why wasn't he talking as soon as he saw me awaken?

"What's wrong?" I asked, sitting up. He didn't answer. "Daddy?"

The smile evaporated. "I keep hearing her voice," he said.

He sounded different, like someone talking in his sleep. I was still quite groggy. Her voice? It took me a second or two to understand what he meant. It brought a flush of heat to my face. Was I imagining it, or did I also smell a whiff of my mother's favorite perfume when she went to dinner or an event, Chance by Chanel?

"You heard Mommy's voice?"

"Did you hear her, too?" He moved closer and then sat beside me on my bed, folding his hands in his lap and looking down.

"No," I said, but I listened hard for any sound of her.

Could she have come home during the night? Was she downstairs? "Did you hear her come home, Daddy?"

He didn't answer. He really did look asleep, even though his eyes were open. It frightened me a little to see him this way. Suddenly, he put his hand over mine.

"Why is she doing this?" he whispered. Again, I listened hard. I didn't hear a thing. "She's punishing us. Of course, she's punishing us."

"For what?"

He didn't answer.

"I'll go look, Daddy," I said.

I stepped out of bed, put on my slippers, and started out, pausing in the doorway to look back at him. He hadn't moved or said anything more. He was still crouched over like someone who had fallen asleep in that position. I hurried on.

The dim chandeliers cast a short circle of bland yellow light over the first few steps of the stairway. We always kept the entryway light on below, but it was barely strong enough to reach beyond the slate floor. My eyes, now used to the darkness, captured the shadowy hallway and the entrance of the living room. A half-moon threw a ghostlike glow from the doorway, probably because it threaded a frail light around the not-quite-closed drapes. As I descended, the weak radiance grew a little stronger. She was there! She didn't want to be in complete darkness.

More confident, I hurried to the doorway and gazed at the sofa, at the place where my mother usually sat, expecting her to be there waiting for me. Maybe she wanted to talk to me first, explain everything, and then go up to my father. He'd be upset, but how could I not rush to embrace her if she had come home?

There was no one. I remained in the doorway, waiting, watching every shadow to see if any would move and open to release my mother, who I dreamed would walk to me, brush my hair with her right palm, and lean to kiss me on my forehead.

"I'm back, my darling Scarletta," she would say. "It was a mistake. Nothing. All will be well again."

In a blink, my fantasy was gone. There were no sounds coming from any other part of the house, not even a creak caused by the wind. For me, silence always seemed to be deeper late at night. Everything that lived in fear of sunshine emerged. Mother had our house treated monthly to prevent ants, spiders, or anything creepy-crawly from establishing a home in our dark corners and especially our basement. Traps were set everywhere down there to squeeze the life out of any rodent that dared venture into our home.

My grandparents had done little with the basement. From the outside, it was approached through a double-panel trap door with a half dozen cement steps leading to the entrance. The basement ran almost the length of the house and contained our hot-water heater and furnace. On one wall, the north-side wall, there were shelves, but only the lower three had anything on them, all tools, wires, screws, and other plumbing and construction supplies.

No floors had been constructed. It was simply covered in silvery gravel. I never had any interest in going down there. It was always cold and damp and had no windows. The ceiling of it hadn't been covered, either. Wires were visible, as was the plumbing, and there were always plenty of spiderwebs the few times I had gone down. It was a womb for nightmares.

Most of the other houses in our neighborhood had finished basements with bars and game areas. My grandparents had dinner parties but rarely anything more and saw no need to develop theirs. The basement was actually the only area of the house my mother had not changed. She wasn't interested in a party room, either.

I turned on a hall light and walked to the kitchen. Maybe something had gotten into our house. Raccoons were capable of it. They could open doors that weren't locked and certainly had more courage than rats. Recently, we had trouble with some raccoons that wanted to establish a family home on our roof. Mother had to call Animal Control to come and take them away. Right now, there were no sounds of anything scratching or moving inside or right outside our windows and doors.

I waited a few moments and then turned off the lights behind me as I walked back upstairs, feeling even more tired.

Disappointment followed me. In my heart of hearts, despite how angry my father was, I was hoping I'd find my mother sitting in the living room, trying to build up the courage to return to her and my father's bedroom. She was never good at apologizing for anything. If she was proven wrong beyond a doubt, she would simply grow quiet. Most of the time, she would change the subject or find fault with something else. She was especially this way with my father. Watching him closely after he had won an argument or a point, I'd see him look satisfied, but he never gloated. He swallowed down his successes as quickly as he swallowed his disappointments.

If my mother said anything at all to me after she and my father had a disagreement, it was usually something like "He's right this time, but he's wrong so much that it's hard to notice or care."

I always believed that my father's love for my mother was stronger than any man's love for any woman because he was so good at not getting upset with her. In the back of my mind, I imagined him thinking that whatever she had said or done paled next to the love she lavished on him when she was moved to do so. Besides, the most important thing to him was pleasing her. Who else would constantly side with his wife against his parents, even to the point of driving them away?

No wonder he was taking her deserting us so hard. There wasn't any way to rationalize it, the way he was able to rationalize or ignore so many other things. His pride was terribly damaged. I was losing a mother's love, but his manhood was seriously wounded. It was why he had put on such a show at dinner. I actually felt sorrier for him than I did for myself.

He wasn't sitting on my bed, so for a moment, I thought he had returned to his. But when I stepped into my room, I saw him lying there, his head on one of my pillows. It was obvious he hadn't simply lain back. He had my blanket over him, too. Did he think he was in his own bed?

For a moment, I didn't know what to do. Should I wake him and show him where he was, explain that maybe he had sleepwalked here? I had no idea whether he had done such a thing in his life. Would suggesting that upset him even more? Should I go to his bed now and just leave him in mine? That was easier, but wouldn't he feel silly in the morning, maybe terribly embarrassed? That would make me feel worse for sure.

I approached slowly and looked down at him. He was so deeply asleep. If anyone had drunk too much, it was he with his martinis, the bottle of wine, and two vodkas with coffee. I stepped out of my slippers and, as quietly and smoothly as I could, returned to my bed. I looked at him so comfortably back into his sleep. I rarely had seen him like this. He seemed younger, almost a little boy again.

Mother was always jealous of Daddy's skin, how smooth it was, remaining untouched by time, not a wrinkle, really. Other men his age had something to mark the years, early crow's-feet, creases around their noses, a deepness or darkness under their eyes, and even more prominent noses and lips. I had heard friends and business associates who hadn't seen him for years call him Dorian Gray. When I asked my mother who that was, she just smirked. Eventually, I looked up the name and saw it was a character in a novel who remained young and handsome while his hidden portrait changed continually to reveal more and more of his aging, tormented soul.

It made me wonder if my father was aging inside, too. Maybe all the suffering and unpleasantness he had swallowed was eating away at him unseen. One day, he would just shatter and fall into all the signs and symptoms of age. He'd lose his perfect posture, walk slower, fall asleep in his chair more often, and have gray hair overnight.

As I studied him asleep, I wondered if he was dreaming. Was he thinking of Mother when they were young together? Was he recalling the day he realized he was head over heels in love with her? Was he remembering a dance, a walk, or a kiss? How long would all the good

213

memories last? How long would they be strong enough to keep him from crying himself to sleep every night? How long would it be before he decided it was time to bury even the vision of her?

One afternoon, I would come home from school and see that her portrait above the fireplace had been removed. In its place, perhaps, would be that portrait of his parents, a painting my mother had quickly shoved into some corner of the attic. I remembered the day she did that.

"Why didn't they take it with them?" she asked my father when he voiced some hesitation. "Do they want to remind us daily how much you owe to them?"

"I earned everything my father has given me," Daddy said, somewhat indignantly. He didn't mean it to result in my mother pouncing and following through on her wish, but she did.

"Good. Then there's no reason to keep it there."

Daddy didn't argue about it anymore. He was never a cowardly man. It wasn't that. It was surely because of how deep his love for her was. Would I ever find a man like him, a man who would be as devoted to me as he was to my mother, a man who wouldn't dream of hurting the woman he loved, even in the smallest of ways? Maybe men like him didn't exist anymore.

When would my mother realize what she had lost when she left him, left us? Sure, she might be with a younger man who lived on the edges, spontaneous and wild, but would that be enough? Perhaps he was so much richer and not only didn't have to work but didn't want to, and therefore she had nothing with which to compete. However, I was confident that after the novelty of it wore off, she'd hope to return. I had to have that hope, and I believed that secretly, my father had the same wish.

I turned over to go back to sleep and drifted off quickly, falling so deeply into it I didn't toss or turn. I woke before he did. Sometime during the night, he had slipped his arm around my waist. The moment I felt it, I was surprised and didn't move. Then I slowly turned and gently lifted his arm away as I sat up. He opened his eyes and blinked rapidly first. I thought the realization that he had crawled into my bed to fall asleep would amaze and even frighten him, but he brought his hands to his face and scrubbed his cheeks.

"What time is it?" he asked, as if he slept here with me every night.

I looked at my clock. "Almost seven," I said.

"Oh, damn. I have a meeting in Summerville at eight." He sat up quickly and brushed back his hair. Finally, he looked at me. "You had a nightmare," he said.

"What?"

He smiled. "You're just like you were when you were very little. You'd never remember them the next day.

215

That's a blessing only a child can enjoy, forgetting dark and ugly things. I'm afraid I have to rush. I'll have breakfast on the road," he said. "Okay?"

I nodded.

He was the one with the blessing of forgetfulness, I thought. I recalled every single moment of last night. Was he forgetting because he wanted to forget or because he really did? Which was worse?

He hurried out, obviously eager to get to work. I sat there amazed but suddenly very worried, too. Most people would probably tell me I should be grateful that he had woken with enthusiasm for his company.

"Your father has accepted his fate and is going on with his life," they would say. "He's not staying home and pining over what your mother has done to him. That would only make things more miserable for you. Follow his lead. Go on with your life."

Daddy was dressed and down the stairs by the time I had showered. I guessed he was really in a rush. He didn't even shout "good-bye," "have a nice day," or "see you later." All I heard was the sound of the car being started. When the garage door went up, the house would vibrate a little. My mother hated that, but there wasn't much that could be done to subdue the sounds.

I chose something nicer to wear today. I was anticipating talking with Chet. By now, Jackie had surely informed him I'd be at the party. When I brushed my hair and checked my appearance, I felt a little guilty. My mother was gone a second day, and I was thinking of a boy, dreaming of a romance. But in a funny way, I thought she might approve. She might think I was growing into the woman she wanted me to be, independent, strong, even resilient enough to deal with what she had done to us. I could see her watching me from a distance and smiling. She had brought me up well; she didn't have to feel guilty about going off. I could handle it.

I paused before going downstairs to make my breakfast and turned to look in at Daddy's room. The bed looked like it had never been used. I struggled to remember more of last night's details. When we came home, he had gone into the kitchen to get a glass of water. I was sure he had said good night before I started for the stairway. He hadn't come to my room before going to his. In fact, I was in bed so fast and had the lights off so quickly I didn't even recall the sound of him coming up the stairway.

Could it be that he had remained below, maybe sat in the living room a while, and then fell asleep in his chair? It made sense. He woke up, changed for bed, and then . . .

Then what?

By that time, had he thought he had heard my mother? Did he come directly to my room and never get into his own bed? Maybe I had jumped too quickly to conclude he was doing surprisingly well since my mother left us. Seemingly, it hadn't disturbed his ordinarily organized life. Sometimes my mother would make fun of that. He had one of these very large calendars with every meeting, birthday, anniversary, car service appointment, dental and medical appointment, just about anything that was set to happen, penciled in. He kept it on a wall in the kitchen.

To tease him, my mother would scribble in some illegible appointment on a date two months or so ahead and then tell him she didn't know what it was. Maybe he had forgotten. She'd look at me with a wry smile. She wouldn't confess it was a joke, either. Eventually, I'd whisper it to him so he would realize what she had done.

"Very funny," he'd say. Then he'd tell her that if it wasn't for him, she'd miss her next dental cleaning or something.

"I'd just schedule another, Raymond. The tail is not going to wag this dog."

She would accuse him of being a frustrated military officer or something, even though he had never been in the service. Everything he owned, all his toiletries, drawers, clothes, and shoes were kept as neatly as by someone who was trained to do it. All was in its proper place. "You can go on living," Mother would tell him sarcastically, but she often praised his personal habits when he wasn't around.

"Most men are slobs," she told me. "They're spoiled by their mothers and expect their wives to pick up after them. Your father's mother was too selfish to be a mother, so he had to take care of himself. Maybe that was good. Now I don't have to do it."

I knew I was quite a bit neater than most of my classmates primarily because of my father's and mother's own personal habits. As far as I could tell, there weren't a half dozen other girls in my class who made their beds before they left for school and made sure all their things were put away, hung up, or dropped in the basket for washing. My mother wasn't gone three days, but I was clearly going to take on most of her household duties. I had done them with her enough times to slip into the role.

What surprised most of the women she did socialize with was that we didn't have a maid, not even once a week like some other families. My mother hated the idea of some stranger—for that's what she would be in her eyes no matter how long she had worked for us—seeing her personal things, touching her clothes, knowing little particular details about her. My father wasn't as concerned about that, and I certainly wasn't. But he didn't see our not having a maid as some sort of negative comment about his success or our standing in the community.

Sometimes I heard him brag about having a wife who could handle domestic chores and still keep herself looking like a magazine cover model.

My father told her that the wives of his associates and friends complained that she was making them look bad.

"They don't need me for that," she told him. "They do a good job of looking bad themselves."

Now I was about to turn to leave my parents' bedroom and go down to make myself some breakfast when I spotted what looked like that envelope my father had waved in the air when he told me my mother had left us. It was on top of his bureau. Somehow I assumed he would have locked it away or at least hidden it in the bottom of some drawer.

I walked to it slowly.

Did I really want to read this? Was there something even more terrible to read, something so terrible that my father had left it out deliberately? Reading her words, even though it had been done on a computer and printed out, would make her desertion more real and more devastating for me. I didn't even want to touch it.

But it was impossible to resist. When you read words written by someone you know, know well, especially your mother or father, you hear her or his voice while you read. I couldn't help wanting to hear my mother's voice, even in my own mind.

I took the envelope, opened it, and pinched the paper within as daintily as someone touching ancient parchment, afraid it might crumble in her fingers. I unfolded it and read.

Raymond,

The nicest way to put this is I've fallen out of love with you. It's the nicest way because it implies I once was. Although you were oblivious to it, it was happening for years. That's not surprising. You're so absorbed in your business that you don't see what's right in front of you. You are a good father, however, and I'm confident you will do right by our daughter. I think she's more like you than me anyway, and I'm sure she will get over this situation, maybe sooner than you will.

Perhaps I could have gone on with you for a while longer, but I've met someone else, someone who lives in the same world I do, hears the same rhythms, and wants the same pleasures. We're going out of the country to start our lives together. He's not as rich as you but rich enough not to have to work, something you could never stand no matter how much money you had. Remember? Your work is who you are? Well, maybe it is, but it's not who I am.

*I don't care what you do with anything I've
left behind. Give Scarletta whatever she wants, or
donate it to some charity. Frankly, I don't want to
carry very much from my old life into my new. It
would take away from my sense of being reborn.*

*You can activate your mother's precious
prenuptial for us.*

See. I finally made her happy.

Doreen

She had even printed out her signature. How cold.

I was surprised by the tears on my cheeks. I hadn't
realized I was crying. Before one fell on the paper, I
folded it and put it back in the envelope.

All my life, I had tried to be like her, and she wrote
that I was more like my father? I would get over her
deserting us sooner than my father would? Was all the
love she did manage to show me all pretend? Was all the
wisdom she wanted me to have really unimportant to
her? It was unimportant whether I absorbed it or not?
What had I done to deserve this indifference? She didn't
write one word of real regret when it came to me. Why
wouldn't she write me my own letter anyway?

I gazed at the framed photo of her that my father was
still keeping next to his bed. She wasn't even smiling in
it. It looked more like the photographer had snapped the
shot while she was unaware, but smile or not, she was

beautiful. Wasn't it painful for him to look at her picture now?

It was for me.

I slammed the envelope back on top of my father's bureau, slammed it so hard that my palm stung.

And then I hurried downstairs, anxious to continue with my own life, enjoy myself, and, if I could, forget her.

Pru

WE COULD NOT get what was happening to me out of our minds. We had our glasses of Graham's Vintage Port, something Chandler had bought a month or so ago, and sat and talked softly, Chandler trying to tiptoe around the subject of my stalker and talk more about his work, a new negotiation involving a large commercial tract of land in San Bernardino.

I didn't want to show him how worried I was about the roses, but I couldn't help glancing at them. If this was Douglas Thomas's work, it meant he wasn't going to stop. He was probably encouraged by the fact that I hadn't called the police. Maybe in his distorted way of thinking, this was proof that I really liked him and wanted him to return. Who knew what he would do next? Perhaps publishing the pictures on the Internet would happen, and one of my fellow employees at the hospital would surely pick it up. Some of them fed off the Internet social media like a newborn calf off its mother.

"You all right?" Chandler asked. He could see I wasn't really listening.

"Yes. I'm sorry. I was distracted for a moment. What did you ask?"

He smiled and stood up. He took my glass from me, took my hand, and said, "Let's go to bed."

When I stood, he kissed me.

We both took longer than usual to prepare for bed. It was as if neither of us wanted to be the first one lying there and then have to look desirable and interested in sex when the other approached. I was in after him. He was under the blanket and had his hands behind his head, staring up at the ceiling, so deep in thought that he didn't notice I had come in.

"Hey," I said, and crawled in beside him. He put his arm around me. "Why are you so pensive? Now wishing you never got involved with someone with all this baggage? Do you regret asking to sit at my table that day? Or are you just dreaming of someone else?"

"You have to be kidding. Dreaming of someone else? We've been on a whirlwind romance for a little more than five months," he said. "I haven't really looked at another woman since that day you and I met in the hospital cafeteria. I look through them and see you standing there."

"How sweet," I said. "If it's true."

"It's true," he protested. "All this time, I haven't suggested a double date with one of my associates because I didn't want to share a minute with you. And I haven't pushed you to introduce me to any girlfriends or remotely suggest we double-date with one."

"I told you. I'm not close with any of the other girls who work with me. I value sincere friendship and avoid acquaintances who I can tell will amount to nothing."

"That's fine. I'm greedy about the time we have together, between your schedule and mine, but I can't get away from the feeling that I don't really have your full attention all the time, Pru. I mean, I have you, but sometimes it's like holding hands with a ghost."

"Boo," I said, and he laughed.

"No, seriously. I think the problem, if I can call it a problem, is that you don't talk that much about yourself, your youth. Sometimes I feel like you're just here, you just arrived as you are. You don't talk about your teenage years and your nursing-school experience unless I ask a specific question. Somehow, most of the time, we're talking about me."

"I know what you're after, Mr. Lawyer Guy," I said. "I can see right through you despite all that sophistication."

I put my right forefinger on the center of his breastbone and pressed.

"Ow. What?"

"You want to know if I had any sort of relationship with another woman in nursing school. I saw how you reacted to what I told you Scarletta was saying on the phone, her sex talk. You think it's possible an old love of mine has reappeared on the scene and this is only about that. I won't face it, and so I've come up with all this other stuff about the other nurses and nursing assistants."

"Has she? I mean, was there someone like that?"

"My father once warned me that the worst thing a woman can do to the man she loves is talk about someone else she loved or attempted to love."

"Was he speaking from experience? Is that what your mother did to him?"

"Maybe."

"All beside the point. I think you're evading the question, Miss Dunning," he said. "There's possible contempt of court here."

"This is my fault. I have no one to blame but myself, starting a relationship with a lawyer. Yes," I said after taking a deep breath. "I experimented a little with lesbianism, but it wasn't enough to result in a deep relationship. I would never call it love. It was only a slight infatuation, the sexual curiosity of a young, impressionable girl, nothing more."

"Maybe that's the way it was for you but not your partner," he suggested. "We often misread how someone else is reacting to what we say and do. How long did this shallow relationship last?"

"Only a few weeks. She was in the experimental mode herself, and we both concluded that we were heterosexuals. When she landed a boyfriend soon afterward, I remember how she looked at me, her eyes full of far more sparkle than they had when she was with me. She looked . . . boastful. She had won the heart of a man faster than I had and had therefore washed away any memory of my touch, embrace, or kiss. Drowned me out."

"Maybe it all surfaced again recently."

"No," I said sharply.

"How can you be so sure? What did she look like?"

"Nothing like the woman I thought was following me the other night. And I certainly would remember what she sounded like."

"What was her name?"

"It wasn't Scarletta or anything like it. Drop the theory," I said firmly, as firmly as one of the judges on one of his cases might say it.

"Maybe she just chose that name for now."

"No. Stop. I told you I'd recognize her voice."

"People can disguise their voices."

I turned away.

"Just trying to figure it out for you," he said. He leaned over to kiss me on the neck.

"I'll figure it out for myself. I'll end it."

"Okay."

I turned back to him, and he kissed me. I wasn't as

receptive as he wished. "Sorry," he said. "I don't mean to upset you any more than you are with all this."

"It's all right. I'm just tired of talking about it. Actually, I'm just tired."

"Of course. There's always tomorrow. We'll make up for it. With a vengeance," he added, with that lusty smile rippling across his lips.

I laughed and kissed him a little better than the last time and then fell back against my pillow.

Neither of us spoke for a few moments. Not surprising—he was still thinking about what I had revealed.

"I think your father was right about what a woman should keep to herself," he said. "Wise man."

"Yes. Wise man. I didn't want to do it, but you wouldn't stop your relentless cross-examination."

"Guilty as charged," he said. "Court adjourned. Good night."

I closed my eyes. Who had left those roses? I asked myself, and then, rushing to escape, drifted into something more akin to a coma.

We didn't make love in the morning as Chandler had promised. It wasn't his fault. I was still too deeply asleep when he awoke. I didn't realize he had risen until he was fully dressed and standing in the doorway, sipping a cup of coffee, and looking at me. He had left some of his clothes here in my closet just so he could go right to work whenever he slept over.

"Welcome to tomorrow," he said when my eyelids fluttered. "I wasn't sure you'd get here."

"Oh. I guess I was more tired than I thought."

"Are you on duty tonight? I forgot your schedule."

"No. I'm on a special from nine to three."

"And when do you have two days off?"

"Tomorrow."

"Good. I decided to take off from work whenever you were off and take us to Palm Springs for at least two nights. You need a change of scenery. Matter of fact, so do I."

"Sounds like a good idea," I said.

"Don't get up. I'll bring you a cup. After that, I have to rush out and get to Beverly Hills. One of the partners just sent me a text wanting to have breakfast with me. I think he's been given the task of either offering me the partnership or letting me go."

"You don't seem too nervous about it."

"I'm not. I have another offer in my back pocket if I need it," he said, and went into the kitchen to get my cup of coffee.

When he returned, I was sitting up. He kissed me and gave me the coffee.

"That was pretty creepy, those roses," he said, watching me take a sip. "Whoever she is, she has a sick sense of humor."

I shrugged. "Nice roses. I'll put them in water."

He shook his head but smiled. "You're a piece of work, Nurse Dunning. I'll call you to let you know how the breakfast conference went. We're meeting at that place close by on Doheny Street. Call me if there is any—"

"I will. Stop worrying," I said. "Concentrate on what's important. Don't let this rule our lives."

"Exactly my thoughts and intentions," he said.

He kissed me again and started out. Then he returned to the doorway.

"You're putting that answering machine back, right?"

"Okay, okay," I said. "We'll do it your way."

"Thatta girl."

I heard him leave. I put the cup down on the night table to my left and leaned back on the pillow. It was then that I looked at his pillow. He had not said a word, not even nodded at it, but lying there on the pillow was the reason for the aborted bottle of champagne at dinner last night, a small box that obviously contained an engagement ring. For a while, I simply stared at it like someone expecting that it would open itself.

I always suspected that most, if not many, women used the words *I love you* too quickly or too matter-of-factly, and I always feared I might be one of them. Some of the girls I knew in high school who had sex, even when they were only in the ninth or tenth grade, wrapped those words around themselves to give some justification for their willingness or eagerness. If I asked them how they could do it so quickly, I'd hear something like "I love him, stupid. And he loves me."

If I asked others whether they loved the boy, some said, "It's just sex." They made it sound like nothing more than having a good pizza. If love wasn't as important as sex, than what was love, anyway? Was it simply words you were supposed to say, like reciting lines in a play?

In a world where divorce was becoming as common as birthdays, piles of those three words discarded were everywhere, and yet they were supposed to be so precious, so everlasting. The essence of them was trust. You were opening the doors to your heart, your emotions, and your soul when you said them. What could possibly hurt more than telling someone you loved him only to have him reject you or casually say, "I'm sorry. I don't love you." You've already gone too far out on that limb. The fall is devastating.

I had no doubt that Chandler had meant it when he said he loved me. The voice inside me that had always come to life whenever I was about to commit to something serious, even my nursing career, was at it again. *When you reach for that box, when you open it, and when you slip the ring on your finger, you will have to smother any doubt. You'll have to trust a man, something you haven't done since you trusted your father. Are you ready to do that?*

Yes, I thought. *This morning, I'm sure. I'm ready to do that.*

Even so, my hand seemed to be the hand of someone else as it moved toward the ring box. I felt like I had stepped out of my body to watch myself. My fingers closed on it, and I brought it to me without opening it.

Don't open it. Put it back on the pillow, one voice said.

Of course, it's time to open it. Don't risk losing him. You won't find another man who will love you as much, a different voice replied.

It's not possible. Don't be foolish. Love is a dream, a fantasy.

Shut up! I heard myself screaming inside. *Shut up, shut up!*

I opened the box and took out the ring. It was beautiful, a twisted infinity halo diamond. It slipped on easily, and when I held my hand up, I was overwhelmed with the beauty. As I turned my hand to catch the light from all angles, it occurred to me that I had no one really with whom I could share my joy. This was the moment most mothers and daughters lived to experience, wasn't it? I didn't have a father to show it to, either.

I had yet to meet Chandler's parents or sisters in person. I had spoken to them with Chandler on Skype, and we were planning on visiting his parents for his father's seventy-fifth birthday in June. His sisters, all his family, would be there. Now we would have this announcement, unless he had already told them.

Of course, I worried about how they would react to me. Would they be instantly comparing me to other girls he had dated, wishing he had given the ring to one of them? And what if I didn't like them? Could I pretend enough to convince them I did? Would I rationalize and tell myself we lived far enough away from each other, so it wouldn't matter one way or the other? Could you love someone and dislike his family? He didn't have that worry. He had only me to like and love. My family was in the ether, adrift in memories, resurrected for only a few seconds or so when I deigned to mention something one of them had said or done. I never did it once without there being a short debate inside me.

The phone rang. I looked at it. I hadn't yet reconnected the answering machine. If I picked up that receiver and it was Scarletta and I couldn't play back what she had said, Chandler would be upset. Another opportunity to put this to an end was lost. *Just let it ring*, I told myself.

But I couldn't resist. *I'll hang up right away if it's her and then reconnect the machine because she'll call back*, I thought.

I brought the phone slowly to my ear and said, "Hello."

"Are you wearing anything new?" Chandler asked. "Maybe on your finger?"

"You sneak."

"It was right in front of you. I couldn't believe you didn't see it."

"I was half awake, remember?"

"And?"

"I'm wearing it," I said.

He was silent.

"You're not regretting leaving it here, are you? Hoping I was going to say no or not yet?"

"Of course not. I was just happily absorbing it all. We'll have a test run of our honeymoon day after tomorrow, then, and when we leave, we'll leave all the baggage behind. Okay?"

"I can if you can."

"Today is different from yesterday. I feel like I can do anything I have to do to please you."

"Have you told your family?"

"I gave Julia a heads-up. I've been closer to her than I've been with Lydia. Julia was more of a big sister, second mother, if you know what I mean. I'm sure she kept it to herself. I figured you and I would Skype my parents, maybe after our short holiday. You can show my mother the ring. I'll call my sister Lydia immediately afterward. But in the meantime, until we leave, let's not forget our little problem and be sure to—"

"Reconnect the answering machine. I know. I'll do it now," I promised.

"Oh, here he comes. He's not smiling. I'll call you again in about an hour with the play-by-play and results."

"Good luck," I said.

Now I was wide awake. I rose, brought my coffee cup to the kitchen, and took the answering machine out of the garbage. After I reconnected it, I stared at it hatefully. *Go on,* I thought. *Call and threaten. We'll get you. We'll make you pay. You're not ruining my life, especially not now.*

I started on some breakfast. I watched local news while I ate. I had a small television set in the kitchen where I usually ate breakfast alone on the maple wood table. While I watched the newscasters go from accidents and fires to murders and rapes, I fantasized my story being reported. *Cedars-Sinai nurse's stalker caught. A tale of a vengeful nurse.* Surely that was worth twenty seconds on the morning news.

After I finished, I cleared off the table the way my mother would, practically sterilizing it, and then started for the shower just as the phone rang. It was about when Chandler was to call, but my hand trembled again as I picked up the receiver. I was poised to hit the Record button.

"Hey," he said. "They gave in and offered me the partnership here. They're sending someone else to run the San Francisco office."

"Oh, how great, Chandler."

"We have a helluva lot to celebrate tomorrow. What are you going to do after work today?"

"Some shopping I've put off."

He was silent.

"Stop worrying. I'll be fine."

"Yes, you will," he said. "I love you, Pru."

There it was, almost like throwing down the gauntlet, not that he was challenging me to do something deadly to one of us. Sometimes marriages turned out to be more like duels, but I truly believed this was going to be different, this was going to be like being reborn. We change so much from childhood to adulthood. Becoming Mrs. Harris had the ring of a real deliverance.

"I love you," I said. I hadn't said it much in my life to anyone, and when I did, I was never sure I was convincing. I immediately wondered if I had sounded too matter-of-fact. *Either sound like you mean it or don't say it*, I thought. *It's not the same as "Have a good day."*

"Love you," I trailed into good-bye. Good rewrite.

When I hung up, I saw those roses on the coffee table in the living room. I had nearly forgotten them and how they lay there at my door.

Why punish them? I thought, and went to fill a vase with water.

Then I showered and dressed. When I put on my uniform, I thought about my affair in nursing school.

My revelations last night had vividly restored the memories. It was truly like putting your life on replay. Chandler regretting making me do it, but it was like releasing a bird from its cage. It was too late to change your mind.

Her name was Natasha, but she was known as Tasha. From the start, I could see how hard it was for her to take her eyes off me. Before long, I couldn't take my eyes off her. At night, I'd see her eyes in my sleep, see her soft smile and the way she held a cup or tossed her hair before she stood. The whiff of her cologne lasted for hours and hours in my mind. I thought green was her color and told her so. I told her she didn't need lipstick, not with those natural ruby lips. Eventually, I counted the freckles on her cheeks and advised her not to powder them until they were unseen. "They're really not unattractive."

Her parents were relatively recent immigrants from Estonia. She was only two when they had come over, so their accent was more influential than the accents of children her age as she grew. She couldn't lose it. She was quite self-conscious about it, but I told her I loved it.

"It makes you exotic."

She had silky Capri brown hair and startlingly beautiful green-blue eyes. An inch or so taller than I was, she looked like a ballet dancer, with her long legs, small waist, and beautifully proportioned breasts. There was something sexy about her long neck. I recalled the first time I touched it and then brought my lips to it.

Right from the start of our friendship, my compliments encouraged her gestures of affection. We were attending Emory University's Neil Hodgson Woodruff School of Nursing in Atlanta, and we each had a one-bedroom apartment at the Exchange, an apartment complex there. Only a week after we had met, we talked about the possibility of sharing a two-bedroom as soon as one became available. We had lunch together daily and separated ourselves from the other girls. When we were together like that, I heard no other voice but hers. I thought it was the same for her.

The first time my fingers entwined with hers, my heart raced. Our mutual laughter was a classical melody. Our groans were equally deep. Emotionally, we were duplicates. I began to have no doubt that she dreamed the same dream. Even our silhouettes clung to each other.

So despite how insignificant I made it all sound to Chandler, it was an experience that had a profound effect on me. I was always challenged by my sexuality, my inclinations. Any failed relationship with a man afterward was most likely mostly my fault. That was why I found Chandler so refreshing, so important. It was truly as if he had restored my confidence in my heterosexuality, not that I wouldn't have had a gay relationship, maybe even a marriage, if that was what I was inclined to do. But I would never say that, never even hint at it now. I was afraid to do even the smallest thing that might put a dent in our relationship.

I had already said too much to him. My father was right. Every reference to someone else you were attracted to was like a needle to the heart of the one you loved and who loved you. Jealousy was an insatiable monster, never weakened, never put aside. It rode unseen on your shoulders and raged in your ear any chance it had.

When I arrived at the hospital today, I said nothing to anyone about my engagement. However, the moment someone saw the ring on my finger, the news was spread. Ironically, it was Belinda Spoon who first approached me, looking like she thought I had succeeded in a major accomplishment. She was genuinely impressed, but the more she asked about it, the more I understood what she was really thinking.

"No one knew you was seein' someone steady like," she said.

They didn't think I was capable of a relationship, I thought.

"Yes." I smiled. "No one knew."

"That looks expensive."

"It is."

"Where'd ya meet him?"

"In the hospital."

"Thought so," she said, smirking. When she smirked, she ballooned her already quite ballooned cheeks.

"He wasn't a patient or a relative of a patient, Belinda," I said pointedly. "I didn't exploit anyone to get engaged."

"So who is he? An administrator or somethin'?"

"No. He's an attorney and has nothing to do with Cedars. What else did they send you to find out?"

"No one sent me nowhere," she said indignantly. "I just come to say congratulations."

"Thank you."

"Yeah," she said, and sauntered off to report.

Now that it was known, however, what little information Belinda had wasn't enough. The questions began coming. *How long were you seeing him? Where does he practice law? Why kind of law? How old is he? Do you have wedding plans set? Is he from here?* Wherever I was on the floor, there was someone remarking about my ring and following it with one of those questions. I wasn't one to be chatty before, and I wasn't going to be chatty now. Like always, I was focused on my work, my patients.

Someone told Dr. Moffet, one of the cardiologists, who seemed truly happy for me. He was very efficient and intolerant of mistakes, minor or otherwise. I thought he had the highest regard for me. When others saw him congratulate me, they seemed to soften. It was as if my getting engaged proved I was actually human or something. Maybe a few were hoping I'd get married and quit.

Almost the moment I ended my shift, Chandler called my mobile. I was almost to my car.

"Hey, how did it go?" he asked.

"Nothing about my work has changed, Chandler. No worries. Except your ring was a hit."

"You mean *your* ring," he said. "I'm glad. I have a dinner meeting in the Valley."

"I'm off to do some shopping."

He was silent.

"Everything is fine."

"I'll be over as soon as I'm done. I've already packed my things. We'll try to get to Palm Springs for lunch, okay?"

"Okay. I'll get my overnight bag done before you've arrived."

"Pre-honeymoon coming up," he said.

I was looking forward to the getaway. The desert promised sunshine, warm fresh air, and lots of spontaneity. It was good to have days with no schedules. It was like unlocking and discarding chains. Right now, I was off to do the shopping I'd told Chandler I was going to do.

I needed some new panties, new walking shoes, perhaps something nice to wear in Palm Springs, and some toiletries. Unlike most women I knew, I didn't like shopping. I hated to be presented with choices. There seemed to be more and more variety of everything, and I didn't trust the salespeople to give me a truthful reaction to my choices. Everything looked good on me as long as I bought it.

Most of the women I knew went on shopping sprees with friends who reinforced their decisions. They had lunch together and shared much of their lives. It was more of a social event. For me, it was more of a chore, something I did rather quickly, focused, with purpose, but from time to time, I envied them, despite how critical I could sound about their chatty gossip and what I considered to be wasted time. I thought about my friends in high school and how different I was from just about all of them. It was never easy for me to make friends, especially a best friend.

On my way home, I found myself actually singing along with Cher and then Pink, until I parked and started up the stairs to my apartment. There was just the slightest hesitation in my steps. I held my breath until I reached the second floor and looked anxiously at my door. There was nothing there and no one waiting, but I didn't take a breath until I opened the door and stepped in. I breathed out but along with a small, birdlike cry that stung like needles in my ears.

The light was blinking.

Chandler would hear her voice for the first time, I thought. Maybe that would be good. I put my purse down and pushed the Play button.

I know what he did to you. He'll pay.

I actually felt myself freeze in place. I seemed incapable of raising my arms. How could she know? Did she follow him and see him come here? Did she approach him afterward? Did she have a way to make him confess? What did she mean by "pay"?

One thing was quite clear to me.

If Chandler heard this message, he would have to be told everything. What would that do to our newborn happiness? How could we go anywhere to celebrate anything? What would he think of me? I had let Douglas Thomas in. I had drunk the champagne with him. I still had his pearls. Did I enjoy his coming on to me? Was he the only patient with whom something like this occurred? I could see the pained expression on his face as he thought aloud, "Do I really know you, know who you are?"

I glanced at my watch. Chandler would be here any minute. "Was there a message?" would probably be his first question when he entered the apartment.

No, I thought. *She will not ruin things for me. NO!*

I erased her message.

Now the only light blinking came from the embers of rage and fear that burned inside my chest.

Scarletta

CHET PALMER WAS eager to talk to me when I arrived at school the day after Jackie's invitation. I suspected that she had probably come close to setting his mobile on fire with her exaggerated description of how eager I was to have sex with him. If he really wanted to be with me at her party because he had genuine feelings for me, why hadn't he said anything to me first? Jackie had said he wouldn't come to her party if I didn't. Why hadn't he ever tried to get to know me before this, even a few days before this? It smelled like a conspiracy. I knew I was the brunt of so many jokes she and her girlfriends often made about me.

If he wasn't part of a plot, perhaps after the first five minutes with me, Chet would realize that Jackie was simply using me as a means to guarantee her path to Sean Connor and that most of what she had said about me wasn't true. Chet knew he was good-looking enough to have any girl in our school, or at least he believed he could.

Maybe I had been too eager to accept her party invitation. I had to seriously consider what Jackie might be telling him about me, possibly describing me as my father had suggested other kids, especially boys, think of a girl from a broken home: an easy girl to seduce. Of course, he might have already convinced himself that was true.

Was it true? Was I so broken and vulnerable that I was easy pickings? Could everyone tell? Was I so oblivious to how I appeared to others? Could anyone read the pain that swam in my eyes and my desperate need to stop it?

When the foundation of your world crumbles, you reach out for anything that will keep you from falling deeper. Would I be like someone so depressed that she turned to heavy alcohol or drugs? Was sex just another drug now? Was that the way it was for other girls in situations like mine? It seemed a natural turn to make once you had lost faith in family and real love. The world was full of hypocrisy, and right now the biggest lie of all uttered seemed to be "'Til death do us part." Why believe in anything more than quick pleasure and satisfaction?

I could almost feel Chet's self-confidence as he was approaching me. Sean Connor had nodded in my direction the moment I came through the school entrance. Chet had instantly broken away from the huddle he and Sean had formed with their friends in the hallway just before homeroom began. They looked like a football team planning their next play. When they all turned toward me and leered, I was convinced I was the new hot topic for their locker-room conversation.

Out of the corner of my eye, I saw him coming, but I didn't slow down or divert my attention from my homeroom doorway. I wasn't going to be some fish on a hook. A part of me wanted to run out of another exit and keep running and running until I had escaped my life as it now was. Since our community had learned what my mother had done, I knew I would feel the sting of eyes on me wherever I went. I thought that at any moment I'd break out in hives, and a chorus of ridiculing laughter would follow me everywhere today, maybe follow me forever.

"Hey, hold up, beautiful," Chet said, and I paused so I wouldn't look like some pitiful, fearful little girl terrified of boys, a wallflower who was asked to dance and would tremble in the arms of any boy.

I turned slowly and tried as hard as I could not to look even slightly impressed and grateful for his attention. "Excuse me?"

"Why are you in such a rush to get in the cages?" He laughed at what he thought was his cleverness.

Despite my effort to be unenthusiastic, I knew I would have to be a stuffed doll not to react to his exquisite grayish-blue eyes. *Sexy* wasn't an adequate description of his way of looking at me. It was as if we were beyond looks and words. Polite preliminaries had been skipped over long ago. Anyone looking at us would easily believe we were already an intimate couple.

Maybe I was being too sensitive, or maybe I was being too hopeful. I could feel that in his mind, he was already seeing me naked. His gaze moved like fingers up my legs to my stomach, hesitating and then going to my breasts as he drew closer, practically bringing his lips to mine. For a moment, I thought he really did mean to cup my face between his hands and kiss me as if we had been going together for months. What would I do then? Be outraged or be flattered? I was in a full-blown argument with myself.

At six foot two, Chet Palmer was a star on our basketball team. Girls might swoon over him, but I believed that most boys would be envious and compete for his attention even more. Maybe they couldn't help wondering why they didn't have his build, his confident gait, his athletic abilities and his good looks. Scholastically, he was an average student, but from what I had witnessed, even his teachers fawned over him more than they did over their better students. He swam confidently through wave after wave of jealousy. In fact, he welcomed all of it.

Why was I surprised at my indecision? He was charming. His smile twinkled with his captivating eyes. You felt more important when he spoke to you, even if it was to ask a simple question, as simple as "What time is the school assembly?" There was no doubt about all that, but I couldn't stop remembering what my father had warned me about, and then I imagined how my mother would react to someone like Chet. Perhaps she would always be my touchstone, and I would never stop measuring myself against her standards. Admittedly, it was comforting.

Arrogant men set off alarm bells in her. She was a woman who always wanted the upper hand, even in a chance meeting on the sidewalk, in a mall, or in a restaurant. If she was in my place right now, I had little doubt that she would give Chet Palmer that side glance and wink at me the way she did when men would come on to her, their compliments cascading around her. Sometimes she would tease them, pretend she was *soooo* appreciative and even overwhelmed, and then she would turn away and laugh, bringing a smile to my face.

"Men like that are the ones who are easy, not us," she would tell me. "You draw them in by pretending you are so dazed by them, and then you sting them with a truthful criticism or a biting comment about their looks, their clothes, or their obvious intentions, and leave them stuttering and stumbling. Honesty is often too big a pill for them to swallow. Unless," she added with that casual swipe of her hand, "you want him. Then you keep your real thoughts behind your smile like a geisha girl keeps her face behind a pretty fan."

Once she even went so far as to confess that was how

she had won my father's love and devotion. Can you love someone you have deceived?

"I'm not in any particular rush," I told Chet now, "and I don't see my classrooms as cages."

Chet widened his smile and moved even closer. The toes of our shoes practically touched.

"Glad you're coming to Jackie's party. I thought you were ignoring me this past week. It almost gave me a complex," he said.

This past week? I thought. Would it break his heart right here and now for me to say I had never noticed, that I had never really thought about him until Jackie mentioned him on the phone? It would certainly give him pause. Maybe that was what he needed, a little weight on his shoulders to bring him back to earth.

"Ignoring you? What would make you think that?" I asked, looking sincerely interested.

"C'mon. Every time I smiled at you, you turned away."

"Probably didn't see anything different from the way you smile at other girls," I said. Good sting, I thought, and imagined my mother smiling.

His smile lost some of its brightness. "Well, what do I have to do, light up like a sparkler?"

"That would capture my attention, yes. Work on it," I said, and he laughed.

Out of the corner of my eye, I saw all the girls with

Jackie looking our way. They giggled and grinned at each other like they knew my inevitable future with Chet Palmer. It annoyed me. The whole school was involved in this little scheme, all of them confident of my gullibility.

I started for my homeroom again, as if I had dismissed him.

That surprised him, but he followed quickly. "I'm glad you decided to go to Jackie's party," he said, rushing his words as if he thought I was about to get on a plane. "I mean, I know how hard it must be at home for you right now. We'll have a good time. I promise."

There was the clear note of desperation in his voice. A girl in this school brushing him off? No way.

I paused and smiled. "It must be a nice feeling," I said. "What?"

"Being so sure you can give someone a good time."

He was speechless, maybe for the first time with any girl here, or anywhere, for that matter. I continued to my homeroom.

"Hey," he called, loud enough to be heard by someone the farthest away in the hall. I turned to look at him. "It is a good feeling," he said, and laughed. Then he shrugged, looking rather innocent for the moment.

Was I overreacting? Should I be so carefree and just dismiss him? *Calm down, Scarletta,* I told myself. *Maybe you're misjudging him. Maybe you're thinking too little of yourself.* Perhaps he would have approached me no matter what. He could have looked at me one day and decided I was truly beautiful, couldn't he? Why belittle myself?

I smiled back at him. I really couldn't help it. If any girl my age could create the perfect boyfriend in a laboratory, he would certainly look like Chet Palmer and have his charm. I recalled Janice Lyn once looking around at the boys in the senior high and asking, "If you had your choice, which boy would you choose to end your virginity?" No one offered an answer immediately, so she looked at us all and added, "Those of you who are still virgins, of course."

If you laughed, you looked guilty; if you seriously perused the boys, you were probably still a virgin.

Now, as the day continued, I was confident that Chet Palmer didn't know what my true feelings were toward him. Perhaps he was now convinced that I wasn't as easy as Jackie had suggested. I hesitated to give him the compliment tickling the tip of my tongue, but truthfully, he was a great distraction at just the right time. Talking to him and being with him all day actually helped me forget about my mother's letter to my father in particular. It was as if our family disaster had been put on pause. I listened carefully to what he said to me and to Sean and Jackie nevertheless, waiting to hear something that would convince me my father's warning was not to be ignored.

"You're doing great," Jackie told me after lunch. I had sat with Chet and her and Sean.

I had to laugh about her comment. I was doing great? The two boys talked to each other almost as if we weren't there or maybe because we were there. They were trying to impress us, performing for us. We talked about the plans for the party, and Chet asked if he could pick me up. I revealed that my father wanted me home by eleven thirty and was planning on driving me there and coming for me after. It brought everyone to a surprised silence.

"He knows it's a Friday night, right?" Jackie asked.

"Of course. My father is very accurate with his dates and times. He keeps a calendar with notes on our kitchen wall."

"Well, I can do eleven thirty," Chet said. "My parents will be surprised I'm home that early, though," he said, laughing. As soon as he started to laugh, Sean followed. They walked in each other's footsteps.

Why, I wondered, did everyone need a best friend so much, and why didn't I have one? Was it me? Had I pulled back every time I began to get close to someone, or did she? My mother never had a best friend. There wasn't one particular woman in her circle whom she favored, spent more time talking to on the phone, or met to have lunch, go to the theater, anything. The only contacts she seemed to have, as a matter of fact, were the wives of my father's business associates. When I gave it more thought,

I realized she never had made a friend on her own. Was that deliberate?

Was I more like her or my father? Which would I rather be?

"I'll ask him to let me stay out later," I said. No one added to that, but from the way the three looked at each other, I knew they thought this early curfew was probably all due to my mother's leaving us. One thing I definitely didn't want was anyone's pity.

"My mother was usually in charge of my social life, time, and transportation. He's just not used to it. I'll speak to him. I'm sure he'll let me stay until midnight at least."

"Cinderella herself," Chet said to break the heavy silence. Sean laughed on cue.

"Just bring a glass slipper, Prince Palmer," I replied.

Jackie laughed, and then the boys did.

"I didn't know you were so witty," she told me afterward, sounding a little more jealous than complimentary.

"How would you? We really don't know that much about each other, do we?"

Maybe that was unkind, but it was truthful, and I was in no mood to be anything other than that with anyone. I was determined not to appear desperate for sympathy.

She thought for a moment. "I guess not. Maybe that will change."

Change? I thought. *Really become friends with you? Would that necessarily make me happier?* How ironic this all was. My family was shattered, but my social life was taking off? Maybe I was reading too much into this, being too hopeful. Jackie's purpose was clear to me, of course. I was merely a means to an end. Once she achieved what she wanted, I had no doubt our budding friendship would quickly wither.

And what about my relationship with Chet? Would that turn into anything more than a one-night sexual encounter? What were his real expectations? Did I want it to be more than a single date? How could I question that? Was there something wrong with me for not immediately falling head over heels? The envy in the faces of other girls was clearly visible when he walked beside me. Or maybe I just wished it was envy. Maybe they were looking at me far differently from how I hoped. Maybe they saw that fish in a net I tried not to be.

"Hey, I can take you home," Chet offered when I stepped out of my last class of the day. There was no track practice, which was something he apparently knew. Again, I wondered whether I should be flattered by his interest or worried. He had quickly left his last class to be waiting near my door.

I had forgotten that seniors were permitted to bring their cars to school, but I did remember that before you could let one take you home in his or her car, your parents had to leave a permission note. It was a particular rule of our school. I reminded him of it.

He shrugged. "So miss the bus," he said.

"What?"

"Go to the bathroom or something. When you come out, the bus will have left. The driver doesn't take attendance. Then start walking home, and I'll come by and give you a ride."

I studied him a moment. "You've done this before," I said.

He shrugged again. "It's not illegal if you do it my way," he said.

Maybe it was clever, but I suddenly saw it as a test. How easy was I?

"Perhaps I'll get my father to sign a note in case you offer in the future. See you tomorrow," I added, and hurried to be sure I made the bus. I didn't even look back at him. It made me feel stronger, more confident that I could handle him or anyone like him.

Today, like yesterday, I didn't run home when I got off the bus. I walked with my head down, thinking. Shelly Myers and Bobbie Lees had sat behind me and tapped me on the shoulder continuously, trying to get me to say something about Chet Palmer.

"Are you the flavor of the day?" Shelly finally asked, tired of my ignoring them.

I spun around. "Is that what you were?"

"She wishes," Bobbie replied for her. I was quite surprised. Both were telling me they wouldn't mind being

Screw of the Night if it was Chet Palmer who would crown you. They had such wishful, matter-of-fact looks on their faces. Ironically, that made me feel better. They weren't condemning me for being easy. They were envious.

"Even if he only pities you, take what you can get," Shelly said.

"She's right. I would," Bobbie said, practically swooning with the idea. "I'd gladly settle for his pity."

"So ask your mother to run off with someone," I told them.

They both looked like I had splattered them with piping-hot water. I turned and smiled to myself. They said nothing more to me. When I got up to get off the bus, I didn't look back. Glancing at Mr. Tooey, I saw him look softly at me, practically giving me permission to do what he complained about each time I had done it, jump off the bus. He wanted me to be my happy-go-lucky, somewhat defiant self. Instead, I walked carefully down the steps again. The only leap I was making was the leap out of childhood. *Thank you for that, Mommy,* I thought.

I wasn't home a half hour before my father called. I had just changed into something comfortable, a pair of sweatpants and a dark gray crop-top sports pullover, the only "slob" look my mother would approve. The house was a little warm because none of the windows had been left open all day, and I had forgotten to lower some shades and close some curtains, almost a cardinal sin to my mother. I took off my socks and put on a pair of slip-on sneakers. As I went downstairs, I was thinking of looking into what my father and I would have for dinner. I heard the phone ring and for a moment froze on the steps.

Could that be her?

I charged down to the nearest phone, which was on a small table in the hallway.

"Hey," I heard my father say. "I wasn't sure if you had track today."

"No. Coach had something personal she had to do after school."

"Oh? What's that about?"

Was my father hoping Mrs. Ward had a family issue, maybe? Was it just natural for someone who had suffered an embarrassing marriage disappointment to seek out others who did? Would he now be getting friendlier with the divorced men he knew? Was it just a matter of time until he, like them, started looking for "hot dates"? How was I supposed to react to all that? Feel sorry for him and understand, or ignore it and maybe be ashamed?

"I don't know, Daddy," I said. I wanted to add that some people were able to keep their family problems secret. Lucky them.

"You okay?"

"Yes," I said. Why say anything else? What good would it do now?

"Stay strong," he said.

"I will. I'll check to see what we have for dinner."

"That's why I'm calling," he said. "I have to go to a very important dinner meeting. Think you'll be all right finding dinner for yourself?"

"Yes. Don't worry."

"Were there any messages on our phone?" he asked after a longer pause.

"No message lights blinking," I said. Was he hoping she would call this soon, her voice full of remorse?

"Okay. I should be home around nine thirty. It's not close by and will probably take more than an hour to drive back."

"I'm fine, Daddy," I said. "I'll wait up to talk to you." I wanted to discuss the party and his curfew. I was also thinking I would like Chet to pick me up and bring me home. I wanted to be treated like a real date and not some event in Jackie's bedroom.

"You got it," he said. "Love you."

"Love you, too."

I heard him hang up, but I held on to the phone as if I expected him to pick up again and tell me more, tell me how much he was suffering and how much he was worried about me.

Silence was painful.

I hung up and went to the kitchen. Now that my father wasn't eating with me, I settled on a salad with

261

some tuna. Sitting there alone with practically the only sound coming from my eating and lifting and putting my glass on the table, everything thundered back at me. I realized I hadn't spent much time thinking about the last time I saw and spoke with my mother. Had I missed a clue? Was she trying to tell me something but I was too absorbed in my own thoughts about myself and this social life I was chasing now?

She had been down earlier in the morning preparing some breakfast for me and my father. Even though I had heard her snap at him when they returned from one of his business dinners the night before, complaining about what he had put her through and what she had to tolerate to help him make money, I had no suspicions about what she was planning to do. I had heard all her similar complaints a number of times. His response was usually to agree that she was making great sacrifices, putting up with the vapid wives of his associates. He would then end up by complimenting her and reinforcing how much he needed and depended on her. In the end, that always calmed her, and they went to bed without any further discussion.

What had made this time any different? At breakfast, she was quieter, but she didn't rant and rave about anything. My father came to the table with his newspaper and read, while my mother and I talked about what I should do about my hair the next time I went with her to her hairdresser. Why did she put on such an act, pretend to be a concerned mother, knowing what she was going to do that day? I couldn't think of one hint. Did she want to avoid any reason to hesitate? She had even stepped up to the doorway with me and fixed the collar of my blouse, something she often did.

"You should have seen this," she said. "Mirrors don't lie; people lie to mirrors."

I nodded and hurried out, afraid she would find something else to criticize or fix. Despite how much she stressed my being independent, she was incapable of not pampering me. I was conflicted about it. Was she merely afraid I would embarrass her, or did she really want me to be as perfect as she was? That was a real question now.

"Beauty doesn't survive neglect," she once told me when she was thinking more about herself and her life, "especially when you're my age."

Thinking about how I was often impatient with her and tried to ignore her, especially when she was all over me with her suggestions and criticism, I realized how much I did remember and appreciate. Now that she was gone, as angry as it made me, I couldn't deny how much I missed her.

I cleaned up the dinner dishes and silverware quickly and went upstairs to start my homework and not think about her. *Fat chance*, I thought, and was actually grateful to hear my phone ring and get a call from Jackie.

"Did you speak to your father?" she asked the moment I said hello.

What was she so nervous about? Did she think Chet would skip her party if he couldn't pick me up and I had to be home by eleven thirty? Or did he tell her how I had left him at school? Did that really annoy him? Was he changing his mind about me? And what about how she thought of herself? Where was her self-respect? She knew she couldn't hold Sean Connor's interest in her if his best friend wanted to skip her party. What kind of a boyfriend is that?

"Not yet. He's at a dinner meeting. Don't worry about it."

She was quiet long enough for me to say, "What?"

"I don't know how I'd be if my mother ran off with someone. Did you know she was going to do it?"

"No. How do you think I should be?" I snapped back at her. "What can I do about it now?"

"Your father seems all right. He took you to dinner, and he's working. I guess it's not like someone dying."

"It's worse," I said, surprised that I was eager to talk about it with her.

"How can it be worse?"

"When someone dies, you don't have to hope constantly that he or she will come back. You know they can't."

"Oh."

She was thinking. I could almost feel it. She was wishing she had never asked and just had gone on being oblivious to anything but her own pleasure.

"Do you think she'll come back? And if she did, would your father take her back?"

"I don't know. That's my point, Jackie; that's why it's more painful."

"Right," she said. I could feel her burst out of moments of seriousness and the darkness they brought. "Well, now you have my party to think about and Chet. Sean says Chet really likes you. He likes you even more after today, too."

"Likes me even more? As opposed to what? You told me he wanted me to come to the party because he was crazy about me, didn't you?"

"Yes. What's the big deal if he likes you even more? You make everything sound like a national emergency. People didn't think you were happy even before your mother left. You're too serious about everything. Chill, at least tomorrow night," she said. "It's not a sin to have fun and be happy, you know. Your mother wasn't worried about it, obviously."

"Okay. I'll go sit in the freezer."

"Huh? Oh. Very funny. I'll see you in the morning. Good luck with your father."

"Thanks," I said, now just happy to get off the phone.

I went right to my homework but had so much trouble concentrating that I knew I rushed it and didn't do as well as I could. My teachers would expect less from me anyway, I thought. None had said a word, but it was easy to see that they knew all. Most avoided asking me any questions. However terrible my work was, they'd be generous, at least for a while. Actually, I hated the thought of that, hated the idea that I was the object of mercy. It resurrected all my rage. I tossed my math book like a Frisbee against the wall and got up.

Despite how I had hated reading it, I returned to my parents' bedroom to do just that, to reread my mother's farewell letter.

I stopped dead in the doorway. It wasn't there. Maybe my father had realized he left it out and had made a special trip home to hide it from me. For a moment, I felt like ripping the place apart until I found it. Maybe I'd burn it. Perhaps he already had. Where would he put it?

I opened the door to his closet and gazed at everything so perfectly organized. Anything out of the ordinary would clearly be seen. I carefully searched the pockets of his jackets and pants. The only thing I found was a receipt from a parking garage.

I went to his dresser. His socks and underwear were folded in such a similar manner they looked painted into the drawers. I hesitated to lift a pair. It seemed wrong to disturb anything, but again, I did so very carefully and found nothing.

I then went to my mother's closet to gaze at what she had left behind. There was nothing on any shelf. I really didn't think he'd hide it there. He probably had trouble looking at her clothes. Like me, I was sure he envisioned her in one of these dresses or outfits, recalling occasions when she wore this or that. The scent of her perfume lingered with such redolence I couldn't help but imagine she had been here recently, perhaps to fetch something she had decided she didn't want to leave behind after all.

Was that possible? It was a stunning, even hopeful idea.

She had come, and then . . . then she saw the envelope out and she took it with her. Why couldn't that have happened? Maybe she was still close by. Maybe she was changing her mind. Perhaps she had been watching my father and me all this time and saw . . . saw what? She didn't see me crying out there. She saw me walking and looking sadder when I got off the school bus, perhaps, but she knew my father and I had gone to dinner. She knew he was still active at work. She even knew he was at a dinner meeting right now. We were surviving. Would that make her angrier or make her regretful?

Maybe she had come to her senses. Why not?

I went to the window and stared down at the street. Was she out there? I didn't see her car, but there were other cars. Perhaps one was her lover's car or she had parked on another street and walked to ours. I studied every shadow and thought I saw something, but that turned out to be just the movement of a cloud through the moonlight, shifting silhouettes.

I returned to my room, still envisioning the possibility. She could return. I lay on my bed and stared at the ceiling, imagining her turning to me and saying, "I'm sorry, Scarletta. I realized very quickly that I couldn't live without you after all. You're too precious to me. We'll be more of a mother and daughter than ever."

The fantasy was so strong that I actually cried. I let the tears trickle down my cheeks, and then, when I heard the sound of the garage door going up, I flicked them off, wiped my eyes, and got ready to greet my father.

"Hey," he said, seeing me at the top of the stairs. He paused. "Everything all right? Something happen?"

"Did you come home today and take the envelope with Mommy's note off your dresser and hide it or destroy it?" I demanded.

"What?"

"Before I went to school, I looked into your bedroom and saw it. I read it, Daddy."

"Oh. I wish you hadn't."

"Well, I did, but I put it back in the envelope and left it there. I looked for it a while ago, but it was gone. So?" I asked, the hope filling my eyes.

He stared at me for a moment. Was he dreading destroying that hope?

"Daddy?"

"I didn't return and hide it while you were at school," he said. "But I do remember leaving it out."

I smiled.

He shook his head. "Why does that make you happy?"

"She's not gone," I told him.

"She's gone," he insisted.

"NO!" I screamed. "She's still here."

Pru

I PACKED MY weekender duffel bag and left it on the table in the living room so Chandler would see it immediately on entering and not, I hoped, look at and think about the damn answering machine. If he asked, I was confident I could convince him I had not received any new messages from Scarletta. Despite his belief that he could read my thoughts, I didn't anticipate his noticing any dishonesty in my face. Maybe, as my father once suggested, I could have become a good actor. A good liar (I hated the word and would rather be known as a good fabricator) had to have the ability to erase the listener's skepticism immediately.

Any good fabricator lies to himself or herself first. If you can persuade yourself something is true, just for a short time, even only a moment, you will be credible. Before Chandler arrived, I went about chanting to myself: "She hasn't called. She's gone. She's given up. There was no message to erase."

But even the best actors, the most experienced performers, are nervous before they step onto that stage. The high school drama coach who had wanted me in his new production told me that if an actor wasn't nervous, he or she was probably a mediocre artist. He was so determined to get me to play the lead female role, Emily Webb in *Our Town*, that he piled on his compliments.

"You have natural poise, a confident air, and a pleasing speaking voice. I like the look in your eyes, your maturity, Pru. I don't confuse being thoughtful with being shy. I've seen that look on your face when you want to be competitive. There's no hesitation. You'd be dynamite onstage."

I thought he was going to say I was beautiful or attractive, too, but with all the fear teachers had of being accused of sexual indiscretion with students, he hesitated to do so. Nevertheless, it was in his eyes. Any other girl would have smothered her resistance, but despite all that flattery, I refused him. He was right about one thing. I wasn't shy. I cleverly used the facade of it to hide fear.

Nevertheless, it wasn't by accident that my father told me I'd be a good nurse because I was a good actress. I hadn't missed his underlying point. He was really telling me I was a good fabricator. In an instant, my face could dissolve into whatever mask was necessary to be convincing. I was comfortable with putting on false faces whenever necessary. It was necessary now.

When I heard Chandler arrive, I quickly emerged from my bedroom wearing my sheer purple lace chemise nightie, something I had not yet worn for him. It was meant to be a little extra distraction. I really preferred that he didn't have a chance to wonder whether Scarletta had called. With him, I'd rather not fabricate whenever it was possible to avoid it.

From the happy, lusty expression on Chandler's face, I knew I was quite successful controlling his attention. If he had been anticipating more trouble, he had forgotten. He looked speechless, mesmerized. I recalled my mother once saying, "Most women don't realize the power they possess or merely don't know how to use it."

"Goes well with the ring, don't you think?" I said, holding up my hand so the ring caught the light.

"I have a feeling that an early honeymoon in Palm Springs might not match tonight," he said, putting down his briefcase. He loosened his tie and started across the room toward me. "But really, why would we wait anyway?" he asked, smiled, and kissed me. "Have to celebrate the moment, right?"

"Who's arguing?"

He laughed and then surprised me by swooping me up into his arms and carrying me to the bedroom. The memory of Scarletta's voice was drifting back like the puffs of a sports car's exhaust as we sped away. He lowered me to the bed I had already prepared, a spider's web with my perfumed silk sheets and pillowcases.

He laughed. I had a condom wrapped in a ribbon on his pillow.

He hurried to get out of his suit, tie, shirt, and pants, rushing as if he thought he might miss the sex train. I lay back, my legs spread, my smile hopefully like cake frosting.

"Just promise," he said, "that you'll greet me like this forever."

"And the day after that."

Naked, he lay beside me, kissed me, and then almost in one graceful motion, when he was ready, turned and slipped into me. Looking down at me, he said, "Oh, sorry. Did I say hello?"

"You're saying it now," I whispered, and he began his erotic thrusts and strokes, his eyes open and fixed on mine.

This was what lovers really meant when they claimed, "We were like one," I thought. Both of us were moving to each other's rhythm, synced into each other's heartbeats, drumming our way toward a moment of real ecstasy like two Buddhists climbing up the four levels to our personal nirvana. Everything around us was disappearing. We were really leaving this world or entering a place rarely visited in it. Neither of us had to speak; no vows were necessary. Yet I heard him repeating, "Pru, Pru." Vaguely, I thought, he was holding on to me as if he was afraid that not only was the world around us disappearing, but I was, too.

Of course, like any man, he wanted to be sure it was him I was making love with and not some past lover or fantasy. Women have that fear, too, for sure, but men want to be the best their woman ever had . . . *Macho, Macho Man.* Even my father admitted that to me once. "For a man," he said, "it never stops being opening night. We're always afraid of the reviews."

Chandler kissed the curve between my neck and my shoulder and then moved his lips up to my cheek and onto my lips. We drew our life forces out of each other like two vampires as our bodies kept perfecting our movements, a continual work in progress, a touch here, a kiss there, all of it building toward a great climax. Yes, this was an early honeymoon, I thought. How could it ever be better? Really, it didn't have to; it just couldn't be much less.

I was moaning with pleasure, and he was licking at my nipples and breasts as if they were two mounds of rich ice cream. I knew he was whispering his love, but I was falling back, drifting to a place where the only sound was the thumping of our hearts, some prehistoric drumbeat, the one that had driven our ancestors toward ensuring the survival of our species. It was raw yet tender, violent but graceful. The taste of his lips on mine, the feel of his stomach against my stomach, and the scent of his very sex filled my nostrils and stirred places in my brain too often asleep, places so surprising that it was as if I had stolen them from someone else.

Although I tried to stop it, I had that too often strange sensation of rising out of my body to stand aside and observe. Maybe I was hungry for every view of him, the way his tight rear end lifted and fell, the tautness of his legs, and the firmness of his back as he arched. His thrusts were suddenly being done almost in a frenzy, more like someone terrified he would not reach orgasm in time. Was it because he sensed I had mine and was afraid I'd be satiated too soon?

Don't be afraid, I wanted to say. *You can never satisfy me too soon and cause me to become indifferent to what remained of our lovemaking. But that insecurity is as it should be. Otherwise, we won't have new discoveries about ourselves. And isn't that what keeps two people together, new revelations? Love must grow, change, turn, and open doors to the wonder of each other. Too romantic? Am I thinking too much at a time when there should be nothing but feeling and pleasure? Tell me to stop.*

His hands moved to my shoulders. He gripped me tightly and lifted his head. It was as if every nerve in his body was exploding, bursting with messages rushing to his heart. For a moment, I really was beyond it. I really was no longer participating. I was now just watching him reaching for the ultimate pleasure. He opened his eyes and saw the smile on my face, but it seemed to confuse him. I knew what he was thinking. How could I be so objective at the most subjective moment our bodies would find in this life?

"Pru?" he said, as if he wasn't sure he was making love to me. Perhaps my face had become unrecognizable.

Before I could speak and reassure him, I heard it, and he stopped because he heard it, too. We were frozen in the act of love, sculpted in passion too hot to touch and yet too cold to melt.

The phone was ringing. He wanted to wait so we could hear what followed when it stopped and my simple message played: *I'm not in right now. Please leave a message.* Was she about to leave another? I was holding my breath.

There was nothing.

That's not like her, I thought. She'd leave something, another warning, another revelation. It was someone or something else.

I relaxed again, expecting he would realize that, too, and return to me, but instead, he asked, "Do you think that was her? Was it her?"

Before I could reply, his mobile buzzed.

"You're not going to answer that, are you?" I asked. I hadn't realized that he had taken it out and left it on the bed. He looked at it.

"Something's up," he said. I groaned when he dismounted and sat up to answer the phone. "Hey," he said. That was almost always his hello when he knew who was calling. He listened. "When? What are they doing now?"

I sat up, too. "Who is it?" I asked.

"Give me ten minutes," he told whoever was on the phone. "Then have them ring again."

He put the phone down, thought a moment, and then turned to me.

"Have who ring again, Chandler?"

"Ben Mallory is parked outside your apartment building's front entrance."

"And he is?"

"My private detective."

"Has he been following me all day since I left the hospital?" I asked. "Was he at the hospital asking questions? I told you—"

"No. He was here when you arrived, though."

"Well, why is he calling now? You're here. What does he want?"

"That ring we heard . . ."

"Yes?"

"He saw two Los Angeles detectives he knows at the front door. They rang to be buzzed in."

"Why? What do they want?"

"I don't know, but we should find out right away. Perhaps it has something to do with her. Mallory says they're homicide detectives."

He slipped on his underwear and pants.

"What are we doing?"

"He's going to tell them to ring again to be let in, Pru, before they go away. Throw something on."

"In the middle of our early honeymoon?"

He smiled. "The night is young." He put on his shirt and slipped his feet sockless into his shoes.

I sat up and reached for my robe.

"What are you thinking?" I asked. "Why have they come here?"

"Maybe they know her and have come to warn you about her. Perhaps she's already wanted for something serious. She might have been harassing another woman and eventually done something violent to her."

"But how would they know she's doing it to me? Did you report it, Chandler? I asked you not to do that. You did, didn't you?"

"No, I swear," he said, raising his hands. "But they could have found something on her, in her possession, that tracked to you. Let's see, but if it is that, I think you'll have to tell them everything, Pru."

I slipped on my slippers and brushed back my hair. A small fire was spiraling in my stomach. This was exactly what I didn't want, a spotlight on me.

"Let's hope this gets us closer to an end to it all. Right?" he said. "Right, Pru?"

"Right, right," I said.

The phone rang again. Chandler looked at me. I lifted

the receiver. "Yes?" I snapped. I didn't have to sound overjoyed, did I?

"This is Lieutenant Julio, LAPD, and Detective Gabriel. We would like to speak with you, Miss Dunning."

I looked at Chandler, who was nodding. Then, without replying, I pressed nine, which buzzed open the door.

"They're coming up," I said, and went into the bathroom to look at my face. I saw I was still quite flushed from our lovemaking, and since I was naked in a robe to greet the police, I was a little embarrassed about what they would have to be dull or stupid not to realize they had interrupted. I splashed cold water over my cheeks and forehead and patted my face dry just as I heard the door buzzer.

"I'll get it," Chandler called.

He was obviously quite anxious to get them involved with my situation and happy something had brought them. In fact, he had seemed too willing to interrupt our great lovemaking. I was a little annoyed at that, but it wasn't really his fault. *Damn her*, I thought. *One way or another, she is tormenting me and ruining my life.*

I stepped into the living room as they entered. Lieutenant Julio was as tall as Chandler. His licorice-black hair was balding, with patches of gray. Like someone who was in retreat when it came to his features, he had the remaining strands cut military-short, very close to his scalp. I didn't think he was as old as the deep lines in his face were advertising. I could see it in his eyes. What he had was the look of someone who had been aged by the terrible things he had witnessed.

Detective Irene Gabriel looked twenty years younger. She was only an inch or so taller than I was, but she had manly shoulders and was one of those women who would have wide hips no matter how severely she dieted. She had remarkably green eyes, though, and a soft, feminine mouth. She looked too innocent and pleasant to be a homicide detective. Whenever I met someone new, I always wondered what made them who they were, maybe because I was always wondering that about myself, despite the good answers I had given Chandler that day we met.

They both turned immediately away from Chandler to look at me. I saw from the way Detective Gabriel was looking over Chandler and me that she had quickly surmised what they had disturbed with their insistence. Perhaps I was imagining it or hoping, but she looked sorry. Or maybe it was just envy.

Lieutenant Julio was all business and couldn't have cared less if he had interrupted a lifesaving heart procedure.

"You're Pru Dunning, a cardiac nurse at Cedars?" he asked.

I started to think that was a dumb question and then realized I could be a friend who was using the apartment.

Establishing identities had to be step one. It was just like us, asking name and date of birth whenever we first met a patient. Forget when you were born, and you were doomed in this new security-conscious world.

"I am. What's this about?" I asked as sharply as I could. Chandler was hoping it was about ending my ordeal, but I wouldn't surrender my right to my privacy so willingly, even if someone was ostensibly here to help me.

"It's about a patient of yours," he said. He looked longingly at the sofa, but I wasn't yet ready to be civil.

"What patient?"

"Douglas Thomas," he said.

I thought I could hear the phone ringing and my answering machine going on. She wasn't leaving a message; she was laughing.

"What about him?" Chandler asked before I could. He stepped forward so as to be between me and them.

"He was murdered today," Lieutenant Julio said.

I gasped. *The bitch*, I thought. *What now?*

Lieutenant Julio looked sharply at Chandler. "And you are?"

"I'm Chandler Harris. Miss Dunning is my fiancée."

"Okay," Lieutenant Julio said, almost as if he was giving Chandler permission to marry me. He looked at my duffel bag. "Are you planning on a trip?"

"Yes, we are," Chandler said. "A couple of days in Palm Springs. What's this about? Why have you come here?" he demanded in a sterner tone. "She was just his nurse. He had . . . what?" he asked me.

"A bypass."

"Right. So why are you interested in Miss Dunning?"

How easily Chandler could slip into his attorney persona, I thought, as easily as I could slip into my nurse identity. We were two chameleons.

I realized I was smiling, and it was not a good moment to be doing so. Lieutenant Julio stepped toward me.

"We're going to have to ask Miss Dunning to come to the station. We'll need fingerprints and a DNA sample," he said.

"What? Why?" Chandler demanded.

"It's best you get dressed and come with us, Miss Dunning," Lieutenant Julio said, addressing me only.

"You'll need a warrant for that," Chandler said. "I'm an attorney with Taylor, Barnes, and Cutler."

"So you'll be Miss Dunning's attorney?"

"Absolutely. Why are you treating her as a suspect? We told you she was his nurse, but did you know she saved his life?"

"How did she do that?" Detective Gabriel asked. Until then, she had appeared to be observing and learning.

"Stopped him from getting what might have been a lethal medicine. You can check on that," Chandler told her.

"The dosage probably wouldn't have killed him, Chandler," I said softly. "It wouldn't have helped, but—"

"Nevertheless, the man was so grateful that he presented her with a gift of very expensive pearls," Chandler told Lieutenant Julio.

He looked at me and then at Chandler before he took out a folded paper from his inside jacket pocket. He handed it to Chandler, who read it quickly and then turned to me, holding his attorney face. My fiancé is fading away, I vaguely thought.

"They have a warrant," he said. "It also permits them to search your apartment." He spun so sharply on Lieutenant Julio that the man took a step back. "How was Douglas Thomas murdered? Why is Miss Dunning a suspect?"

"Person of interest," Detective Gabriel corrected.

"I think it's best for us to continue this at the station, Mr. Harris. Miss Dunning, will you get dressed, please? Detective Gabriel will go with you."

"Why do I need her while I'm getting dressed?" I asked.

"To be sure you don't hide anything," Chandler answered for Lieutenant Julio.

He nodded.

I started to return to the bedroom.

"Pru," Chandler called. I turned back. "No more answers to any questions without me present."

I nodded and continued. I didn't like the idea of another woman coming into my bedroom with the bed the way Chandler and I had left it. My intimacy was being invaded. Detective Gabriel's eyes went everywhere but settled quickly on the creased silk sheets and blanket bunched at the foot of the bed. Chandler told me not to answer questions, but he didn't say anything about not asking them.

"Are you married?" I asked as I opened my closet. I reached for a mocha-colored glitter lace jacket and then paused because I thought it was a bit too *I don't care*. I took out a more elegant three-piece rhubarb-colored outfit that gave me more of an executive look.

"I'm not the center of attention here," she replied. She stood there with her arms folded under her small bosom. She wore a light blue shirt under a gray jacket. Her knee-length skirt revealed her chubby calves. She was wearing a pair of black-laced Skechers with gray socks.

I glanced at her, started to smile, and stopped to put on my nurse's face.

"Are you having some thyroid issues?" I asked.

"No," she said.

I shrugged. "I suppose you have frequent physicals in your line of work."

"Just get dressed, please, and don't concern yourself with me. There's a lot ahead."

All my moves were deliberately exaggerated and slow. I took an inordinate amount of time choosing my panties and bra. Every time I looked at her, I saw she was a little nervous.

"I'll bet you haven't been a detective that long," I said.

"Long enough."

I smiled, one of those sickeningly sweet ones, put on my clothes, and then spent time choosing a pair of shoes. I finally settled on a pair of dark blue shoe boots. When we emerged from the bedroom, I saw that Chandler had put on his socks as well as his shoes, tie, and jacket. He had just finished speaking to someone on his mobile.

"You'll have to ride with them," he said. "Ben and I will follow. You're not to say anything until I'm there, too, and we find out what this is all about."

I nodded. The phone rang. I looked at Chandler. He was obviously wondering if it was Scarletta.

"It's our forensic team," Lieutenant Julio said, and picked up the receiver. "What's the number for the front door?"

"Nine," I said.

Chandler took out his mobile again. "I want my man here," he told Lieutenant Julio. "Police have been known to plant evidence."

"As long as he doesn't get in the way," he replied. If he was insulted, he didn't show it. Experience gave you the skin of a reptile, I thought.

"Change of plan," Chandler told Ben Mallory when Mallory answered. "You're up here to observe while the apartment is searched for I don't know what."

He returned his phone to his inside pocket and then

asked Lieutenant Julio for the address of the station. Before we left, two men from forensics entered, and Chandler's private eye, Ben Mallory, followed on their heels. He and I had yet to be introduced, but Chandler didn't make any effort to do that. Mallory looked at me and almost smiled. He was a stout, six-foot-four-inch-tall man with curly dark brown hair and an unshaven face. Wearing a black trench coat, he looked more like the traditional image of a detective than Lieutenant Julio did.

Chandler whispered something to him. They watched as Lieutenant Julio and Detective Gabriel led me out. Chandler was right behind us.

"I'd rather take the stairs," I said when they approached the elevator.

Lieutenant Julio nodded, and all of us descended. When we stepped outside, Detective Gabriel put her hand firmly on my right arm and directed me to their black Lincoln. She opened the rear door. I glanced back at Chandler.

"I'm right behind you, Pru," he said. He looked sick with concern. It wasn't until that moment that I thought about our two-day holiday. At the moment, that seemed to me to be the biggest threat, not being able to go.

Was I being too frivolous?

"One moment," I said, turning back. Chandler paused. I stepped up to him to whisper, "You know she's done something to involve me in this."

He shook his head. "Why would I know that?" His face brightened with soft anger. "What haven't you told me?"

"A lot," I said, and returned to the detectives' car.

As we pulled away, I felt myself begin to tremble. The earthquake began in my heart and rippled through my bones.

You should have killed her the night she was out here, I told myself.

And then I leaned forward to look out the side window, searching to see if she had been watching all of this and was now smiling as we passed pedestrians.

She was there. Surely she was.

Gloating.

Scarletta

I SLOWLY FOLLOWED my father down the stairs. Obviously, he'd had quite a bit to drink at his dinner meeting. He swayed with every step and realized he had better cling to the banister, but I didn't rush forward to help him. Alcohol had clouded his eyes. I wondered if the subject of my mother's leaving us had come up with his business associates. If they had sympathized with him, it would only have made him drink more.

At the bottom of the stairway, he hesitated, and then, without looking back, he went to the bar and poured himself what looked like nearly half a glass of bourbon. When he looked up and saw I had followed him, he stared a moment, took a long sip, and then came around the bar and sat precariously on a stool. I was still standing in the living-room doorway. There was something about the look in his eyes that kept me from drawing too close.

Behind me, my scream was still resonating. My bones continued to tremble with the reverberation. I had never yelled at my father that way. The shock on his face would linger for a long time on the doorway of my nightmares to come. Very quickly, however, his expression had changed from alarm to anger, his lips white; but when he had turned to leave me, he moved more like someone in fear than in rage or disgust. He looked like he was fleeing.

I told myself that all the whiskey and wine he had drunk was mainly responsible for his mixture of emotions swirling so quickly on his lips and in his eyes. What else would explain such a change in his usual calm, quiet manner? Normally, he would be comforting me, not trying to get away.

As we continued to stare at each other, my father wiped his mouth with his jacket sleeve, nothing I had ever seen him do. If he ever had done it in front of my mother, she would surely have howled like a wounded beast. He was always fastidious about his clothes and his habits, knowing how important that was to her. I remembered her bawling him out for spitting in our backyard once. He was raking up some leaves, and the dust probably had gotten into his mouth. He never anticipated her watching him through a window. She was like that with both of us, never missing a mistake. But I always had the sense that she was doing it to keep us from being, as she often accused others of being, common.

After a few more moments, Daddy closed and opened his eyes, nodding and looking more composed. Nevertheless, I could sense the rage still rumbling within him. His eyes were steady and his shoulders relaxed, but his fingers were so tight around his glass of bourbon that I could see his whitened knuckles straining against his skin. I anticipated the glass shattering in his hand. He was like a stranger. Cold fear washed over me. My blood felt like it was pooling at my feet.

"I know what you're doing, Scarletta," he said in a coarse, loud whisper. "I understand, but you've got to stop it."

I shook my head slowly, hoping he would see my innocence, see that there was nothing sly or deceitful in me. "What am I doing?"

"Denying reality doesn't help us," he declared. He took another sip of his bourbon and looked around as if just realizing where he was. "We have to face the truth head-on, bravely and together. Have you forgotten everything we promised each other at the restaurant? I was so proud of you, proud of your courage."

"Daddy—"

"NO!" he screamed.

Everything in the room seemed to tremble. I tried to swallow but couldn't. I couldn't move a muscle.

"No illusion, Scarletta. No more pretending. Bravely and maturely, you look people in the eye and say, 'Yes, my mother is gone, but we're fine. We're fine.' Do you hear me, Scarletta? Do you?"

I simply stared, almost afraid to breathe. He looked like he would leap off the stool and seize me to shake out of me what he didn't want me to think. He relaxed, took a deep breath, his shoulders rising and falling, and then gazed around the room again.

"We should think of changing things, I suppose. It will help us both face the truth. I'll start replacing this furniture. I have some newly designed modern pieces and more attractive colors. I don't think either of us particularly liked her taste, but we were both afraid to utter a word. Now it doesn't matter. It will never matter again."

"Stop talking about her as if she's gone for good," I said, gathering my courage. "You even said she might call one day and beg to return. I know you're very angry, but you would take her back, wouldn't you? You loved her too much. Right, Daddy?"

Without answering, he finished his bourbon in one gulp and slammed the glass so hard on the bar's granite top I was sure it would shatter. Then he leered at me. He looked distorted, with his right shoulder turned in and his back rising, like a hawk about to pounce.

I heard myself gasp. Daddy was so good-looking. How could he metamorphose into what looked more like a creature so quickly? His face was redder than before, and his eyes were ready to pop. His handsome, manly mouth was twisted, and the veins in his temples looked embossed. Any other girl would think she was gazing at a man who hated the air she breathed.

"What'ja do with her good-bye note, Scarletta?" he asked with a cold smile. "Huh?"

"I didn't do anything with it," I whined, now speaking through an onslaught of cold, stinging tears. "Don't you see? If you didn't come home and find it, then she—"

"Stop it!" he screamed, clapping his hands so sharply I winced. He sat up straighter. "Stop," he continued in a much calmer tone. "Don't you see? You're making this worse than it has to be."

"I'm not. Really, Daddy."

He smiled, but it was a stony, hateful look. "You're just like her right now, stubborn, stubborn, stubborn. I don't think I changed that woman's mind about anything in all the years we were together. She wouldn't grant me this much," he said, holding up his right hand and pinching his thumb against his forefinger.

I was speechless but still crying silently.

His angry face suddenly softened into a warmer, more recognizable Daddy smile. "But I loved her no matter what. You saw that, Scarletta, right? You saw it every day, saw that I would do anything and everything for her, didn't you? Didn't you?"

"Yes, Daddy."

He nodded, and then his smile flew off his lips like a

frightened bird. For a moment, he simply stared at me, his eyes blinking slowly, like someone fighting to keep awake. I was thinking I should stop talking and simply leave him alone. That was the best solution. He'd fall asleep soon. It was better to bring this weird conversation to an end.

But then his eyes opened fully, and he was nodding as if he was hearing someone whispering in his ear to tell him something. He was agreeing, agreeing with his own thoughts, and looking like someone who had another person inside him.

"Yes, yes, exactly," he said.

"What?"

"Do you know what other men called me behind my back? Huh, Scarletta? Did you know? Have you heard people talking about me?"

"No, Daddy. I don't know what you mean."

"They called me henpecked. Some even went so far as to say your mother wore the pants in our family. How'dja like that if you were me, huh? A man who has built all this, who employs so many people, henpecked, weak? Huh? But did I stop loving her because of it? No. And now what? She's made a bigger fool of me. And you, too! And you're not helping any by refusing to face up to it. You're helping her. That's what you're doing, helping her destroy us. Is that what you want? Are you doing her bidding?" he asked, pointing his accusing right forefinger at me. "Were you always conspiring with her?"

Tears came to my eyes. He looked so riled. I couldn't recall him ever looking this angry at me. He might pretend to be upset about something I had done or said because my mother was, but as soon as he could, he'd wink at me. This whole conversation was better conducted in a nightmare than in real life. I only hoped I could forget it, wipe these images and words out of my mind.

"I'm not doing anything like that, Daddy," I said softly. I was exhausted. My emotions were so twisted inside me. I felt my heart straining to break loose so it could beat and keep me alive. Maybe he saw the terror in my face now. He sat back, looking more relaxed, returning to himself.

"Your mother decided to leave us and start a new life with someone else," he said, like a reporter describing events on television. "She's gone. Pretending she isn't won't bring her back. I'm sorry. If there was one thing more I could have done to keep her, I would have done it, and don't be blaming yourself, either. Don't ever think you did anything to drive her off. Hear? You'd be sorry quickly. You'd feel like a real fool in the end."

I took in his words like bitter medicine. He was giving me a prescription for the rest of our lives. My eyes felt like broken faucets. The tears that had come and gone wouldn't stop coming now, and I didn't make any attempt to wipe them away. I let them drip off my cheeks.

"Damn!" he suddenly cried. He pressed his palms

against his cheeks and looked like he was trying to crush his face. Then he suddenly stopped and leered at me again, stared so long that unbridled fear rose inside me once more. Once again, he was listening to a voice I couldn't hear. "No, no, Scarletta. It's too soon," he said.

I finally wiped my eyes with my palms. "What's too soon?"

"You going to some party. It makes it look like you don't believe this thing your mother's done will last much longer. It makes you look all right with it because you believe it's only temporary. Why be mournful or ashamed about what she has done if it's just some little episode? That won't stop you from having a good time. That's the way people will see you. That's what they'll believe you are thinking."

"But you said I should go to the party. I don't understand, Daddy. We went to dinner to show people that we were all right. You told me to go to school and be strong. Now you're—"

"I said too much. I wasn't thinking straight. And that was before this. I didn't expect you to do something like this. It's . . . a little sick."

"What's a little sick? Do something like what?"

He put up his hand like a traffic cop stopping cars. "I'm tired of talking about it. You'll come to your senses, but it takes time. I know that. I was a little blind to how it was affecting you," he said. "I'm sorry. I was thinking too much of myself and not you. My eyes are opened now. It will be all right. I'm thinking straight again. No worries."

He slipped off the stool and staggered. How could he be thinking straight now?

"What are you talking about?" I asked in a much more demanding tone. His jumping from one thing to another had exhausted me. I knew I sounded more like my mother, but I felt I had to. "What are you saying? Doing something like what? What's sick?"

He narrowed his eyelids and stood firmly, no shaking, no unbalance, stern.

"It's time you stopped this pretending. Go on up there or go to wherever you have it and get that goodbye note, Scarletta. Before I go to sleep, I want to see it exactly where I accidentally left it today. And until you put it back there, you don't leave this house, not to go to school, not to go anywhere. Understand? I don't want you on the phone talking to any of your friends, either. I'm warning you. Don't dare disobey me," he said, wagging his finger.

He stepped forward. I gasped and stepped to the side to get out of his way, because he looked like he was going to walk right into me or through me. I watched him pull himself up the stairs, grasping the banister and nearly tripping on one step. For a few moments, I couldn't move. I followed him but didn't get too close. When he reached the top, he tottered for a moment, looking at my bedroom. Then he walked to his and my mother's bedroom, leaving the door wide open.

As if the heavens had decided to support what was happening, there was a boom of thunder. A heavy downpour started, the wind and rain scratching at our windows. I saw a streak of lightning through my open door as I walked in a daze to my bedroom. What had just happened? What was happening to us? The thunder was so loud, the lightning so close, that it seemed like it would come stabbing at me through my windows and set my room, my bed, and me on fire.

My mother was never frightened by the weather. When I asked her how she could be so brave, she said, "There's no point in being afraid of things you can't control. Just be afraid of making your own mistakes."

I tried to be as brave as possible for her, but that didn't stop me from quivering in the wake of my father's frightening words and threats. He was almost unrecognizable. It was as if my mother's leaving had permitted his truer self to emerge. All these years, she had kept it under lock and key. Maybe he had been fighting that from the moment I found him crying over the note she had left, and now that battle within him was over, and the part of him I had grown to love and cherish was dying away, dwindling like a lovely song falling far behind me in the darkness.

Nevertheless, hope popped up again, fighting the attempt to drown it. Maybe in the morning, Daddy would forget everything he said while he was drinking, I thought. He'd be sorry and surely make it up to me. I'd be forgiving. We did need each other. *Think of all this as his suffering, too. Help him, Scarletta*, I told myself. *Help him.*

I sucked in my breath, squeezed my hands into fists to get myself to be determined and crush the memory of what had just occurred, and then I went to the bathroom to prepare for bed. There was another boom, shaking the house. Lightning flashed brighter than before. The rain sounded like hundreds of whips snapping over the roof, the sides, and the windows. Trying to ignore it, I concentrated on washing up, brushing my teeth, and putting on a nightgown, this time deliberately avoiding my mother's.

After I had put out the light, I slipped into bed but lay there staring up at the ceiling and listening to the rain until it slowed and the lightning was gone. I was afraid to close my eyes, afraid that I would see my father's grotesque expressions and anger displayed on the inside of my eyelids, streaming like film images projected from the deepest dark places in my memory to keep me soaking in a pool of cold fear. Eventually, my emotional exhaustion took control, and I closed my eyes. Sleep came with the finality of a coffin lid.

I had no doubt that I would have slept through the night, slept even past my time to get up to go to school, something he had forbidden me to do until I produced my mother's good-bye note, but I was suddenly awoken with the feeling of lips on my neck. For an instant, I thought it was a dream, and then the scent of whiskey swirled under my nostrils, and I shuddered and turned to see my father beside me, his eyes closed.

His hand moved up my stomach to my breast. It resembled an independent creature cupping and gently massaging, the fingers slipping over my nipple. I was too shocked and frightened to move or speak, especially when I realized he was naked.

"I'm sorry, Doreen," he whispered. "Forgive me. Come back to us."

His lips were on my neck again, and his hand slipped off my breast and down to my thigh.

"DADDY!" I screamed.

He stopped. I remained still, frozen and frightened. He did not speak. He turned, and then, rising like someone about to begin sleepwalking, he started out of my bedroom, the weak illumination of the hallway making it look like I was witnessing everything through a sheet of gauze, his naked body ghostlike as he appeared to float through the door and disappear.

For a few seconds, I lay there questioning whether he had been here beside me, touching me, or if I had dreamed it. There was a lingering scent of the whiskey to convince me it had really happened. I sat up and listened.

I didn't hear any footsteps or any door closing, so I rose and went out to the hallway. He wasn't there. I walked to his bedroom and looked in. Because the sky had not yet cleared, there was almost no illumination. I stepped in to get a better view of the bed and saw he was not in it. For a long moment, I stood there in the dim light borrowed from the low-wattage hall chandelier and listened. The bathroom door was open, but I didn't hear him in there.

And then my eyes drifted to the far left corner near my mother's closet, and I saw him sitting on the floor, his arms around his knees, his eyes open.

"Daddy?" I said, stepping toward him.

"Get away!" he cried. "Away!"

I stopped, terrified. "What is it? What's the matter? Why did you come to my room? Why were you in my bed again? What are you doing?"

"Away," he said. "Just stay away."

He lowered his head.

He's still drunk, I thought. *He's just drunk.* I felt sorry for him, but I didn't want to disturb him any more, so I turned and left. When I crawled back into my bed and thought about what had happened and what I had just seen, my body felt like it was made of fine crystal that had been so shaken it had hairline cracks up and down and across it. If I moved too quickly, I would shatter into pieces.

I didn't move, and I didn't fall back to sleep. I lay

there with my eyes open, anticipating my father realizing what he had done and what had happened. He would come to my room to apologize. He might even be crying like a baby when he asked me to forgive him. I would, of course. I wanted that to happen so much that I was afraid if I fell asleep, he would see I wasn't awake and return to his room. He, too, would then lie awake, full of regret.

But he never came. The light of morning came instead. It was then that my exhaustion took control, and I closed my eyes. When I opened them and looked at the clock, I saw it was nearly noon. Groaning, I sat up, ground the sleepiness out of my eyes, and rose, putting on my slippers. Daddy must have overslept, too, I thought, and I went to his bedroom. The door was closed, but I opened it and stepped in. He wasn't in his bed, and he wasn't in the bathroom.

I hurried back to my room, got into my robe, and started down the stairs, listening hard for any sounds coming from the kitchen. The house was silent. Nevertheless, skeptical of his leaving without speaking to me, I hurried to the kitchen and saw he wasn't there. There were no signs of his having had breakfast, either. I had started to turn away to look in the living room when my eyes caught sight of the paper on the kitchenette. Slowly, I approached and then picked it up and read. There were only five words.

Return your mother's good-bye note.

My fingers stung as if the paper was electrified. I dropped it on the table and went to the door to the garage. His car was gone. He had left for work.

Still quite dazed, I started to return to my room but paused to look in the living room. It was as if I had to check every place in this house every day forever to be sure my mother had not returned. I saw no one there, but my gaze drifted, and then I lifted my head and looked up at where my mother's beautiful portrait had hung.

It was gone.

And in its place was the old picture of my grandparents, my father's parents. He had said he would do that, but I didn't think he would. It was as if someone had thrown a pail of snow and ice over me. Why had my father done this now, this morning? Was it because of the missing good-bye note, to drive home my mother's desertion? Was it because he couldn't stand the sight of her looking down at him anymore? Was it to convince himself it was over? Where had he put her beautiful picture?

I went from room to room downstairs searching for it, wondering if he at least had decided to hang it somewhere less conspicuous, but it wasn't anywhere, on any wall. I rushed to the garage, thinking he had put it against one of the walls, but it wasn't there, either. I ran up the stairs. He hadn't put it in what had been my grandparents' room and, of course, not in his. I thought of the attic.

Our house had a retractable stairway to the attic. There was a hanging strap that you pulled to lower the ladder steps. I hadn't done it by myself ever. My mother wasn't fond of going up there but occasionally did, and often she did with my father. It was then that I would go up, more for the excitement of doing it than interest in the attic. It was far more than a crawl space. The roof was high enough for my father to walk without having to bend over, and it ran almost the length and width of the house. Twice that I could remember, handymen had to go up there to repair some areas of the roof that had leaked after a heavy rain.

Most of what was stored up there had belonged to my grandparents. If it wasn't such an effort to bring it all down and throw it away, my mother would have done so. She said she didn't consider one thing up there to be a valuable family heirloom. "It's all junk, the sort of stuff a serial hoarder keeps to gather dust. Your grandfather wouldn't give anything away. He was so stingy he wouldn't give someone his cold."

She went off on how petty my grandmother was and how she lived in a world of illusion, believing that just because it had belonged to her or her mother, it was valuable.

When I pulled the strap and began to climb the ladder,

I realized how hard it would be for my father to carry up the large portrait of my mother by himself. It had a thick ivory scrolled frame. It was too heavy and wide. After the night he'd had, I couldn't imagine him navigating with it in his hands. And I couldn't imagine my sleeping through his having one or two of his workers come here to carry it up, either.

When I rose through the opening and gazed around, I saw nothing new. Still there were the old trunks my grandmother and grandfather had used for their many cruises, as well as other luggage and some dark wood cabinets. There was a mirror on a wooden stand, the glass caked with dust, black metal file cabinets, old standing lamps, and piles of fashion magazines. There were books scattered about as well. I remember my father insisting some of that was really worth money.

But as I panned the whole attic, I did not see the portrait. I saw no point in walking around to look further, so I carefully backed down the ladder and then sent it up to lock in place. For a moment, I stood there, thinking. The portrait really was too big to fit in my father's car, backseat or trunk. It struck me that he could have put it outside, perhaps in the rear of the house. I hurried down the stairs and to the rear entrance.

The moment I stepped out, the bright sunshine blinded me. I covered my eyes and gazed around. There was no sign of the picture leaning against a wall or lying off somewhere. What a horrible thing to do with it anyway, I thought. If it rained on it, it would be ruined. I thought how nasty and vengeful it would be to leave it in the sunshine, too, recalling how strict Mother had been about those UV rays. She was always on my father about it, almost as much as she was with me.

I'd have to wait until he came home or called, I thought. Surely he would call to see how I was or if I had disobeyed him and left the house. But it was too late to go to school anyway. Vaguely, I wondered what everyone was thinking. In a little while, when lunchtime would start, I had no doubt Jackie or maybe even Chet would call to see where I was. Jackie had probably been worrying all morning. Tonight was her party, and if I was indeed sick, what would happen to her plans for her great night? That would be more important than my being sick, of course. Would Chet simply choose another girl?

Considering what was happening here, I felt stupid for even thinking about it. Maybe my father was right in his drunken lecture last night. Maybe I should act more upset about my mother's leaving us and stop smiling for a while. Perhaps he was accurate to say I was refusing to face reality.

As if my thoughts organized the way things happened in the world, the phone rang as soon as I reentered the house. I debated answering it. I really didn't want to talk to Jackie or Chet right now, but of course, if it was my father, my not answering it would convince him I had disobeyed his orders.

"Hello," I said even before I had brought the receiver to my ear.

"Where the hell are you? What are you doing?" It was Jackie. "Don't tell me you're sick. There wasn't anything wrong with you yesterday. Well?" she demanded when I didn't respond instantly.

"I am sick, sick from our personal family problems," I replied. I thought that would just end it, but Jackie wasn't buying it, and sympathy wasn't her strong point.

"That's crap, Scarletta. Everyone knows you and your father are not devastated. And you certainly didn't seem very sad when you were with us, especially when you were with Chet."

"I'm not the sort of person who likes sympathy, especially from people who are phony about it. I had a very bad night."

"Well, are you still coming to the party?"

"I don't think so," I said.

"What? You don't think so? I did a lot to convince Chet you'd be fun anyway. Even if we didn't consider what your mother did, it would still be hard to get him to believe me. I set you up. It was a lot of work. This is some gratitude."

"Set me up for what, Jackie?"

"A good time, stupid."

"I guess our definition of a good time is quite different after all," I said.

"You are nuts. You know that? Boy, did I make a mistake."

"Well, don't worry," I said. "You'll make plenty more."

"Fuck you, Scarletta," she said, and hung up.

I held the receiver for a moment and smiled. It was the first time in almost a day that I did. But I wasn't really feeling as good about it as I pretended. Why wouldn't I want to have a good time, too? I felt like I had been dragged underwater and given a chance to rise to the surface to take a breath, only to have my head pushed down before I could.

I stood there in the rear of the kitchen, staring down at the floor. I was exhausted again. Suddenly, my eyes went to the basement door just inside the rear entrance of the house. Nothing personal was kept there. It was damp and very poorly lit. If he had brought the portrait down there, he might as well have broken it up, torn up the picture, and shoved it in the garbage can. Maybe he couldn't get himself to do that, so the next best thing in his mind was the basement.

A part of me fought going down there to look. He'd be so angry again, and he'd accuse me again of not facing reality. He might be devastated if I dared to suggest that I keep it in my room. But what was I supposed to do, throw out every picture of my mother? If I could keep any, why not keep this one, the best one? Every time I had looked at it, I had dreamed of being as beautiful. Maybe she was different now, but she was my mother. The great picture was as important to me as it had been to my father and to my mother. It was as much a part of who I was as anything in this house ever could be. I wouldn't let it rot away in our damp, dark basement.

To my surprise, the door was locked. I went to the drawer where keys and batteries were kept, but I couldn't find the key. Why did he lock the door to our basement? I grabbed a screwdriver and returned to pry at the tooth of the lock. It took me a while, but after pushing and pulling, I managed to get the door opened. Because there were no windows below, I looked down into pitch darkness. Fumbling on the side, I found the switch that would light up the stairs. I hesitated, thinking I would surely surprise rats or something. Carefully, I started down.

When I reached the bottom, I looked for the chain that had to be pulled to turn on the basement ceiling light. Nothing happened. I looked up at the fixture and saw there was no bulb in it. Why take out the bulb? Did it blow and my father forgot to replace it or knew we didn't have any? I hurried up the stairs to the kitchen pantry, where I knew we kept light bulbs. There were at least a dozen. I grabbed one and went back down the stairs. I wasn't tall enough to reach the fixture, but there was a small ladder. I unfolded it and climbed up to screw in the new bulb. Instantly, the basement was lit enough for me to look at the length and width of it.

I didn't see the picture anywhere, but I stepped off the ladder and walked slowly over the gravel floor. The damp, rancid smell turned my stomach. As I looked around, there was at first nothing in the basement I didn't recall. Then I saw the shovel against the wall on my left. When I looked at the floor in front of it, I saw there was less gravel. The area looked like the width and length of my mother's portrait. How bizarre, I thought. Daddy had buried it? How could he do such a thing?

I seized the shovel and began clearing away the gravel that looked swept over the area. Then I began to dig carefully, not wanting the shovel to go through the picture if it was really there. After a few minutes, I saw the ivory frame. My stomach churned. This was crazy. How could he do this? I dug carefully all around the picture until it was no longer covered. He had buried it facedown. My hands were trembling. *I'll clean it up*, I thought, *and I'll put it in my room*. He'd be upset, but I would not give in. I could hate what my mother had done and not hate her. Even he had said often that we had the same face. I was cloned, right? *So don't make me forget her as well as hate her.* I would do neither.

Carefully, I reached down and, grasping the top of the frame, pulled the picture back and up.

And then the world caved in on me. My scream was so shrill, such a strain on my vocal cords, that I went mute.

My mother was looking up at me. She was lying there with her eyes still open, and she was wearing the gown she had worn on her anniversary, the gown she wore in the portrait.

Pru

THEY LED ME directly to the interrogation room. Before I could take a seat, Chandler was at my side. Lieutenant Julio and Detective Gabriel left us, telling us they'd be right back.

Chandler spun around as soon as the door closed. "What didn't you tell me?" he demanded.

How do I put this gently and make it sound less than it is? I wondered. *How do I keep from hurting him?* She had put me in this place. She had designed a way to destroy my relationship with him. It suddenly occurred to me that she might be someone who worked in his office, someone who had a terrible crush on him. Hadn't her calls begun about the time Chandler and I first met? Her jealousy was like a sharp knife cutting into my heart. I had gone too far out alone. She had baited me, drawn me into her world, a world where she had more control, and I had let her do it, never anticipating she would go this far.

"Well?" he said. "They'll be back any moment, Pru. Talk. I have to know everything in order to represent you right now."

"He might have raped me," I said.

It always amazed me how quickly blood could rise into someone's face. I saw it often when a doctor related undesirable results to a patient or informed him or her how something serious, something invasive, had to be done. The crimson in their faces was darker and lasted longer than a blush from embarrassment. Chandler's face was almost ruby red.

"Who?" he asked, pulling back as if I had contracted something contagious.

"Douglas Thomas," I said.

He knew the answer, but like anyone who was hoping it wasn't true, he'd asked as if he didn't.

"What are you saying? When? In the hospital?"

"No. He came to my apartment. He was waiting at the door with a bottle of champagne. He said he had returned to work and wanted to celebrate with me. I told him he was wrong to track me down, but he pleaded for the opportunity to share his joy with the nurse who he still believed saved his life. I think he had been waiting there in the hallway by my door for more than an hour. Who would do that? I thought the fastest way to get rid of him was to have one glass, toast his health, and send him on his way. I told him I had to clean the apartment because you were coming very soon."

"What do you mean, he might have raped you? How could you not know if someone raped you? Did he attack you?"

"Not attack. He wanted a picture with me holding the glass of champagne and wearing the pearls, so I went to get them, and while I was gone, he must have put something in my champagne, maybe GHB."

"How do you know that's what it might have been?"

"I had it once as a teenager but not that great a dose, of course. Some call it the date-rape drug. When I awoke, I was naked on my bed, and Douglas Thomas was gone. I went to the bathroom to look at myself, and I saw a used condom floating in the toilet. I thought he might have deliberately left it so I'd see it."

"Why?"

"Perhaps he was bragging. I had no marks on my body and no awareness of penetration."

"Why didn't you call the police? Go to have a rape-kit test?" Chandler asked. He was firing his questions at me as if I was on the witness stand in a trial.

"I thought about it, but if he did rape me, he used a condom."

"Yes, exactly, but you had it. It surely still contained enough of his sperm to reveal his DNA. Why not use it?"

"That's true, but . . ." I hesitated.

"But what?"

"He did more. It's almost indescribable."

"Describe it, and quickly."

"I was washed clean, almost sterilized, so there wouldn't be a hair, even a skin cell, left behind on my body. In fact, the entire apartment had been cleaned, vacuumed, every glass and dish washed, the coffee table dusted. It looked polished. I realized that there would be no fingerprints. He even had changed my sheets and pillowcases and washed the previous set. The bottle of champagne was gone. There was no trace of him having been there. Everything was pristine. I was afraid you might notice that and start asking questions."

Chandler stared at me for a long moment, so long I thought he didn't believe me.

"I know how bizarre it sounds, but it all happened just as I described, Chandler."

"You still should have called the police and explained. It's important to report something like this as close to the crime occurring as possible. How could you not?"

"I did think about it, but in the end, I realized what they might think, how they would respond to my claims. I had let him into my apartment, I still had those pearls, and there was nothing that indicated force of any kind."

"Why do you still have the pearls?" he practically screamed.

I shook my head. It was difficult to explain. I didn't understand it myself, but there was something about those pearls that kept me from getting rid of them, and it wasn't just how valuable and pretty they were.

"You're a nurse, Pru. You know you could have had blood taken and have proven you were drugged?"

"The window was closed on discovery. I know the limits of the drug when it comes to toxicology. And just because it's in your system doesn't mean you were drugged. People overdose, get too excited about it. The ER is often busy with teenagers who do it."

He grimaced, shook his head, and thought. Then his eyes widened with an idea. "How did he get into the building in the first place? If you told the police, they could have started with that."

"I did think of that, but then I realized that even if they discovered how, like followed someone in or pressed other tenants and one let him in without questioning, that would only prove he was there, nothing more. And they could very well think I buzzed him in to begin with, and I didn't, as I described, find him already there at my door. The building has no cameras, lacks security."

"So then what happened after he did this? Did he call you, try to visit you again?" he asked.

"No. I tried to forget it. I thought if he posted pictures on the Internet, then I might do something, because then I'd have some sort of proof of his maliciousness at least."

"And he didn't?"

"As far as I know, no. Believe me, if he had, there are

people at the hospital, especially on my floor, who would have had them circulated by now."

He thought a moment. "That night at dinner, when I had the champagne brought to the table . . . is that why you acted like that?"

I nodded. "It happened to be the same champagne."

"You could have told me then."

"I knew how much it would upset you, how angry you would be at me for letting him in. You'd be like you are now. Blaming me."

"I'm not blaming you, but, Pru, this is different. They're considering you a suspect in a murder."

"I know. I was hoping I could just forget it all. And I probably would have managed to do that, but today . . ."

"But today what, Pru? For God's sake, what else?"

"She called and left a message. She said, 'I know what he did to you. He'll pay.' "

"Scarletta?"

I nodded.

"Christ. Why didn't you show me that message?"

"I would have had to tell you everything and I was hoping—"

"How could she know what he had done to you?" His eyes lit up. "Maybe she worked with him. That's how she knew what you had done for him in the hospital. He bragged about your stopping the wrong medication. He might even have told her or others that he had given you those pearls. Maybe she liked him and thought you were taking him away from her."

"Maybe," I said. That did make more sense than her working with Chandler and being in competition with me, but in any case, she was driven by jealousy.

"This is so twisted, but we can play that message for the police and get them off your tail."

"No," I said. "We can't."

"Why not?"

"I erased it."

He simply stared as his lips moved. The words wouldn't come.

"How could I play it for you and not tell you everything? Don't you see?"

Before he could answer, the door opened, and Lieutenant Julio and Detective Gabriel returned, Lieutenant Julio carrying a folder. They sat across from us, and Lieutenant Julio pressed the button on a recording device, beginning their interrogation with the time and who was present.

"We'll do your fingerprints and your DNA sample after this," he said. "Unless you make it unnecessary."

"We will not respond to any questions until you reveal how and when Mr. Thomas was murdered," Chandler said, gathering his thoughts and sitting up firmly. "I'm not going to permit Miss Dunning to be a part of some fishing expedition."

Lieutenant Julio nodded, turned to me, and then, as if

Chandler hadn't spoken, asked, "Did you have anything to do with Douglas Thomas after he was released from the hospital, Miss Dunning?"

"I just said we're not going to respond unless—"

Lieutenant Julio put up his hand to stop Chandler, opened the folder, and, like someone laying out cards in solitaire, spread out pictures of me naked on my bed, the pearls prominent between my breasts. There were different views, pictures taken from different angles. It was clear that in one, he had been standing directly over me, shooting down, and in another, he had been lying beside me. After those were displayed, Lieutenant Julio put out an additional one with me facedown but my legs spread as far apart as they could be. The photographs were better quality and more graphic than pictures in porno magazines.

"I have placed photographs collected as evidence from Mr. Thomas's apartment," Lieutenant Julio said for the recording. "They are pictures of Miss Dunning nude in her own bed."

Not only could you hear a pin drop, but you could hear particles of dust colliding with the walls.

"As you can see," Lieutenant Julio said, "this is far from a fishing expedition."

Chandler turned to me. "Tell them all that you told me," he said. "In as much detail as you can recall."

Before I began, he added, "As you can see, her eyes are

closed in all the pictures where you can see her face. Keep that in mind as she explains."

Neither Lieutenant Julio or Detective Gabriel changed expression, but both turned to me and waited.

I began by describing my stepping out of the elevator, explaining why I had decided to take it and not walk up the stairs as I usually did, and my shocked reaction at Douglas Thomas's presence. From there, I included every moment, every word spoken between myself and Douglas Thomas that I could recall. Neither detective interrupted me with a question, so I went on to describe the aftermath, how I had found my body and my apartment immaculate and then explained why that, plus what I knew about the drug he had used, had convinced me it would be useless to call the police or go to the hospital.

"Without a shred of evidence to prove what he had done to me, it would end up being one of those he said, she said things," I said, and looked at Chandler to see if he was satisfied. I guessed my describing it all in such detail had left him stunned again. He just stared at the detectives, his face still crimson.

"So you were angry, enraged?" Lieutenant Julio asked, smiling.

Chandler realized why he looked so pleased before I did. I had just established motive and made their job easier. He leaped on it.

"There's more. Miss Dunning has been stalked for

some time. It's been mostly through phone messages, but on one occasion, the stalker, a woman, was waiting for her outside her apartment and followed her. She lost her, but the stalker continued calling and leaving messages."

"Threats?"

"All sorts of things," Chandler said. "Implications, sexual innuendos. We know only her name or the name she used, Scarletta, but we have suspicions that she is somehow involved with the hospital or perhaps works at Mr. Thomas's firm and maybe was unhappy he was talking about Miss Dunning so much. She had obviously been watching Miss Dunning's every movement and haunted her apartment building. She knew Douglas Thomas had been there to see her."

"And you know she knew this how?" Lieutenant Julio asked me.

I repeated Scarletta's last message.

"She even sent Miss Dunning a bouquet of roses," Chandler told them.

"Do you still have the card?" Lieutenant Julio asked.

"There was no card. It was just there at the door, so we know she knew exactly where Miss Dunning lived."

"Maybe Douglas Thomas sent it," Detective Gabriel suggested.

"He would have put his name on the card. He told everyone at the hospital how indebted he was to Miss Dunning. He gave her those pearls," Chandler said.

"Why would he hide the fact that he had sent her roses? It has to be the stalker." His voice was straining like someone struggling to keep relevant.

"So you think this stalker is also a nurse with a crush on you or, what, a jealous lover angry at Douglas Thomas for being with you?" Detective Gabriel asked me. She was grimacing skeptically, her tone quite condescending.

"Possibly," Chandler said. "We're not sure about her motives, but she's certainly a more likely suspect."

Both detectives were silent. Then Lieutenant Julio took out his mobile.

"I'll have the answering machine brought here," he said. He rose to go make the call.

"Unfortunately, Miss Dunning erased the messages, even the last one," Chandler revealed, painfully.

"Why would she do that?" Lieutenant Julio asked, lowering himself to his seat.

"She didn't want me to know what had happened to her. I didn't know all this until a few minutes ago," Chandler said. "We both realize that was a mistake now, but her intentions are understandable. She isn't the first woman to hide being sexually attacked or abused for fear of how she would be viewed by other women and men or what it would do to her current relationship," he said, directing himself more to Detective Gabriel.

There wasn't an ounce of sympathy in her face.

She'd probably enjoy being raped, I thought, and said as much through the expression on my face. She looked away.

Lieutenant Julio thought a moment. "This message was left on a landline?" he asked me.

"Yes," Chandler replied for me.

"We'll pick up the machine and check it out. Maybe there still could be something if it's digital. I have to call my team over at her place anyway to see where they're at with the search. Just sit tight," Lieutenant Julio said, turned off the recording device, and left the room.

I smiled at Detective Gabriel, who looked uncomfortable being left alone with us.

"Could you leave us for a moment?" Chandler asked her. She stood up fast, obviously delighted to do so, nodded, and left.

"Pru, did you have any contact with Thomas after the incident, anything else you can remember? Did he try to call you at the hospital, for example?" he asked as soon as the door was closed.

I shook my head.

"And you never called him and threatened him with prosecution?"

"No. I'm so sorry now that I kept it all from you, Chandler," I said.

The pictures were still on the table. He looked down at them, thought a moment, and then turned to me.

"We've got to locate Scarletta. I'll have Ben Mallory check out the other employees at Douglas Thomas's firm, and I'll get a new answering machine for your landline since they'll hold on to your present one, and we'll—"

He stopped when Lieutenant Julio and Detective Gabriel returned.

"We'll need that DNA sample and we'll be taking your fingerprints, Miss Dunning," Lieutenant Julio said. He looked at Chandler. "We'll be booking her."

"Why? We just explained that—"

"You asked how he was killed. Friends at work were concerned when he didn't arrive. His secretary, Florence Wilson, who had a duplicate key to his apartment, was sent to check on him. They knew about his surgery, of course. She discovered his naked body on his sofa and immediately called for an ambulance. The paramedics couldn't revive him. The police were called as well as the medical examiner. My team," he added proudly, "is headed by a sharp guy, Dr. James Gaede. He's been featured often in the *LA Times*. He spotted the localized irritation from the injection at the heart and got the body into a toxicological examination as quickly as possible.

"Douglas Thomas was killed with an injected overdose of propofol, an anesthetic. The overdose would cause respiratory failure." He looked at me. "Get the idea from Michael Jackson's death?"

"Now, just a minute," Chandler said. "Just because Miss Dunning is a nurse—"

"A small box containing syringes and two vials of propofol were found in a corner of the floor of Miss Dunning's clothes closet in her bedroom," he said.

Chandler turned to me, the fear visible in his eyes, hoping I had an explanation.

"She must have gotten in and planted it," I said.

Lieutenant Julio smirked. "Do you want to explain to your client how much better it would go for her if she offered a confession now, especially after the events she described?"

I looked at Chandler. He was juggling everything in his mind.

"I didn't do it," I said. He nodded.

Lieutenant Julio opened the door. "Let's go," he said.

I rose slowly. Chandler did not, as I was anticipating, take my hand. He stood back so I could walk ahead of him, and he was looking down at the floor as if he was afraid to look me in the face now. Detective Gabriel quickly gathered up the photos and shoved them back into the folder Lieutenant Julio had brought with him.

"I've got to make some calls," Chandler told me when we had stepped out of the interrogation room and he had pulled me aside. He was speaking quickly, his voice devoid of warmth. "We'll have to wait until your arraignment before we can ask for bail. I'm not really a criminal attorney, but we have two good ones at the firm. I'll get right on it." He looked at his watch. "You could be spending forty-eight hours in jail before your arraignment, Pru. We can ask for bail then."

I just stared at him and turned my engagement ring around on my finger as I waited for some sign of affection. He realized it and hugged me, kissing me quickly on the cheek and squeezing my hand gently.

"Stay strong," he whispered. "And don't answer any more questions or make any more statements about the situation. Okay?"

"Okay. I really don't have anything more to tell them anyway. I'm sorry, Chandler, sorry we'll miss our early honeymoon."

He looked caught between a laugh and an expression of utter shock. Then he squeezed my hand gently again and started away.

"Miss Dunning," Detective Gabriel said as I continued to watch Chandler leaving. I thought it looked more like he was fleeing.

I turned to her. "Left with the grunt work, Detective," I said.

Her eyes widened. "This way," she said. "And if I were you, I would stop being a smart-ass now."

Of course, she was right, but I didn't want her or anyone to know how loud and hard I was screaming inside myself, and for the moment, being a smart-ass, arrogant and confident, was the armor I had to wear.

All the way down the hall, I could hear someone else, too. I could hear Scarletta's laughter after she said, "And you thought you could get away from me."

Scarletta

I REMEMBER RUNNING up and down the center of the street, my arms flailing about as if I was some large bird trying to lift off the ground. Drivers either had to stop and wait for me to pass or turn into the other lane quickly. I vaguely saw or heard them open their windows and lean out to shout something nasty at me. A cacophony of horns blared. Later I was told that most assumed I was high on some drug. One of the neighbors who lived farther down the street and really didn't know us very well called the police. When I made a turn to start back, a patrol car with two policemen stopped ahead of me, and both got out to wait as I continued running toward them.

Scalding tears were flowing, and although my legs felt like two saplings hard to bend, I kept going. I could hear my lungs going in and out like a fireplace bellow pushing the air up through my throat. My mouth was wide open, the sound of my desperate breathing like a dying animal gasping for breath. The weight on my chest was as heavy as it would be if an iron breastplate had been fastened on me. I had not yet regained my voice, although I was going through the motions of screaming. My face surely looked like the face of someone whose head had been stuffed in a plastic bag, my eyes popping wide, my mouth twisted and distorted, and my nostrils wider than they had ever been. I was scratching at the air the way someone would if she was trying to claw her way out to breathe.

The taller and older-looking of the two patrolmen stepped in front of me, his arms out. Maybe I thought I could run through him. I kept going. From the look on his face, I could see he was surprised and quickly braced himself for a collision. With my momentum, I did almost bowl him over, and the second patrolman quickly came to assist him. He wrapped his arms around me firmly, locking mine to my sides, but my legs were still moving, my feet kicking against his legs.

The two of them got me to the ground, and the younger one turned me so that he could fasten handcuffs around my wrists. When I felt them, my voice returned, and I could hear myself screaming.

"Hey, hey, hey," the older patrolman said when they turned me on my back. He was kneeling beside me and had his hands on my legs to try to stop me from kicking. In my mind, I was still running. He was strong, but my strength came from somewhere so deep inside me I couldn't recognize or explain it. My legs continued until he leaned over me, putting the full weight of his body behind his effort to stop my kicking.

I finally did. I was gasping harder, though, and fighting to stay conscious.

"What do you think you're doing?" the older patrolman asked.

"Did you take something?" the younger one followed. "Are you high?"

I looked from one to the other, and then, when the full realization of who they were occurred to me, my whole body started to melt. It was as if I really had taken some powerful drug, because I was under the spell of something far beyond my control. Now my crying was different, more of a dry sobbing and gasping.

"My mother," I said. "My mother."

Still kneeling beside me, the older officer asked, "What about your mother?"

"She's . . . looking up."

"Looking up where?" he asked.

"Looking up, looking up. She was under the picture. When I took it off her, she was looking up."

The two policemen glanced at each other, and then the younger one assisted the older one in getting me to stand. Out of the corner of my eye, I saw people had come out of houses along the street. There were three of them standing on the sidewalk across from us, whispering to each other and watching.

"Okay," the older policeman said. "Just relax." He nodded at the younger one, who opened the rear door of their patrol car. They led me to it and sat me, keeping the door open. "Now, tell us what you're talking about," the older cop said. The younger one stood beside him.

"My mother can't get out."

"Out of where?"

"The basement," I said.

"Your mother fell down in the basement?" the younger patrolman asked.

I shook my head. "I don't know if she fell down. She was buried under her portrait, her beautiful portrait with her in her silk and taffeta gown, wearing her pearls."

"Buried?" the younger patrolman said.

Instead of answering, I sobbed and said, "I knew she hadn't gone away for good. I had to convince Daddy, so I hid the good-bye note. I was right to do that, wasn't I? Daddy was very angry, but I had to do it. He wants to change everything. That's why he took down my mother's portrait and put his parents' back up."

They both stared at me a moment, before the older policeman stepped away and spoke into a radio on his shoulder and then returned.

"Which house is yours?" he asked.

"The most important house," I said. "The most historic house."

"Well, we don't live on this street," the younger cop said. "So you'll have to give us your address."

"It's right there," I said, nodding at my house. "See the Duke and the Duchess?"

"Huh?" He looked.

"The two oak trees," I said. "My father says one is feminine, and so it is the Duchess. My mother says that's silly, but I think my father's right."

They looked at each other, whispered something, and closed the rear door. Both got into the police car. I sat and watched as they backed up the street and pulled into our driveway.

"Who's home?" the younger patrolman asked me.

"Just my mother," I said. "My father is at work. I didn't go to school because I overslept. He took down my mother's portrait and put my grandparents' back while I was still sleeping, so I went to look for her portrait."

"What's your name?" the older policeman asked me.

"I'm Scarletta Barnaby. My father owns Barnaby Furniture."

"I know it," the younger patrolman told the older one.

I could hear sirens and turned to see another patrol car and an ambulance pull in front of our house. The two policemen got out of the car we were in, and the younger one opened the rear door.

"Show us where your mother is," he said. He reached in to help me get out. "If you're calm enough, I'll take off those handcuffs. You think you'll be all right?"

"Daddy says we'll be all right," I said.

He looked to the older policeman, who nodded, and then he unlocked the handcuffs. Even though he did, my wrists still felt like they were around them. Two more policemen joined us, followed by two paramedics.

"She says her mother is down in the basement, buried," the older patrolman told the others.

"C'mon," the younger cop said, gently taking my right arm. "Show us where your mother is, okay?"

"Will you help me bring up her portrait, too?" I asked.

"Sure," he said.

I looked back up the street to the corner where the school bus would stop and imagined myself jumping out and running toward my house. I was taking big strides. I had won a race, and I couldn't wait to get home to tell my mother, even though she never seemed that interested. I knew my father would be. Usually, I could smell the smoke of disagreement between them. "Running and leaping like that. It's so unladylike," she would say.

"There are female cheetahs, Doreen," he would reply.

So much of what they said to each other seemed to have been written down and rehearsed and rehearsed until their words didn't change and the way they said them was identical to the way they had said them previously. Sometimes I felt like the three of us were in a play, and one day, when I turned to the left or the right, I would see an audience and hear applause.

"You okay?" the younger patrolman asked when I stopped in the open doorway.

I looked at him and nodded.

"We're all going to be okay," I said.

He smiled, and I entered the house, aware that everyone was following me.

That's good, I thought. *There'll be plenty of help to get Mother's picture back up from the basement. What we'll do is put it where it was hanging before. We'll take my grandparents' picture down again. Daddy will be upset at first, but then I'll explain. Mother is here; she didn't go away after all. We had better get the picture back up. She'll be so upset otherwise, and we both know you don't want that.*

They followed me to the kitchen and the opened basement door.

"Maybe you should sit with her, Jerry," the older policeman told the younger one.

He nodded and pulled out one of the chairs by the kitchenette. "Yes, sit here until we figure it all out," Jerry the policeman said, smiling at me.

I did.

Everyone else went down into the basement.

It wasn't often that we had guests, but when we did,

my mother was the perfect hostess, even if she didn't particularly like the couple my father had invited to dinner, mainly because of business interests.

"We must always be better than those we are better than," she told me. "Put aside your feelings so that you never give them an excuse for their inferiority."

I really didn't understand it fully, but I knew she meant to be polite always.

"Can I get you something to drink?" I asked Jerry the policeman.

"No, thank you," he said, smiling. "How about you? I bet you'd like a glass of water?"

I nodded, and he got up, found the glasses quickly, and poured me some cold water. I drank it all in one gulp. I heard footsteps on the basement stairs and turned toward the doorway. The older policeman came up first. He looked very upset, and I thought maybe he should have a glass of water, too, but I didn't have time to ask.

"Take her to the station. Elaine Small from social services will be there to greet you."

"Bad?" Jerry asked.

"Worse," the older policeman said.

Jerry turned to me. "Hey," he said. "We're going to go for a short ride. Okay?"

I looked at my watch. "Today's Friday, right?" I asked.

"Sure is."

"I'm supposed to go to a party tonight, but I still have to talk my father into letting me go."

"That's fine. There's time," he said. He reached for my hand.

I looked back at the basement door. "Can they bring my mother's portrait up, please?"

"We're doing that first thing," the older cop said. "Don't worry about it."

"Thank you."

I walked out with Jerry, who kept his hand on my arm but didn't squeeze very hard.

"Hey," he said. "Tell you what. You ride with me up front, okay?"

"Okay. I didn't like the back of the police car."

"Naw. I'm not crazy about it, either."

He stepped forward to open the front door on the passenger's side for me, and I got in. Then he hurried around to the driver's side. When I looked back, I saw many more people on the sidewalk, on both sides of the street. They were all talking and looking at our house.

"I don't see people come out of their houses this much usually," I told Jerry as he backed out of our driveway.

"That's people," he said, as if that would cover all answers.

I looked ahead as we drove away and didn't turn to look at anyone looking at us.

"Penny gossips," I remembered my mother saying.

"They love to hear 'a penny for your thoughts.' They feed on scandals, especially family scandals, so keep our problems to yourself."

That's what I would do.

Keep our problems to myself.

There was a very nice woman waiting for me at the police station. She wasn't any taller than most girls in my class. She had very kind, soft cerulean eyes and very neatly trimmed hair the color of hay after a rain. Whenever I was someplace where the air smelled fresh and cool and the patches of clouds looked whiter and fluffier, I would have that image of wet hay in my mind. I thought I had seen it on some trip we took when I was very young. In a field we were passing, the tied-up bales looked like sleeping animals. I might even have said that, because I remembered my father laughing. I thought my mother might have smiled. It was often hard to tell if she was amused or annoyed.

"She certainly sees things we don't," my father remarked. My mother grunted, looked back at me, and then gazed out the window as if she wanted to see the things I saw, too.

"Hi, Scarletta," the nice lady said now, reaching for my hand. "My name is Elaine Small. Now, don't you go telling me my name fits me," she said, smiling.

She did have petite facial features and was doll-like. Her hands were smaller than mine, too.

"We're going to go to a room here, just you and I, and talk a while, okay? Do you want to go to the bathroom? Can I get you something cold to drink or even something hot like tea?"

"Something cold, please. I like lemon and lime, orange, or ginger ale."

"Oh, I'm sure we'll find one of those," she said.

"I don't have to go to the bathroom yet," I said.

"Okay."

She took my hand, stopped to get me my drink, and took me to a room where there was a small settee and two chairs with a light wood table between the chairs and the settee. There was just one window behind the settee, but it was high, almost to the ceiling. There was nothing on the walls, and the floor was a light brown tile. I sat on the settee and drank my ginger ale.

"So," she said, "why don't we talk about today and what happened?"

I sipped my drink and looked at her. She didn't look like a penny gossip, but I couldn't be absolutely sure.

"I have to go home soon," I said. I looked at my watch. "I have to explain everything to my father first, and we have to put my mother's portrait back where it was above the fireplace. It's important that I explain. I don't want my father to be angry ever again."

"Sure. That makes sense," she said, nodding. "I just want to understand everything so I can help you."

I nodded, put my glass of ginger ale on the table, and stood. "That's exactly what a penny gossip would say to get me to talk about family problems. My mother wouldn't like that. I have to go home."

I started toward the door, and she grabbed my arm. She wasn't smiling, and her face changed. It became bigger, and she grew a few inches in height, too. I tried to break free, but she held me tightly. She was talking, but I wasn't listening. I started to scream. Another woman in a police uniform came in quickly. She took my other arm. I twisted and turned and screamed and screamed, until I felt myself sinking and everything darkening.

When I woke up again, I was in an ambulance. The two paramedics beside me were talking, but it was difficult to hear them. There was something in my left arm, and my arms were strapped down so I couldn't lift them. I could hear the beep of some sort of monitor. Moments later, I was asleep again, and when I woke up the next time, I was in a hospital room. My arms were still tied down, and there was still something in my left arm.

Vaguely, I recalled the words "shock," "murder," "therapy," but they seemed part of a dream. A nurse came in with a tall, stout man with grayish black hair and black-framed glasses. He pulled up a chair beside my bed and asked me how I was doing.

I looked at the nurse and at him. "Where am I?" I asked.

"You're in a hospital. You've had quite a shock, and we're going to help you get better. Can you tell me your name and where you live?" he asked.

I thought for a moment and then shook my head.

"Don't worry about it right now," he said, patting my hand softly. "You'll be fine. You have a little journey to make, and then we'll see."

"Where am I going?" I asked.

"Back," he said. He smiled. "In time."

Later I was in a place where time didn't seem to matter. I was never uncomfortable until the day I left. I was given medications, spent many hours talking to very nice doctors, both male and female, began to read magazines and books, took walks, and listened to music until eventually I felt the thick fog begin to thin out.

All that had happened to me and to my parents returned in the form of a jigsaw puzzle, a piece here, a piece there. My main doctor, a woman named Dr. Nettles, carefully worked it all together with me after I was able to recall most things myself without screaming and crying.

Gradually, I was fed the facts. My father, in a rage during an argument, had struck my mother. He had never hit her or me ever, but according to Dr. Nettles, all that my father had kept pent up inside him had exploded. The story he created about her leaving us with a lover was how he dealt with fatally injuring someone he did love.

His behavior with me was another way for him to tolerate his tremendous guilt. He was hoping I'd accept her being gone. That would help him live with it.

Dr. Nettles thought that somewhere deep inside me, I had known all this, and my refusal to accept my mother as being gone for good was my way of keeping the truth buried, maybe alongside my mother in the basement.

For weeks afterward, I struggled with it all, but then one day, I awoke and began caring about my appearance, my hair, and my clothes, everything I used to care about. I wondered what had happened to my clothes, to our house. I asked more sensible questions, until finally, a week or so afterward, my aunt Rachel and uncle Benjamin came to see me. They had been waiting for Dr. Nettles to tell them I was ready.

She brought me to her office in the clinic and left me sitting on the settee. The door opened, and they entered, almost on tiptoe, I thought. I hadn't seen them in so long. They looked much older. My aunt had dyed her hair a more brassy-like blond, and my uncle's dark brown hair was quite gray on the temples. He always kept his hair short. They both looked a little terrified, but my aunt quickly smiled and rushed over to me.

"How are you, darling?" she asked. It was comforting to see the resemblances to my father in her face. When I didn't stand, she knelt to hug me.

"Hello, Scarletta. It's good to see you," my uncle said.

He stood by, obviously waiting for my reaction to seeing them.

My aunt stood up, looked at him, and then smiled at me.

"I'm okay," I said.

"You look very good. You're as pretty as ever. So," she added, slipping on a serious face the way my father would, "we're not going to go over it all with you. We're never going to talk about it in any detail unless you want to," she promised.

"Nora is really looking forward to seeing you," Uncle Benjamin said. "With her sister off to college, she's eager to have a new buddy in the house."

That was the way they were telling me I would live with them.

My aunt explained that she and my uncle had gone to my house and packed as much of my things as they could. Everything had been brought to their new house, a bigger house than the one they had after they had gotten married and moved to North Carolina. I was going to have my own room, a room no one had yet used, even guests. I would start school there, a new school, a private school that their daughter, my cousin Nora, attended.

"You'll find it a lot nicer than the school you were in," my aunt assured me.

"What about my house?" I asked.

"It's been sold, as was the furniture business. We've

set money aside for you, of course," Uncle Benjamin said. And then he smiled and added, "You'll never have to worry about your teeth." It was his way of joking about his being a dentist.

No one here had told me anything more about my father, so I thought I'd ask. They looked at each other first, and then Aunt Rachel said he was in prison and that he'd be there a long time, maybe forever.

"But we'll deal with all that later," she added. "First things first, and the first thing is to get you home and help you get started on a new life."

"A new life?"

She smiled and nodded.

Could you have a new life? Where do you put your old life? I wondered.

Dr. Nettles came in after that, and we all sat in her office and talked about the steps to my adjusting to this so-called new life. I was still going to be on medication for a while, but she was convinced I was ready to move on, to what I really would have to consider being reborn.

Although you don't know it, the day you're born, you have your name. It's rare that your parents wait to give you that, unless they're arguing about it. The day after I had arrived in North Carolina and had been moved into my aunt and uncle's beautiful new home, my rebirth began. They had brought most of my clothes, and every-thing was hung up and neatly put in my dresser drawers in my room. I didn't say it, but I liked this room much more than my room back in our historic house in South Carolina. The walls were papered in a pink texture, and all the furniture was a pink-tinted white. I had a king-size bed with oversize pillows and a ruched rosette quilt. There was a computer desk with a brand-new computer in the right corner. The room was bright, with two large windows that looked over the east side of the property. I had a plush pink shag rug.

I thought to myself that they were determined to make everything bright for me, down to the colorful hangers in my closet. Neither my cousins nor I had television sets in our rooms. My aunt and uncle told me they encouraged their girls to watch television with them, either in the den or in the living room.

"We've always tried to be a real family," Aunt Rachel said. "To be a real family, you have to want and like to do things together."

I didn't know all that my cousin Nora had been told about me, but either she was excited about me living with them because I'd be a project for her, or she was genuinely lonely with her sister gone. I wasn't to begin school for a while. Dr. Nettles had described it as being like lowering yourself into a hot bath, getting used to it, and then just soaking it all up with delight. She was sure it would be that way for me.

It was a three-day weekend for Nora, so she and I,

practically strangers, really, had time to get to know more about each other, Nora carefully skating around all that had happened to my parents. Her questions were mostly about my friends at school and boys there.

On Sunday night, after dinner, we adjourned to have what my aunt and uncle called a family meeting in the den. Nora had filled my head with stories about her friends and the boys in her class and the class above. She wove a picture of small romances, parties, picnics, rowing on the lake, and hanging out in the mall on Saturdays, where they could meet boys they liked. She talked quickly, incessantly, really, like someone afraid of any silence between us. In a matter of hours, I knew her favorite songs, singers, movies, colors, and fashions.

I thought she looked more like her mother, just like I looked more like mine. She wasn't beautiful or stunning, but she was cute and energetic, with her short bobbed light brown hair in a simple side twist. She had her father's friendly hazel eyes and her mother's nose and mouth, and she expressed her thoughts and feelings with her mother's expressions and gestures. I was about three inches taller than she was and still quite thin.

Although we were close in age, I thought she was a lot less mature, but I also thought that the maturity I had was not what I'd want for anyone else, especially her. I felt as if I had already skipped my childhood. Everything she was excited about seemed terribly unimportant and juvenile, but I smiled and did my best to be as enthusiastic as she would like me to be.

At dinners and when we all went for rides, everyone was as kind and considerate of me as could be. My uncle proudly bragged about their community, showing me where improvements were either made or under way. It was apparent that they wanted me to feel at home as quickly as possible. I did my best to show my appreciation, but getting excited about anything was like climbing a very steep hill. For now, I thought, my smile would have to do. No one seemed disappointed. They appeared overjoyed at my having an appetite, wanting something new to wear, and being eager to watch television, listen to music with Nora, and especially sleep through the night in my new room and surroundings.

"You're doing so well," Aunt Rachel began when we all sat down for the family meeting. "I spoke with Dr. Nettles, and she says she's going to wean you off the medicine soon."

I nodded. I saw how the three of them were looking at each other, so I readied myself for the next statement, request, or announcement. I had thickened my skin for when sudden news and revelations were sent my way. I had gotten so I would do no more than blink at a hydrogen-bomb explosion.

"Unfortunately," Aunt Rachel continued after her short pause, "the events, the horrible events that occurred, attracted great interest, salacious interest. It went national and was highlighted in one of those network dramatizations of terrible crimes. Fortunately, your picture was not shown."

"But the family name was," Uncle Benjamin inserted, obviously impatient with my aunt's lengthy prologue. She gave him a sharp look, but he explained that Dr. Nettles thought this was fine, was necessary. She took a deep breath.

"It's known as the Barnaby Furniture Murder," he revealed.

"And with the Internet being what it is," my aunt followed, "even though your name and picture were kept out of most news stories, for now, I'd like to take you to my hairstylist and change your hair color . . . something you would like, of course, just a little added protection. Later you can return to your natural color if you want . . ."

"So what we were thinking, so as to make things even easier and more comfortable for you and for Nora," Uncle Benjamin said, "was we would enroll you under a different name as well. Because this is a private school, we have more cooperation from the administration, and secrets will be well locked up."

"What name?" I asked.

My aunt smiled. "Well, that's the biggest surprise of all, dear," she said. "Benjamin and I have decided we'd like to legally adopt you and therefore give you our name, our surname, Benjamin's family name, Dunning."

"We've got all the legal documentation started," Uncle Benjamin said.

"However, we left something big for you to decide," my aunt said. "If you want, of course. We think it would really help."

"More added insurance," my uncle said, smiling.

I looked at Nora. She actually seemed very excited by all this. She thought it was a wonderful adventure. Her mind was already running away with scenarios, cover-ups, ways to invent a new former life for me.

"And what's that?" I asked.

"You can choose your own new first name and a middle name if you like."

"I'll help you," Nora blurted. "It's like you'll be the star in a great big play. I'll be costar."

"Play?"

"You have to do a lot of acting," she said. "But we'll sit down together and invent everything."

"Yes." I turned to my aunt and uncle. "What happened to my fake parents?" I asked. "The Dunnings."

"I thought car accident on vacation in Europe," he said. "Your father was the son of my father's brother. You and Nora are still cousins."

"You don't have to start school until you're comfortable with it all," Aunt Rachel said. "We'll keep

Tess informed about everything, every little detail, of course," my aunt said. "She knows most everything up to today, so when she comes home for the holidays, she'll help."

"I'll help you right now," Nora said. "I have lists and lists of great names, names I wish I had."

"So I really am being reborn," I thought aloud.

"We're all so sorry you have to go through this," Aunt Rachel said.

Nora didn't look at all sorry. "We can start right now," she said.

My aunt and uncle were silent. They both looked like they were in real pain, suffering for me. I did appreciate that, but I also thought that what they were doing would make things easier for them, too. Maybe that was their chief reason, but why should I blame them? I didn't want to blame anyone for anything anymore, and becoming someone new did seem like the easiest and quickest way not to do any of that.

"Okay," I said, smiling and thinking. I had to create a different smile, a different voice, and maybe a different walk, too. I would need Nora's help to build my new background, listen to her music and read her magazines. Together, she and I could create a past romance for me. I'd be reborn a little more every day.

Nora clapped her hands together. Everyone in my new family was smiling.

Fix your posture, my mother was telling me in my mind. I was leaning awkwardly forward.

You're talking to the wrong person, I replied.

I heard her laugh. *You'll never be free of me, Scarletta. No matter what they tell you or do for you, I'll always be there.*

Pru

I WAS SITTING in the same interrogation room by the time Chandler and one of the criminal attorneys at his firm, Anthony Basso, arrived. Chandler hurried over to me to kiss me and introduce Anthony.

"Tony will take over from here," he said, "but I'll be right beside him as much as possible, Pru."

Lieutenant Julio and Detective Gabriel entered. Lieutenant Julio was carrying my answering machine under his arm. He turned on the recording device for the interrogation room as soon as the two of them sat across from us. He then explained what he had and what he was presenting to me and my attorney.

"Is this your machine?" he asked me.

I looked at Chandler, who nodded slightly.

"Yes," I said.

He then lifted off the cover of the machine so that the

parts were visible. He took his pen out of his top pocket and pointed to something.

"We have had the machine examined, and as you can see here, one of the elements is burned out. We can tell that it has been burned out for some time. It was not possible for anyone to record anything on it during the period you claimed to have received messages from a stalker you call Scarletta," he said.

"We'll have that property analyzed by our own technicians," Anthony Basso replied.

Lieutenant Julio nodded at Detective Gabriel, who took the machine, put the cover back on, and pushed it to the side. She then handed Lieutenant Julio a folder, which he opened in front of him.

"Miss Dunning," he began, his eyes on his paperwork, "how long have you been Pru Dunning?"

"What?" Chandler exclaimed.

Lieutenant Julio glanced at him and then looked at me. "Is Pru Dunning the name you were given at birth?"

"Yes," I said.

He smiled, but something he saw in my face made that short-lived.

"We have done a full background check on Miss Dunning," he told Anthony Basso and Chandler. "Pru Dunning is not her given name." He looked at me again. "Were you not born Scarletta Barnaby? Are your real parents not Raymond and Doreen Barnaby?" he asked.

"Let me see that," Anthony Basso demanded.

Lieutenant Julio passed the documents to him. Both he and Chandler read them.

"It's a very clever way to cover your actions," Lieutenant Julio said. "You have created a new life for yourself. You did well in high school and went on to nursing school. Considering what your father did to your mother, I don't blame you for assuming a new identity, but . . ."

"She did this," I insisted. "She's very clever. She's always been jealous of me. She never wanted me to succeed at anything."

No one spoke for a moment.

"Some of the news clippings are in there, too," Lieutenant Julio told Anthony Basso.

Chandler was still perusing the documents.

The two of them looked at some of the news stories.

I sat back while they were reading and closed my eyes. Scarletta was smiling at me. She was in my mirror. She would often slip in behind it and turn it into a window.

"You hid the good-bye note," I said.

"Excuse me?" Lieutenant Julio asked.

I opened my eyes.

"Under the circumstances," Anthony Basso said, "we're going to ask for a psychiatric."

"Oh, the DA's anticipated that and is going to do the same."

"Then there is no reason to continue," Anthony Basso

told him. He looked at Chandler, who had the appearance of someone just struck in the back of his head with a brick.

Lieutenant Julio took back the paperwork and put it in his folder. Then he and Detective Gabriel stood.

"We'll have the answering machine available for your technician," he said, and Detective Gabriel picked it up.

Neither Anthony nor Chandler replied. We three watched them leave the room.

"Do you realize what they are accusing you of doing?" Anthony asked me.

"I'm sick of her," I replied. "I want her gone from my life."

He nodded and looked at Chandler. I thought there were tears in Chandler's eyes.

"I'll wait outside," Anthony said, rising. Chandler nodded, and Anthony walked out.

Chandler moved to the seat beside me and took my hand. "It's going to be all right," he said.

I smiled. "Yes. My father always said that."

He leaned over to kiss me. The door opened, and the female officer who had brought me to the room stood there. Chandler sighed and stood up, reaching for my hand so I would stand, too.

"I'll be there for you every step of the way," he promised.

"She won't like that," I said.

He smiled. "She'll have to get used to it or maybe . . . maybe leave you alone."

I nodded. We walked to the doorway together. He turned to say something else, but I had something more important to tell him. I was thinking of him, but I was really thinking more of her.

"Do you know what is the hardest word to utter?"

He shook his head. "What?" He smiled.

"Good-bye," I said.

Author's Note

DISSOCIATIVE IDENTITY DISORDER (DID), as defined by the American Psychiatric Association, is a severe condition in which two or more distinct identities or personality states are present and alternately take control of an individual. This disturbance is not due to the direct psychological effects of a substance or of a general medical condition. When in control, each personality state, or alter, may be experienced as if it has a distinct history, self-image, and identity. Certain circumstances or stressors can cause a particular alter to emerge. The various identities may deny knowledge of one another, be critical of one another, or appear to be in open conflict.

DID reflects a failure to integrate various aspects of identity, memory, and consciousness into a single multidimensional self. Usually, a primary identity carries the individual's given name and is passive, dependent, guilty, and depressed. When in control, each personality state, or alter, may be experienced as if it has a distinct history, self-image, and identity. The alters' characteristics—including name, reported age and gender, vocabulary, general knowledge, and predominant mood—contrast with those of the primary identity. Certain circumstances or stressors can cause a particular alter to emerge. The various identities may deny knowledge of one another, be critical of one another, or appear to be in open conflict.